# Covert Avengers
## By Jess Parker

PublishAmerica
Baltimore

© 2002 by Jess Parker.
All rights reserved. No part of this book may be reproduced, stored in a retrieval system, or transmitted in any form or by any means without the prior written permission of the publishers, except by a reviewer who may quote brief passages in a review to be printed in a newspaper, magazine, or journal.

First printing

ISBN: 1-4137-0559-6
PUBLISHED BY PUBLISHAMERICA, LLLP
www.publishamerica.com
Baltimore

Printed in the United States of America

Also by Jess Parker:

Detachment X-Ray

To my wife Judy, for her help and love for almost 50 years.

# Acknowledgements

Judy Parker:
my wife, and number one editor and reader.

Tom Parker and Lori Neagle, my computer support staff.
They helped me with many problems
including some "Parker goofs."

The Staff at Publish America:
Their help and understanding has been invaluable.

My Children:
Tom Parker, Clay Parker, Sheila Stone, Karen and Mike Pruett,
Erin and John Sackman, and nine grandchildren.

When I thank people,
I always have to thank my doctor, Victoria Allen MD.

And of course my cheer section
at the Rowdy Table, Kitsap Mall, at Silverdale, Washington.
Some are: Ralph Strickland, Joe McManus,
Linda Tecson, and Wes Morton.

# Foreword

He grabbed for a gun but was too late. I watched his surprised eyes as the first of nine bullets slammed through his body. There were shouts from other parts of the house, and I beat it out the door and headed for the plane at a dead run. It was rolling as I jumped through the door and pulled up the steps and could hear bullets hitting the fuselage.
After getting airborne, Birdman asked calmly, "Where to?"
I answered, "Northwest, I will know when we get there."
We rotated out of the CIA airfield outside Huntsville, Alabama, and I rotated out of Detachment X-Ray. (Detachment X-Ray)
The plane banked over a bend in the Columbia River, and I knew I was there. Birdman gave me a thumb's up, after I pointed down, and he turned toward an open stretch of highway and made his landing. In a few minutes the airplane had disappeared over the nearest ridge.
I was on the road hitchhiking again. The landing area was about two miles from the bridge that crossed the river. There was little traffic and I didn't hold out the thumb. I walked the bridge on the Columbia River and thought about a trip across the Tennessee River but only for a moment. Those days were over, and I had to arrive and make an early blend into the population of Venture, Washington. A stranger would cause a stir for a short time, but a few months of talking and salmon fishing should soon create the blend I was hoping to achieve. The General had recommended going deep into the population. (Detachment X-Ray)
In a very short time I became "the fisherman" instead of "the stranger." After moving into a local rooming house, I made sure the people would see me fishing or talk to me about fishing on a daily basis. In less than six months

my new friends were introducing me as a neighbor to the surrounding ranchers and farmers. After a few more months had passed I became a "native." One morning I walked into the coffee shop and sat at "the table." This table is in all small towns where stories are told often, the lies were such whoppers no one would believe them and that was the way we wanted it. I also enrolled in a high plains university to finish my education. One Saturday morning I was pointed out to a couple of tourist as the best fishing guide on the river—my acceptance was complete.

    I bought a small house down by the river and asked one of the boat builders to build a boat for river fishing. By the end of the first year, I was a part of the village population and my friends were actually proud of the fact that I enrolled in college and commuted rather than move away from home. The unrest of the Vietnam Era had spilled over the entire country, and at times, if you knew what to look for, it was possible to see the footprints of Detachment X-Ray. By the middle of the 1970's most of the unrest had settled, and a student of my ilk could get his work done without campus politics. I finished four years at Central State College, and then transferred back to the big city for a master's degree followed by a doctorate. This was a rewarding time for me because after the PhD, Central State hired me on the first application as an associate professor. I taught Political Science and become a consultant for state and local elections. One of the state senators talked me into coming to the Capitol to work for the Senate Majority Leader. This put me in touch with many high-powered politicians, and one of them, from a neighboring state, became a very good friend. Sam Martin had lived in the northwest most of his life, but he sounded like a 'good old boy' from Mississippi. We kidded him about his accent because his family left Tupelo when he was seven years old. He was completely enamored by my hometown of Venture, especially by the caring nature and the strength of the local citizens. My house, down by the river, had become a neighborhood stop when I was in residence. After major renovations, the small house had become the big house down by the river.

    Over a few years, I had piled on my cover until an investigator would have a hard time finding me out of the Northwest. In some of my introductions my neighbors stated many times that I had always lived in Venture. According to them, the only time I was gone for a major length of time was during the Korean War. Most of them remembered when I left for Korea, and when I returned home. This type of cover was possible because of "the table." I told many stories about Korea and the other parts of the Far East. My narration always ended by saying how good it was to get back home in 1954. On some occasions, others repeated my stories and they all remembered when I returned in 1954. It seems as if I had hitched hiked all the way home from Seattle, because I wanted to blow the stench of the world out of my system. I had become a native, both in fact and lore.

During a fishing trip with Sam Martin, the Governor, and the Dean at Central State College, the Dean had let it slip that I would be offered a new position at the college. Sam Martin spoke up, "Dean, y'all better git yer offer straight 'cause ah'm gonna ast him to move to Washington and head up my research staff."

The school official responded, "Senator, we are prepared to offer him the History Chair at the school with full professorship."

The Dean looked at me and winked, "And Senator, if he will accept the offer today we will allow a year's sabbatical before taking the chair"

Sam jumped all over the sabbatical and said that there wasn't any reason for me not to accept both offers.

The Governor caused a relaxing laugh when he said, "Jake, it looks as if you can take your pick of two great positions. Now tell us, are you staying in Washington or are you going to Washington?"

The following Monday I accepted both positions and after a conference with the school and state officials, they granted my request for the sabbatical to start the first day of the Fall Quarter. They were also surprised and pleased when I suggested that my salary should commence after the sabbatical.

It had taken some deep thought and soul searching for me to make the decision to leave my part of the world for the bright lights of a big city. There was another consideration, what if I was identified with Detachment X-Ray? I couldn't answer that and Sam Martin was relentless in getting me to move to Washington, D. C., and work for him while the Senate was in session. I finally agreed and went back to big city life. I arrived on Friday, rented an apartment and went to the Senate Office Building.

Sam rushed out from behind his desk and said, "Hey boy, hits good to see ya. Yuh got here jest in time. We is leaving fer New York this evenin'. We is a part of a trade delegation meetin' with the Chinee. Boy, don't even unpack. You jest need a couple of weeks worth of clothes."

# Chapter 1

The doors opened simultaneously, with the Chinese delegation filing in from the left, and their American counterparts from the right. Everyone took assigned seats after the leaders bowed and sat opposite of each other. United Nation employees were busy with water pitchers, glasses, and ashtrays while the junior members of the delegations crowded in for seats.

I took a seat behind and to the right of Senator Sam Martin. He had asked me to head his research staff for the present session of Congress. After I agreed to this, all of his talk was about a longer commitment because of the sabbatical at the College—but I wouldn't go any further. We had a standing joke that I was the highest paid research staffer in Washington because my compensation was living quarters in DC. Sam had brought most of his staff to the meetings with the Chinese. The Peoples Republic of China had surprised the world by asking for the meetings to be convened at the United Nations Headquarters in New York City.

As with any meeting between international parties, this one was getting off to a slow, but political, start. All delegates on the United States' side of the table had scheduled a welcoming speech. Across the table the Chinese delegates were accepting and responding. All eyes turned toward Sam Martin as he started speaking. I was watching the Chinese, and they either listened on the simultranslator or to the personal mutterings of a translator. My eyes swept across the sameness of the oriental faces—crossed and immediately returned to one of the delegates near the end of the table. Recognition?

"Not really, just another gook."

The passing thought startled me because that word had been dropped from my vocabulary for many years.

Senator Martin's counterpart, Chin Hau, was responding and my attention returned to him. Sam had asked the staff to pay special attention because Chin Hau was considered the most important member of the delegation. He was a small, wispy individual, but with eyes that appeared to see everything. The speech was directed at the Senators, but the eyes were watching the staff assistants. A slight smile showed, as our eyes caught and held momentarily.

I slid a note to Sam, "Watch this cat, he is the turnip salesman."

I caught Sam's chuckle. Before leaving DC, the United States Delegation had been warned by the President that we didn't need to trade hi-tech and machinery for rice and turnips. Chin Hau finished speaking—looked directly at me—to the note, and back to me with a slight bow and the hint of a smile.

My attention returned to the end of the table. I had an uncomfortable feeling of recognition. The seating chart did not help. He was identified as Mr. Hsu Dong Ping of Peking. I moved my chair and could see that Hsu Dong Ping was a tall, well built, and an obviously in good shape Chinese man. The only other distinguishing feature was a goatee, and I continued to study him. He appeared to be listening intently or was slightly deaf because he was holding the earphones to his head. Every so often he would question and listen closely to his interpreter. Then I noticed that the earphones were not covering his ear.

"Mr. Dong Ping, you understand English, don't you?" I mused.

The speakers changed, and his eyes traveled up the table—crossed me—and then swiftly back. Our gazes locked and held. Neither of us changed expressions and he finally broke the look, as the speaker from his side began speaking.

"You son-of-a-bitch."

I almost jumped. Why would Mr. Dong Ping cause such a reaction from me? None of the other delegates caused me any grief. What was it? The speeches wore on and my stare would return to him from time to time. As often as not, he was looking at me. My attention came back to Chin Hau who was trying unobtrusively to find the focus of my attention. Hau looked across the table with a sort of musing, questioning glance, until the blank oriental expressionless manner took over.

The first session of the trade mission closed, and the Chinese Chairman invited the Americans for cocktails in his legation's anteroom at the United Nations. The refreshments would be ready in a half an hour, so it was a busy, bustling few minutes as the assistants gathered brief cases, papers, and books to be stored in a safe provided by the United Nations.

Senator Martin and I made our way to the reception after discussing Chin Hau with John Stone of the United Nations staff, who told us that the Chinese Chairman was only a title. We were advised that any agreement would have to be with Chin Hau's approval. "He is a tough nut, Senator. Watch him. He will proverb you to death," said Stone.

Our hosts were in a receiving line. When we got to Chin Hau, he stopped Sam for a moment. Each of the statesmen tried to size up the other while engaged in small talk. The Senator moved away, and the fragile looking old man took my hand in a cool but firm handshake.

The faint smile broke with, "Oh ho, my colleague Senator Martin's right hand."

I acknowledged with a smile but before I could move, he continued, "Remember a turnip is good when it is with other good food."

In my mind I knew he couldn't have seen the contents of my note during the meeting.

Trying to appear casual—not sure I made it—I replied, "A turnip with good food causes as much gas as one with bad food."

He actually smiled and said softly, "Ho, Ho, an American who understands proverbs. One we will have to watch."

We had a break in the line, and Sam asked what that was all about.

I answered, "Remember the note? That old man used a proverb about turnips."

"Hmm," was the Senator's only response as we approached Dong Ping at the end of the line. The Chinese delegate acknowledged us and stared at me through a brief handshake. I turned out of the line and looked quickly over my shoulder. His head snapped back from watching me.

These receptions are typical mix and mingle—mix and mingle were the instructions to the aides and assistants. The delegates from both nations were in the center of small unmoving islands of people. When a delegate would move, it would cause a chain reaction around the room.

As if by law—no more than one delegate from the two nations could be in a single group. Only the staff level people were moving freely, around the room. I noticed that as I moved from one group to another, Chin Hau's top aide would soon appear. Upon leaving a group I waited for him. He stepped around a couple and smiled when he saw me waiting.

He extended his hand and said, "My name is Chow Ling, should we mix and mingle together?"

"You bet," I said, "It'll be easier on both of us if we travel together."

For the next three quarters of an hour we moved around the room, all the while sizing and assessing each other. We had a pleasant but guarded time, and later I described him to Sam Martin as a "sharpie."

I broke away with an offered and accepted handshake saying, "My boss is ready to go. I will see you at the next session."

Chow laughed quietly and responded, "Senator Martin is no more your boss, than Chin Hau is mine."

Raising an eye brow, I saluted him and we both laughed when I retorted, "Chow Ling, I don't know what the hell you are talking about."

He turned away laughing, and I felt a presence at my side.

It was Dong Ping and his interpreter who said, "Mr. Hsu Dong Ping wonders why you stare."

My eyes were holding Ping's as I answered, "My apologies for staring. I hope the delegate is not fearful."

The interpreter gasped before speaking, and I caught a glint of something in Ping's eyes that he immediately veiled.

He spoke for a couple of seconds and was interpreted, "I am not fearful of a Senator's assistant. Should I be?"

Turning away, I said, "No, not yet."

A slight hesitation from the linguist, and I heard no reply as I joined Sam Martin. When we reached the door, I looked back and Ping had joined Chin Hau but was staring over the crowd at our party.

I was sure he was looking directly at me, and mused, "Who in the hell is that gook?"

I tried a brief memory search but no Hsu Dong Ping. The antagonism I was feeling bothered me because I held no prejudices toward the Chinese, but here I was, thinking in racist language.

"Hell, Chow Ling and I were almost buddies, and I liked old Chin Hau, even with his turnips. How in the hell did he come up with that?"

Sam broke into my thoughts, "That big Chinee bothering you ole buddy? Go git into yuh best overalls. We is havin' supper with El Presidente. Come by our place 'bout eight."

# Chapter 2

The President and First Lady were hosting a dinner for the Senate Trade Delegation at the United Nations Ambassador's residence. I tried to refuse but Sam was adamant. These occasions normally called for the top people, and I was a second level staffer. I decided that it was the long-term friendship that rated the invitation because I was certainly new to the Washington scene. John Moody was Sam's Political Assistant and Chief of Staff and was normally the only staff member to attend such occasions.

John and Valerie Moody were at the elevator and held it for me. At Sam's suite the real boss of the operation, Susan Bonnet, Executive Secretary, greeted us. Our host and his wife Dorothy welcomed us. A bar had been set up and soon there was a glass in our hands. Most of the talk was about the upcoming visit with the President, but I detected an undercurrent of excitement. Susan and Dorothy would not be cornered—they disclaimed knowledge to what I was referring. John Moody shunted the questions aside with a knowing and satisfied smile. Before I could corner Sam, the door opened and the suite filled with legislators, staff members, and media representatives.

The Senator got attention by standing on a chair and saying, "Friends, we ain't got much time. So quieten down and listen up. A good friend of mine has sum'n interestin' to say."

John Moody stepped forward and said, "Thank you, Senator Sam. It is an honor to be called your friend.

He continued, "Folks, I have been on Sam Martin's staff for many years, but I am leaving."

He was interrupted by a buzz of conversation.

Holding up his hands he continued, "I'm leaving the Senator's staff but don't plan to leave Washington. With Sam's blessing and advice I will be declaring my candidacy for Representative from my Congressional District. Valerie and I are leaving for home tomorrow morning for formal declarations throughout the District. My only regret is that I will no longer working in my present capacity. There have been long discussions with Senator Martin and others back at home. We feel my experience would better serve the people if I were in the House of Representatives. I will be my own man, but certainly I would expect to have a close relationship with the best Senator in Washington, my friend, Sam Martin. We have just a few minutes for questions."

The few minutes ran for almost half an hour. Sam Martin's staff was always news, especially John Moody. He had recently been the subject of a couple of feature stories. One of the columnists had boldly predicted that John Moody had found his "niche in life" as Martin's right arm and had no other ambitions. Many of the questions concerned that statement. Some of the reporters appeared insulted because neither Moody nor Martin had told them of John's intentions.

Susan Bonnet smiled as I move alongside and whispered, "How long have you known about this? Who is going to replace John?"

She replied, "I've known of John's decision for six months. You will have to ask Sam about the replacement."

Before she finished, a reporter had asked the same question, "Senator Martin, who will replace Mr. Moody as your Chief of Staff?"

The slick talking politician drawled, "Well ah really don' know yit. Got a couple of people in mind."

I had an uncomfortable feeling when he looked over and smiled broadly at my raised eyebrow and continued, "Got some good people right now. May not look far. Course hit's gon' be hard to replace Ole John, but I look for'ard to him coming to the House. He'll do right smart for our people."

The other reporters did not let up, "Senator Martin, you must know, who will be your top assistant?"

"Oh, I do have a good idee, drawled Martin, "Just cain't 'nounce it right now. But when Ole John gits in Congress, the people of his district of our gret state will have some good representation. Sorry folks, tha's all. We have a dinner engagement wif de pres'dent. Cain't afford to keep him waitin'."

# Chapter 3

The President was entertaining some of the Chinese Delegation at the dinner. From my table I could see Chin Hau and Dong Ping and two Chinese women who I surmised were the wives of the delegates. After catching Dong Ping's eyes one time, I studiously ignored him. Susan Bonnet was with me and I found that she was enough to keep my attention. Sam had hired a delightful lady as his secretary, and according to her she had been in the same position for almost twenty years.

I broke her up when I said, "Twenty years! I hope that cheap bastard has given you a couple of raises over the years."

She laughed and said, "Only a couple but Dorothy has forced him to make them good raises. How long have you known Sam?" she asked.

"About five years," I answered.

The President called for attention to introduce his guests. Dong Ping was looking at me while he was being introduced. I caught his gaze and immediately recognized him! I knew him as Long Ball Kwong from the Korean War! (Detachment X-Ray). I had to suffer some but I threatened to gut him on a number of occasions. Susan noticed the change in demeanor but I wouldn't discuss the reason. After the dinner she invited me to have a drink and I refused with an excuse of having to leave for a meeting in Kansas City.

After kicking myself a couple of times for not accepting her invitation, I headed west the next morning to attend a seminar for congressional aides. During the drive, plans were considered and discarded for approaching Dong Ping. I wanted him to know that the possibility of the promised gutting would be seriously considered. His security was continuous with agents from both countries guarding him. My decision was to approach him in some manner after returning from the seminar.

The seminar ended Thursday evening and early Friday I was on the way home from Kansas City. The weather was threatening and caused me to break a standing rule of not picking up hitchhikers. I passed a youngster with his thumb up, and as I ran by him a few drops of rain splashed on the windshield, accompanied by lightning and a rolling crash of thunder. I stopped about a hundred yards away and watched him race the rain. Just as the door opened, the bottom fell from the clouds and for a few minutes it was like having a broken water main directly above the roof of the automobile.

It was impossible to see, not only because of the rain but also for the lightning. I pulled over to the shoulder and we waited silently until it let up to a heavy downpour. After about an hour of travel and still under the torrents of water, my passenger told me about a cutoff that headed into the Ozark Mountains. I asked, as we slowed, if the road would bring me back to the interstate highway. He assured me that it would and thanked me profusely as we turned off the freeway. After twenty some miles the road started winding up to the foothills, and a few miles further he asked to be dropped at a crossroad service station and grocery store. He told me to continue in the same direction for "jest a little piece" to get back to the main highway.

I was still traveling the "little piece" at noon. This was after leaving the hitchhiker at 0900. A hill was crested and the road started dropping rapidly into a valley. I rounded a long curve, crossed over a bridge, and was in downtown Larkspur. The natives evidently didn't believe in signs because no warning had been given approaching the community. Larkspur was a small mountain town nestled between the mountain slopes with Main Street following a small river. There was a combination general store, a café, tavern, and a service station taking up one side of the Town Square. When I pulled into the gasoline pumps, all movement in the village stopped. A man of indeterminate age ambled out and only grunted when I asked him for a fill up. As he was filling the tank, I inquired about the distance to the interstate highway.

He showed some surprise when I laughed at his answer, "Jest a little piece down the road."

The communications system in Larkspur was very efficient. After servicing the car, I pulled in front of the café for lunch. The place soon filled as the stranger was inspected. No one was speaking except for a conversation that could be heard from the tavern.

My seat was next to the pass-through window, and I almost dropped my fork when I heard an answer to a question, "You cain't live ferever."

It had to be! A voice out of the past, but only Carpenter could say those four words with such meaning. I hadn't seen or heard from him since December 1950. He was the first one to be reassigned after our escape from the North Koreans. The voice immediately brought back memories that had all but been suppressed until the past few days. Those memories flooded back and I was positive that Hsu Dong Ping was Long Ball Kwong. He was waiting for me in New York, and I still planned to gut him (Detachment X-Ray).

I paid for lunch, and under close scrutiny, walked into the tavern. The Sniper was sitting alone at a table and did not move as I walked toward him. In retrospect him moving would have been a surprise. Every eye was on me, and all conversation ceased.

"Hello Carpenter," I said.

He did not even look around when he responded, "Navy, whut the hell you doin' heah?"

His expression changed only with a faint grin upon hearing about the hitchhiker's, "jest a little piece down the road." He indicated a chair. Before I got settled, the bartender brought two glasses—one with water—the other with whiskey so white, I had to identify it by smell. He had not changed because his half of the conversation was grunts, monosyllables, and full statements of three or four words.

The surrounding conversation picked up after Carpenter stated, "I know 'em."

Some of the people moved in from the café, but there were no introductions. We sat for a while sipping the whisky, and he almost broke a grin when I strangled on the potent potable.

His eyes hardened and expression froze, when I leaned closer and said softly, "I have seen Long Ball Kwong."

Nothing was said for a long moment, he then muttered, "Wheah he at?"

Before I could answer he stood up and said, "Les talk in heah," and led me into the tavern office. We sat down with another glass of the white brew—this time with no chaser.

I did not feel the need for chaser with his statement; "Les kill 'em."

His suggestion firmed the resolve that had been forming in my mind after I reached the conclusion that Mr. Dong Ping was my old nemesis Long Ball Kwong. This conclusion happened after the dinner with the President. Susan and I were walking to her room when Dong Ping stepped out of a room in front of us. When he turned away, I knew why this particular delegate had troubled me. There was no doubt; he was Long Ball Kwong. I stopped in my tracks and watched him walk to the elevator. Susan appeared concerned but didn't question me.

To Carpenter, I said, "I plan to."

He did not acknowledge my answer indicating that I was planning to kill Long Ball Kwong. The Sniper reached for the telephone, and I could tell he was dialing long distance.

In a couple of minutes he said into the telephone, "Kin I talk to the Cap'n?"

After a moment of listening he continued, "Yes'um hit's me."

Then— "Cap'n, Navy is heah. He seen Long Ball."

Again— "Uh huh, O. K., see you."

The telephone was replaced and he said quietly, "Cap'n and Sarg will be on the way. Be here bout six. Sarg is callin' Josephs. Les go."

He assumed that I was in agreement because he was out the door before I could retrieve my coat. I followed his pickup truck down a narrow, two-lane road that at times was dangerously close to the river. We drove for about ten miles and the road ended in front of a beautiful mountain home. My host still acted like a hillbilly, but the outward appearances of his lifestyle disputed all thoughts of his being a hillbilly. Without waiting for me, Carpenter went in and was pouring more of his firewater as I came into the room.

I sat at the kitchen table and he muttered, "Be back."

Without another word he left me sitting at the table trying to get up nerve to take a drink. I was still squeezing the glass when the truck returned. Voices could be heard and the kitchen door opened and the most gorgeous woman I had ever seen, walked in ahead of the fabled Marine Sniper.

She was just over five feet, maybe a hundred pounds, alabaster skin, long, shining black hair, and flashing black eyes. Gorgeous was the only description that fit.

She walked over and took my face in cool, strong hands, and said, "Navy, I'm Lydia."

She kissed me and I felt like a clumsy teenager in front of that beautiful smile. What a contrast for a tall, lanky hillbilly like my friend from long ago. We sat at the table with Lydia and me talking—hearing Carpenter grunt every once in a while. She had a full-throated, infectious laugh. It was demonstrated often, when I told some of the tales about her husband. In her presence Carpenter was almost animated.

She reached over and took my knurled, crooked left hand and gently kissed the deformed knuckles and scars.

"Carpenter told me about this," she said with moist eyes.

I smiled and said, "That is the best it has felt in years."

"Huh," Carpenter grunted, "Tol you he's a slick talkin' dude. Nex, he will tell some real war stories."

Lydia squeezed my hand and said, "I had better start cooking if the Silvers' and Jacobs' are going to be here."

I offered to help, but she refused, saying, "You guys go ahead with your drinking."

They both laughed when I retorted, "That is what I'm afraid of, Carpenter, where did you make this stuff?"

She giggled and her husband said, "Huh, jes lak a swabbie. Cain't drink man likker."

Soon, delicious odors were wafting from the pots and pans as Lydia quietly, and almost ghost-like, moved about the kitchen. Carpenter and I sat drinking with no real reason to talk. The corn whiskey had smoothed out, and I was able to drink his "man likker."

We were interrupted by the telephone, and Lydia said, "All right, Caleb, we are expecting a car with Iowa license plates. What do they look like?"

She listened and then continued, "O.K., those are the guests we are expecting. Thank you, Caleb. Tell Mary I was asking for her."

She looked in the door and said to us, "They just turned down our road. John is driving and Sarg is sitting in front."

Carpenter signaled for me to follow. We could hear the automobile, and he told me to stay on the porch. He took a position where the car and the road could be observed without the observer being seen. I wondered about the obvious precautions until the car stopped. Captain John Silvers got out smiling. He had not changed that much. Sergeant Jacobs was entirely bald but obviously the same strong man I had known years before. We were still shaking hands when our host materialized from his observation post.

Silvers laughed and said, "We are safe. Carpenter has recognized us."

The women had been ignored as we renewed our acquaintances, but as I was introduced they greeted me much the same way as Lydia.

Samantha Silvers kissed me and said, "I have heard a lot about you, Navy. It is time we met."

"Me too, Navy," Darlene Jacobs continued, " We have talked about you often. The Old Sarg has wondered many times what happened to you."

I answered, "Same here. When we left the hospital everyone disappeared. I have been afraid that you guys were dead. I don't know if you are aware, but your military records are buried with a red flag. The Navy did the same with me. What we did in Korea did not happen. I have tried to trace you. No one would discuss your records or explain the red flag. It is the same in my case."

Lydia came out and after greeting her guests, she directed us in for dinner.

As we sat down, Jacobs said, "The Josephs can't make it until about midnight."

Lydia picked up the telephone, dialed, and said, "Caleb, we are expecting an Oklahoma car sometime before midnight. Should be a man and a woman—after that—no one else."

She listened a moment, then, "Sure, tell Mary I will get her the recipe."

I remember thinking that my old buddy was living under strange circumstances, but he and his wife didn't appear to be under any pressure. It was an enjoyable meal, and no one mentioned Korea or Long Ball Kwong. We were old friends at a reunion trying to size and assess each other, after a number of years in my case. It was apparent that the Marines were able to maintain contact over the years, but today was my first contact with them since the end of 1950.

After dinner the men were dispatched to the family room. We settled in without much talk. The women were different. They were enjoying themselves as if no one had a problem. I thought that maybe they hadn't been told the reason for the unexpected reunion. But observing my companions and the obvious relationships with their wives, I discarded that notion. John Silvers broke the silence by asking what I had been doing over the years.

I answered, "Cap'n, you called it very close. I didn't go to the Marines, but did stay in the Navy for a while—worked for another agency for a few years—went to school—taught a college class, and thought everything had settled down for me. Then Senator Sam Martin asked me to work on his staff for a short time. Now the old codger wants me to go full time when the Senate goes into session after the first of the year. I'm not sure I want that—DC is a shit hole, but Sam will be hard to turn down. He and I go back a while. He is a good friend."

Silvers broke in with a grin, "What about Norma?"

"She married some jerk back home," I laughed. "He is a nice guy and a good friend. It is funny but after leaving Korea, she was only half as pretty, and just another girl when I got home."

"Sounds like most of us," Jacobs said, "I was in love with the only girl in the world. She introduced me to Darlene, and I couldn't wait to get off that date, so I could call Darlene."

The conversation livened and I found that John Silvers was a Department Head at the University of Iowa, and Jacobs was the Senior Military Advisor at Iowa State's ROTC unit. Jacobs also told us that Josephs had recently been elected to Oklahoma State Senate.

"Ah'm jest a pore old country hillbilly," Carpenter drawled among the hoots and laughter from us.

I looked around the room and said, "You may be a hillbilly, but a poor one doesn't own this house and pour good corn whiskey—much less have a watchman on a private road."

He grinned and said, "Jest good neighbors lookin' out for a pore old boy."

Lydia came in and said, "It's snowing and the Josephs have been in a wreck. They are fine. Major Sanders is bringing them in."

"Who is Major Sanders?" Jacobs asked.

"He is from the State Police," she answered.

I peered over my glass and said, "Jest a pore old country boy, hunh?"

Silvers and Jacobs laughed as Carpenter, with a straight face, muttered; "Jest good neighbors."

In a short time we heard an automobile coming up the road. Our host waved us back to our seats and went to greet the new arrivals. We heard the vehicle leave and soon were involved with greetings of Josephs and wife Linda. The other women appeared in command of the situation. Linda Josephs reminded me of a bird poised and ready for flight after being disturbed by a noise. She reminded me of a lady I had known many years before in the cold climes of the South Atlantic.

That lady was fingering her knife and said "Let him try. I hope he tries. I hope anyone tries." (Detachment X-Ray).

When he tried, she slashed his face, and later pinned one hand to the deck with the same knife.

Linda's most distinguishing feature was long red hair. Josephs was the same unflappable Marine who had raised his face out of the mud and joined others who were disobeying an order by the North Koreans. Under threat of death he had sat up cross-legged waiting for what was to come. He accepted congratulations for winning the state senate seat with a shrug of his shoulders.

Lydia Carpenter put us to bed at 0100, and there had been no mention of why we were together. I was tired and worn out, but sleep didn't come. Just as the clock struck 0200, I heard a faint noise outside. The moonlight was causing shadows among the trees and new snow. As I neared the window, I was sure that two armed men had crossed my view. Keeping watch from inside the room—sure enough there was movement by the garage. Four heavily armed men were talking and turned as Carpenter approached from the house. He spoke for a couple of minutes, and his visitors nodded, waved, and took off in four directions. *Guards for us? Probably not because this meeting came without notice and it must have something to do with good corn whisky or a hillbilly who could command chauffeur services from a State Police Major without having to ask. Who in the hell cares?*

I interrupted my own musing and went back to bed.

# Chapter 4

I awoke with a start—a common occurrence when one wakens in a strange room. It was 0530 and no sounds were coming from the other parts of the house. After a shower and shave, I still didn't hear anyone and made my way to the kitchen. The house was cold, and in the pre-dawn light there was a definite feel of impending bad weather. Lydia had left the coffeepot ready and in minutes the burbling sounds of the percolator broke the stillness of the mountain ranch house.

As I sat waiting, the central heating system came alive.

I was pouring my first cup of coffee when Lydia spoke from the door, "What service this is, I get up to find my coffee ready. How long have you been up?"

"Not long," I answered and handed her a steaming cup, "I cook too—what do you want for breakfast?"

Over her objections, I insisted and soon the house was permeated with the smell of frying country ham. We had finished eating before the first of the late risers came in. She took over the toaster, and I noticed that Carpenter was not in the kitchen.

I started to speak, and Lydia said softly, "He will be here soon."

She had hardly finished speaking when he walked in, looked at me, and said, "OK, Messcook, gi me mah breafas,"

The Carpenters exchanged looks and he shrugged his shoulders. I couldn't help but wonder how he got out without me hearing—and why he was out. Later that morning the news broke that Major Sanders of the State Police had been ambushed and killed by unknown assailants. Our hosts weren't surprised at the announcement and didn't participate in the speculative conversation.

Without any suggestion the men dressed for the outdoors, and helped

Carpenter with chores. At 0800 John Silvers suggested we go for a walk. Carpenter led us down to the river and turned upstream. Snow had started falling—I watched the flakes settle and wondered about our possible mission. Did any of us want to expose ourselves by killing a man who was expected to vie for the leadership of the largest nation on earth? Was a wartime experience one that should cause a meeting like this? If I had left the hitchhiker in the rain—we would not be here. If I hadn't heard Carpenter in the Larkspur Tavern—we wouldn't be here. Maybe I should leave—they should not be involved—they were leaders in their communities, with family responsibilities.

None of the questions had been answered when we entered a small clearing. Without a word Carpenter took a seat on a fallen tree. The rest of us explored the river for a few minutes. Josephs was the last one to take a seat. As he did, all eyes turned to me and I passed around a number of photographs.

While they were passing around the pictures I said, "This Hsu Dong Ping of China."

Josephs spoke up, "Lot of people think he is going to be the next Premier of China."

"I know," I said, "But take a good look. Did we know him at one time as Major Long Ball Kwong?" This caused a stir and I continued, "John, you knew him best. Is it Long Ball?"

Silvers responded, "It has been a long time, but it sure could be. Yes, it's got too be him."

Carpenter retorted, "It's him."

The other two weren't sure and nodded when Silvers suggested I tell what I knew.

I related the facts, including my confusion and the conflicting thoughts that I had had about Dong Ping.

In continuing, I said, "I haven't confronted him yet, but the son-of-a-bitch knows that I suspect there is no need for his interpreter. I have made it a point to speak directly to him and watch any response of understanding. He doesn't know who I am, yet, but our confrontations are becoming more and more adversarial. He has run a background check, but my records don't mention our little sojourn in Korea. I have no doubts because the name Long Ball came to me without prompting of any kind."

I stopped for a few minutes and then said, "On our way up here, I was beginning to wish I hadn't heard Carpenter in the tavern. You guys, with your positions, shouldn't be involved in this kind of crap."

Jacobs piped up, "Screw you, Navy. I want to be included if you are after that prick."

Silvers, always in charge said, "Let's not get hasty. Before we do anything we have to be sure this is Long Ball. Navy, can you get us into position to see him?"

I indicated I could get them in viewing range and he continued, "If it is Long Ball, then what happens?"

Carpenter started to say something. I stopped him by placing my hand on his shoulder, and said, "I told that bastard, the day before we escaped, that some day I would gut him. I think I've found him."

Carpenter and Jacobs stated that they agreed with me that he should be killed.

Josephs spoke up, he simply said, "I want to pull the trigger."

He surprised us with his statement that he wanted to be the triggerman.

With all of us agreeing that we should kill Kwong, Silvers sealed it, "That's it then. Navy, when can we see him for a positive identification?"

I replied, "The next session of the trade commission convenes on Wednesday morning at the U.N. Building. They'll break at 1045, and Mr. Dong Ping always comes out the front door then down the steps at the middle handrail to his limousine—which will start moving when he appears at the top of the steps. There are four aides who will escort him to his transportation. Two get in before him and two after."

"Hunh," grunted Carpenter, "Good thing he picked up the hitch-hiker or he woulda killed 'em hisself."

No one seemed confused by Carpenter's use of pronouns. It was a silent group who started back down the river. Just before we got to the house, I broke the silence again with my reservations about their getting involved. They would have none of it, and the conversation turned to them ribbing me about needing protection again by the Marines. The good-natured ribbing didn't last long. A man's life was being threatened by our decision, which in retrospect, was as cold as the local weather. That decision would likely lead to other deaths, with the possibilities of wrecking many families—

ours included—yet none of us appeared to have second thoughts or the lack of resolve.

The drifting spits of snow had increased to a full and heavy fall. The yards and fields were completely blanketed when we left the tree line by the river. The temperature had dropped below freezing, and the clock chimed ten as we entered the yard. The chores were finished and none of us appeared ready to go inside but all wanted to be alone. Without a word, Carpenter left in a four-wheel drive vehicle. Silvers, Jacobs, and Josephs took different paths to the river.

Left alone, I took a walk around the Carpenter home place and explored the barns, tack room, and other outbuildings. The wood shed was near the house and the wood yard was full. Someone had left a splitting maul in a block of wood. I freed the maul and started splitting the blocks sitting upright. The first few swings of the tool caused the features of long Ball Kwong too shatter as the wood fell apart. Soon the exertion of unaccustomed labor took over and all thoughts of what was likely to come, faded. After splitting a few blocks, I removed the parka and steadily and mindlessly continued swinging the maul. The wood was clean, and with the low temperature, would fall apart at the point of impact with the blade. I vaguely remember that Lydia Carpenter came out and approached the wood yard. She stopped and watched a few minutes, turned and went back inside. The snow continued to fall and every so often, a muted laugh could be heard from the kitchen.

Slowly my awareness returned; I was surprised to see the other men stacking the split wood. Each moved as if alone—two of them collided and moved apart without speaking. I was splitting the last block when the attitude was broken by Samantha Silvers' call to lunch. That broke the spell because we relaxed and were chatting as we stacked the last few sticks in the woodshed. Most of our conversation was about the weather. Snow was drifting and there were four or five inches covering the region. The wind was beginning to blow and the porch thermometer was hovering close to zero. I predicted a major storm, which brought some laughs and was confirmed by the women. The forecast was calling for twenty-four to thirty-six inches before the weather front cleared the mountains.

At lunch we enjoyed the chatter and gossip. Every once in a while I would catch Lydia Carpenter studying one of us with a questioning expression. She had caught the undertones of our morning actions. First, the walk by the river, and our solitary retreats, followed by a frenzy of work—was enough to call many people's attention. We had a long way to go in controlling our own emotions as we continued plans involving the next Premier of the People's Republic of China.

I caught Lydia's eyes and smiled. The look was held as if those piercing black eyes were trying to search my soul. I maintained the contact and they softened into a smile. Samantha Silvers also picked up on the undercurrents and started to ask a question. I interrupted her by inquiring if preparations were needed for heavy weather. Samantha looked at John for a few moments, and they shrugged their shoulders as if too say we will let it pass for another time.

Lydia asked that we run safety lines to the outbuildings. The ropes were already made up and the rings for tie down were installed on the buildings. With the deteriorating weather, it took us most of the afternoon to run the lines, bring in wood, and feed the livestock. The visibility was so low that at a hundred yards the barn was a dim outline. I was on the back porch waiting for Josephs and he materialized out of the snow less than fifty yards from the house. Unless the weather cleared by Sunday, there would be no way we could be in New York by Wednesday. On this Friday afternoon, there were no indications that the storm would clear.

After the chores we came back into the house, very much in need of hot drinks

Darlene Jacobs got a laugh when she handed her husband a cup and said, "Here, Honey, drink this like a good boy and then I will really warm you up."

He said with great expression, "If you are ready for that I don't need a cup of coffee."

She archly replied, "No, no, I was suggesting a drink of Carpenter's white lightning."

Silvers said to Lydia, "It's bad out there. Heard from Carpenter?"

"He will be along," Lydia replied, "As a matter of fact he's on the way."

I don't know how she knew because I was getting my second drink when the growl of an engine was heard over the storm noises.

The Sniper came in and before removing his coat; he looked at his wife and asked, "Ever thin awright?"

She responded, "Yes, these guys rigged the lines, fed the livestock, and even split and stacked your firewood. They have been working hard all day."

"'Bout time," he growled, "All been happenin' is them eating mah food and drinkin' mah likker. See, hits mos gone."

I caught a couple of looks between the Carpenters as they communicated without speaking. He shrugged slightly, and she invited us to dinner. We moved toward the dining room, and she was smiling but her eyes gave away the worry she was feeling. As the others settled around the dining table, the Carpenters remained at the sink talking quietly.

I moved toward them and said, "Carpenter, you sure have a gorgeous wife."

In a whisper I asked, "You folks have a problem?"

"I sho do," Carpenter responded to the comment and question at the same time.

"Need any help?" I whispered, and covered it by hugging Lydia.

The other couples watched and were amused and were unaware of the "might" from Carpenter.

The meal was enjoyable. We were relaxed and Josephs started tales about his adventure into politics. His wife no longer appeared nervous and for the first time was taking an active part in the conversation. She had an infectious giggle, and all of us were being entertained by the Oklahomans. During a lag in the conversation Carpenter asked me to help bring in some firewood, and he invited the other men to mess cook. I knew that the woodbin had been filled but made no comment. When we were alone, he offered me a snub-nosed .38 special. I shook my head and showed him the automatic that was a holdover from Detachment X-Ray. My old friend showed no reaction except a nod and a shrug. He dropped the revolver in my parka that was hanging at the back door. Maybe they did have problems!

At 2130 the Josephs went to bed, followed shortly by the Jacobs'

Samantha Silvers broke the silence, "You guys ready to tell us what is going on?"

A few minutes passed and John took his wife's hand and gently said, "Not yet, babe, not yet. It could be nothing."

Lydia spoke up; "We want to know before you take any type of drastic action."

Silvers simply said, "We will tell you."

That ended the conversation until Samantha asked her husband to take her to bed. Then Lydia identified their nemesis to me as a family named Gorman, who had been feuding with the Carpenters for years.

# Chapter 5

The Carpenters and I sat without talking, and they appeared to be waiting for someone or something to happen. I started for the bedroom but was caught by Carpenter's action. He stood and said that someone was coming and headed for the front door. He asked me to go to the garage through the back door. It wasn't until I opened the door that I heard faint engine noises. The snow was still falling, and on the way to the garage I realized that the years had taken their toll. There was no comfort from the feel and weight of the weapons, and the fear was real, even with unknown circumstances. I wasn't doing any good trying to convince myself that Carpenter was waiting to greet a friend. Another concern was that we were waiting for an enemy to arrive, and there had been no advance warning by the people on the road.

I slipped into the garage and watched two snowmobiles glide into the darkened yard. Three men got off the vehicles and were surprised by floodlights that lit up the scene. Two of the men were big, but the third was huge—made larger by heavy, outdoor clothing. Carpenter had their attention from the shadows, and I could see the glint of his gun as he spoke to them. I heard the voice of the leader and it was surprisingly high-pitched for such a mountain of a man.

He said, "Hell son, invite us in so we don't freeze."

Carpenter indicated the garage, and I backed in behind some machinery. The fear had left; I was waiting for the action to start. It was apparent that our visitors were a family. The huge man appeared to be about sixty years of age, and as it turned out, his sons were twenty-five and thirty. The older man overwhelmed everyone by his size. That could have been a factor in

Carpenter's mistake. He stumbled as he came through the door. The two younger men were like cats. One grabbed the shotgun, and the other slammed my friend into the fender of a four-wheel drive vehicle. The fear and nervousness had vanished, and I was looking forward to the confrontation because they weren't aware that I was in the garage. On Detachment X-Ray missions, we were always looking to surprise and ambush without any notice.

I tensed as the Mountain Man drew his revolver, but he let it drop to his side, and said, "Now that's better—we can be comfortable."

He continued addressing his captive, "Son, I knew your daddy and his daddy before him. Our families have always had our differences, but we got along."

He smiled and continued, "But now son, I can't abide by what has happened in the past couple of days. What have you to say?"

Carpenter did not respond, just calmly returned the gaze of his adversary. One of the younger men restlessly started to say something, but just a motion from the father stilled the protest. During this interruption Carpenter sat up on the fender of the vehicle. This apparently satisfied them because it put their captive at more of a disadvantage, but then they aligned Carpenter's new position, all their backs were to me.

"Now son," the big man spoke again, "I can abide what happened to the State Policeman. He was on his own. No one told him to do that, but what happened today—I can't put up with. If I let it pass I'll have all sorts of problems. Son, I like you, so I'm going to give you a chance." One of the brothers snorted, but the older man continued, "You move out of Larkspur and Evergreen County, and I will forget it. My boys don't like that. They want to take you out tonight, but I am willing to take your word that you'll leave—your word is good. Tell me now that you will do as I say, and we will get on our machines and leave."

He chuckled, "Of course, after a drink of that good whiskey."

Carpenter had kept his silence, and I slowly straightened up.

He saw me and spoke, "Whut happens if I don' leave?"

The big man laughed, "Why son, I'll let the boys take you out, and I hate to think of that pretty girl becoming a widow woman. She… "

I interrupted him by slamming the heavy automatic against his back and said, "Drop the gun or I'll blow your back bone through your belly."

Then, "Carpenter if those two clowns move a muscle say 'shoot', and I'll blast this tub of guts."

The surprise was complete, and when the gun dropped I kicked it behind me. One of the brothers started to move, and I told his father what he would get if his sons moved any more. He motioned for them to be still. Carpenter casually slid down from his perch—regained the shotgun and moved further into the garage so we would have a safe crossfire if things started happening. I backed away and tapped the youngest brother on the shoulder and ordered him to assume the position for a search. His brother started to bluster and paid for it by getting the automatic alongside the head.

I heard Carpenter say, almost gently, "Don move Mistah Gorman, don move."

We restrained them by pulling their parkas down to the elbows and buttoned the coats. The younger men were ordered to lace their fingers behind their backs and lean forward against the vehicle. Then I turned to their father and called him 'fat man' and the oldest boy started to take exception, and Carpenter slapped him alongside the head with the shotgun—both sides of his head were bleeding because he was more brave than smart. There was a noise outside that caused tension too rise, but it was Lydia and two friends. The one named Caleb offered an apology for allowing the trespassers to get around the checkpoint. Carpenter just waved it off and told them to forget it.

With the two extra men, the prisoners were allowed to stand straight and pull up the heavy coats. Carpenter asked Lydia to take me back into the house because according to him, I was in the way and would probably wet my pants. I stopped at the door and looked back at the Gorman men. The boys were angry, embarrassed, and scowling at me.

Their father's face split into a wide grin, and he said to me, "Son, I don't know where you came from, but I like you. So you better leave when the weather clears—and Son, don't come back."

I acknowledged his clear, friendly warning with a finger to the brow and followed my hostess back into the house. All of the other guests were up and wondering what was happening. Lydia offered no explanations nor did her husband. He had returned after the snowmobiles roared into life and left the yard. The guests were told that the trouble stemmed from a friendly old mountain feud.

Carpenter looked at me with a raised eyebrow and asked, "Wheah you been? You din't learn things like dat in a swabbie school."

That was all he would say about the incident. I was surprised to see that the action lasted about forty-five minutes. It felt like two hours—the excitement was drained and I went to bed.

My last conscious thoughts were, *What in the hell is Carpenter into— this wasn't a friendly mountain feud. The Gormans were ready to kill. Oh well, when he wants me to know—he will tell me."*

I awakened with a start, soaked in sweat, just before the rifle butt hit my hand. It took a few minutes to sort out the confusion, and remember that I was in the Carpenter's home. The confusion was caused by the dream. I lay there looking out into bright sunlight. The snow sparkled and glistened, but the dream kept me from enjoying the scenery. The dream had occurred before, but this time the Gormans were my tormentors and not Long Ball Kwong and his soldiers. Finally, everything was sorted out. It was Saturday morning—we were snowed in—and I am supposed meet Senator Martin on Monday morning. We were planning to work on the final response for the U. S. Trade Delegation. Murmurs of conversation drifted in from the kitchen.

The smell of food and coffee helped clear my mind. I received hoots and comments about my late appearance, upon entering the kitchen.

"Is there a way out of here?" I asked, attacking the food. "I am supposed to be in New York on Monday."

Lydia said, "I will call the airport."

She left for a few minutes and returned with, "Charlie Daniels will pick you up about noon. He is one of our local helicopter pilots."

The morning passed quickly. Our hosts offered no explanations for the night before, and no one questioned them. The clock was striking noon when we heard the beat of helicopter rotors. Carpenter agreed to take care my car until I could pick it up at a later date. The next few minutes were taken up with good byes.

Carpenter, Silvers, and I walked into the yard, and the Captain said, "Navy, we will be in New York sometime Tuesday evening, weather permitting."

"Call me when you get in," I responded, "Don't identify yourself on the telephone, and I should know where you can see our friend. If I don't say differently, it will be on the front steps of the United Nation's building."

Silvers turned back after shaking hands.

Carpenter stopped before reaching the helicopter and said, "Mistah Gorman is runnin' dope—blowed up two stashes. The Majuh was takin' dirty pictures with young 'uns."

He didn't wait for a reply or to shake hands. I wasn't surprised. It would have been a surprise had he taken different actions. The flight to the airport was uneventful. The pilot refused any payment and he stayed close by. When my flight was called, he acknowledged my parting salute with a slight grin. I had a feeling that he had been told to make sure I boarded safely.

# Chapter 6

Senator Martin's staff was busy Monday and Tuesday preparing the final statement to the Chinese. The Senator, himself, could hardly speak because an attack of the flu had left him with a very sore throat. Tuesday morning I brought him the final draft and was told to be prepared to read it Wednesday morning. I hated to see my old friend sick, but it would give me a pretext, or reason to speak in front of Hsu Dong Ping. Without some justification I couldn't accuse him of being Long Ball Kwong because his staff wouldn't allow me to approach. This situation wasn't all bad because I wanted him in a quandary before seeing John Silvers and the others. He might not recognize any of us, but he would know his old classmate from the University of Chicago. Shortly after arriving in my room Tuesday evening, Silvers called with "we are here" and hung up without comment when he heard that 1030 would be a good time. I had no reason to believe anyone was listening, but a recording at a later date would certainly have to be included, with many other facts, before the conversation would have meaning.

The Chairman of the United States Delegation greeted everyone with a long rambling statement and finally closed, saying, "Ladies and Gentlemen, Senator Martin's statement will denote the position of the United States. Senator Martin is with us in body, but we've finally got him. He can't talk."

The Chairman bowed to the Chinese and continued, "For our friends from the Peoples Republic of China, it isn't often that Senator Martin is speechless."

The attempt at humor caught well with the Americans and a few of the Chinese. Most of them had puzzled looks on their faces—they didn't understand what the laughter was about. It was decided to hear the Chinese position, and then I would read Martin's statement into the record.

The Chairman of the Chinese Delegation began speaking. And I caught and held Dong Ping's gaze, until he looked away. Chin Hau noticed the by-play and whispered to Chow Ling who immediately left the room. The aide returned as the delegate was closing his statement. A slight negative nod was directed at the old Chinese Statesman. There was no chance for me to consider what might be going on because I was introduced and directed to read Sam's statement for the record.

When the paper was read I looked up and continued, "Ladies and Gentlemen, if you would allow me a few seconds, as a staff member, I would express our appreciation to our opposites from the Peoples Republic of China. They, like the delegates, came well prepared, showed us every courtesy and I feel that both nations gained through the mutual respect and the understanding the two staffs achieved."

I had allowed my eyes to rest on Dong Ping's aide as I spoke. Then acknowledging Chin Hau, I continued, "If it hadn't been for the good people on both sides, there could've been times when we would have found ourselves between the proverbial rock and hard place." I casually flexed the scarred hand before continuing. "But each time a problem surfaced, a long ball was hit, and in all my years in the Navy…"

Dong Ping's earphones falling interrupted me. He had recognized me, that I was certain. The interpreter apologized and I bowed in his direction, while holding the eyes of Long Ball Kwong. His eyes were the same as they had been, so many years before, when Long Ball Kwong said, "Navy, when I see you next, we will have a long talk, and I know your name, rank, and number."

I knew that I had been promised a bad time and his expression let it be known that I would be a guest for a long time. One of the saving graces though, was the hint of fear at my promise; "I will gut you some day, you son-of-a-bitch."

On this occasion, I was pleased to see the same fear light his eyes. I left the room as the final comments were being made with announcements where and when the following meetings would be convened. At the door I looked back and smiled at him as he quickly avoided my look. Chow Ling was waiting in the hall with an appraising, questioning stare, which flashed into a smile when I offered my hand. Without a word we turned for the front door of the building. As we walked through the door, John Silvers was standing near a group of tourists who were listening to a guide. There was no sign of recognition between us as his eyes swept past the front door. Dong Ping's party appeared, and the future Premier of China rocked back on his heels when he saw Silvers. The recovery was immediate, and he spoke to an aide who in turn spoke into a radio. The party's pace quickened, and Ping's eyes followed Silvers, who casually glanced at the group and then turned back to the tourist guide. I looked down the steps and ten or twelve Chinese were alertly closing the escort party. Two of them actually brushed Carpenter as he ambled up the steps. Ping's shoulders tightened. He had recognized the sniper. By this time, the entire party was rushing toward the vehicles waiting at the curb. One of them surprised me. A tall, very attractive, woman reporter was desperately trying to question the Delegate. Her questions were being ignored, but she was not ignoring the pistol in her purse—another, but unexpected, aide to Ping. I remember thinking that she may be the most dangerous of all. Ping and his guards walked between Jacobs and Josephs, and his head snapped back and forth between the two casual tourists.

Chow was taking in all the moves of the different groups. He didn't rise to my bait when I commented that the future Premier seemed to be in a hurry. His only comment was after I asked if the Delegate had seen a ghost. He said that he was wondering about that also, and turned toward Chin Hau who had appeared at the door. Sam led his colleagues out. No one was aware of anything out of place.

Sam started looking around when a reporter said, "Senator, we have a definite impression that someone or something has caused alarm for the Chinese."

The Senator, of course, had no clue why the reporters were making such statements.

During the short delay with the media, I watched Silvers and Carpenter get into an automobile—Jacobs and Josephs were picked up by another vehicle. They were traveling different directions and no one paid any attention. We had pulled it off, and I was sure no one could connect the five of us— except for Long Ball Kwong. Would he be willing to tell the world of our connection? I didn't think so, and we were betting on his silence. I couldn't help smiling when thinking about his peace of mind, or what he must be thinking.

Sam Martin had invited his staff to dinner before departing for Washington, D. C. Susan Bonnet greeted me at the elevator, and we made whispered plans for the evening, if time and circumstances allowed. Susan had become a very good friend, and in the short time we had known each other, at times, she became a very special friend. The elevator doors opened and the tall, strikingly beautiful Chinese television reporter who carried a gun in her purse greeted us. Susan introduced her as Tsu Pei Li. She flashed a gorgeous smile with a proffered hand.

Beautiful Chinese women in native dress are the sexist women in the world. This lady filled all the bills. She was tall, close to six feet, and the dress fit like a glove—not a rumple, line, or bulge was apparent except where bulges are meant to be. The dress was buttoned to the throat, but did not hide, in fact accentuated the rise of her breasts. The green and gold fabric was broken only at the sides of the skirt—as she moved, a long expanse of honey colored thighs were exposed. She and Susan were chatting and I was probably drooling. When we approached the bottom floor, she turned to me and asked if I would sit for an interview on Chinese television. I tried getting out of the offer by telling her I would be on the way to DC on an early morning flight. My excuse didn't take. She said she was making plans to fly to our Capital City.

We parted at the elevator door, and I was thinking as she walked away that if she were carrying a gun in that outfit, it would have to be very, very small. Susan took my arm and accused me of drooling and then stated that the reporter was a gorgeous woman. She almost choked when I stated that I hadn't noticed. Before we arrived at the dining room door, Cliff Grogan, of Senator Jeremiah Cotton's staff called to me, "Hey, let's get together in a couple of days."

Grogan had joined the Tennessee Senator's staff just before the delegation left for New York. I knew something that probably not many would have any need of knowing. A few years back, Cliff Grogan had been pointed out as a CIA operative—I knew him and he wasn't aware of my knowledge.

"Sure are popular, aren't we?" Susan quipped, as I held the door.

"You bet, lady," I retorted, "You walk with me and you walk in tall cotton."

She answered by giving a long sigh and an exaggerated grimace. Her response didn't change my thoughts that in less than ten minutes I had received invitations to meet and talk to the Chinese Secret Service and the United States Central Intelligence Agency.

*Got to walk carefully in this company,* I mused.

The arrival of the Senator's party caused a stir. Sam was his jovial self even with a croaking voice. He and Dorothy were in company of Mr. and Madam Chin Hau. All of the staffers were introduced to the Chinese statesman and his wife. The youthful Americans received effusive greetings by this sprightly couple. I had pegged Chin Hau to be in his seventies or eighties, but his wife could be anywhere between forty and ninety. We stood as they approached.

Chin Hau said, "This is the one I have been telling you about."

We broke up as Madam Hau looked at Susan and replied, "Yes, I can see why. She is lovely."

She looked at me with twinkling eyes and said, "Oh, you refer to this one, the one who was kind to our people."

To me she continued, "For that kindness, we thank you."

She turned her attention to the young people, and her husband was smiling as he watched her capture the Martin staff. Sam Martin, as noted before, was a good politician. He asked me to tell the visitors to have a good time and there would be no speeches. They responded with a standing ovation. Chin Hau commented that it was too bad all staffs were not as enthusiastic. He looked directly at me when he said that some of his people were pulling in all directions. When I asked the problem, he offered one of his enigmatic shrugs and dropped the subject.

During the meal, Dorothy Martin informed the table that Chin Hau had been posted to Washington as his country's Ambassador. Amid congratulations and welcomes we were somewhat surprised to learn that, Sam Martin had been invited to accompany the Ambassador when he presented his credentials to the President. I remember thinking that "an old turnip salesman" was planting a new crop. The planting continued. Susan and I were invited to visit after they were ready to receive guests. Madam

Hau centered her attentions on me with an invitation to discuss western governments. She continued the conversation by asking for my favorite contemporary political author, and then said it was common knowledge that I was a Political Science Professor. I was somewhat surprised, she had stated a fact, but I was willing to bet that not over five people knew that I was a teacher. I had requested no public attention because Political Scientists were a dime a dozen. That was probably true but I didn't want attention because I didn't want to become well known in DC circles. I was momentarily taken aback by her knowledge.

My question was: "Who informed her of my background?"

On her request I said, "I recommend Alan Drury as a contemporary writer. He is a media analyst turned novelist, who had written a great body of work about the United States Government. Sometimes, he's not kind to your country, and never is he kind to Russia, and he's very critical of the news media. His first book of the series is *Advise and Consent,* centered on the United States Senate."

Madam, Hau smiled and said, "I will obtain his books."

Then she leaned closer and for my benefit only, she whispered, "I too am not very kind to the Russian Bear, and your news media is for the shits."

I suppose my mouth fell open in surprise as this personification of Chinese gentility straightened with a slight smile. Her eyes were twinkling with amusement at my obvious reactions. I was going to like Madam Hau, while realizing that she was a brilliant lady who was representing her country. I would have to be very careful around two turnip salesmen.

The Martins and Haus left at midnight. Susan and I remained as hosts and instructed the band to wind down by 0200. Later at her door, she asked if I wanted to come in for a nightcap.

I said, "Friend, if I do, there will be an attempt at seduction."

I put my hands at her waist and she leaned back, laughed quietly, and replied, "Friend, go to your room but remember that thought for a later date."

As she entered the door, she leaned back out and said in a stage whisper, "We'll see who seduces whom."

The telephone was ringing as I entered my room.

"Yes," I said into the mouthpiece.

I recognized Joseph's voice, "We are home," and he broke the connection.

I was packed but took a second look around the room. Nothing was missing, but I had a definite feeling that someone had been there. The bedspread was wrinkled on one corner, an unused drawer was slightly open, and there was an extra click on the telephone when I called the desk for a taxi. A feeling of paranoia slowly spread.

Was I being watched? If so, by who? Why?

The ride to the airport was uneventful. As far as I could see, no one was following the taxi very closely. My feeling of paranoia had eased until we reached the airport. The driver was oriental, and in my mind he was Chinese. His name tag read Tony Agowa, which probably was Japanese, but in my state of mind—who knows?

At the check-in counter, there were no Japanese taxi drivers, but even from a distance, with car coat and slacks, Tsu Pei Li was gorgeous as she proceeded down the loading ramp. I presented my ticket and said, "That sure was a whole bunch of pretty woman."

The agent grinned and answered, "She sure is. The aisle seat next to her is vacant."

I looked at his name tag and said, "You are a good man, David Manning, and you should go far."

He refused the offered gratuity and with a leer, said, "Good luck."

The plane ride from Kennedy to Dulles was short but enjoyable. Tsu Pei Li appeared to be pleasantly surprised when I took the seat next to her. She led a lively conversation during holding and take off. When the plane was airborne, I jacked my seat back to take advantage of the lovely view without craning my neck. She pushed her seat back also, but obligingly kept it in front of me. The conversation lagged and she leaned back and closed her eyes. What a sight—she had raven black hair, smooth, honey colored skin with no blemish even under close scrutiny. Her nose was small, well formed, and set perfectly, above lips which appeared moist, yet, uncolored except for natural beauty. The rise of her breast filled a western styled shirt that showed no wrinkles or bulges as it covered a flat, firm belly. Her slacks were as smooth, and caressed the slight curve of her body down too long, well formed legs. She shifted position and the buttons on the shirt were strained. From my vantage point there was no evidence of sag in her breast line. A gap between buttons indicated no bra, and an inviting jiggle would occur when the aircraft encountered turbulence.

The fascinating daydream ended with the pilot's landing instructions. She declined my offer for a ride, indicating she would be met. We set an interview date as the plane rolled to the landing gate, and we walked through the terminal with her still in lively conversation. For a newcomer in this country, she was certainly appeared comfortable in her surroundings. I remember thinking that she had already been to Washington before this visit, and I wondered if the plane ride had in some way been staged for my benefit. If so, she was certainly succeeded in getting my attention. A car was waiting for me, but I dawdled putting away the luggage and watched as she was met. Her car passed as I entered mine, and I was sure that her driver was friend Chow Ling. I instructed my driver to keep the Chinese vehicle in view, without taking chances in traffic.

In a short time the driver said, "He's got turn signals on. Want me to follow him?"

"No," I answered, "Just watch for his exit.'

Moments later, I was informed that the automobile, a gray Buick, was heading south toward Richmond.

We pulled into a loading zone at the senate office building, and the driver was instructed to take the luggage to my apartment.

Before I could leave, the driver said, "I took the Buick's license number. Want me to trace it?"

It was the first time that I was aware that the driver was female. She was looking at me with green eyes, surrounded by freckles, and close-cropped red hair.

She grinned broadly and her eyes sparkled with excitement, when I answered, "You bet. Be casual and don't make any waves. If you get the information, bring it to me."

I hoped she would take me at my word and not call the office until it had been swept for bugs. Paranoid? I suppose so. It was early in the game, and the people I would be facing "got up early and stayed late." Another problem, I didn't know who all the players might be in this game. It was early for Sam Martin's Saturday staff to be working. I expected to be alone, but there was a light in John Moody's office—nope, not Moody's office—Sam had been on the telephone—John's name was off and mine was on. I had told the Senator that I would only take the job on an interim basis. He had evidently paid a lot of attention to me. That was Sam though—full speed ahead at all times.

I shoved the door open and heard an irritable female voice, "Some bitch."

Sally Gordon, Moody's secretary, was at her desk with boxes and papers strewn over the floor. A broken bra strap had caused the expletive. She had her shirt unbuttoned and was trying to repair the damage.

I stopped her with, "Not a bad sight to start a new day."

She recovered after a moment of confusion, and retorted, "Whut I git fer buyin' cheap shit."

I was surprised at her language and grammar because of John Moody's bent for excellence.

Looking around at the confusion, I asked, "What are you doing?"

"Packin' my junk," she answered.

"Going to work for John?" I asked?

"Nope; jest gitten outen yore way."

"You are not in my way," I said, and asked, "You want to stay and work for me?"

Her eyes filled, as she turned away and mumbled with a trembling voice, "Yes sir."

"Well, get this shit cleaned up," I said, going into my office.

She paid me with a delightful smile when I turned back and gruffly said, "Then bring me all the crap that Moody has piled up for me." In a few minutes she came in with an armload of files.

In her phony and exaggerated dialect she said, "Dis is whut Mistah Moody lef fo yuh. An' I sho do thank you fo lettin' me stay. Ah'm a hard wukker."

She broke up when I answered, "Well all I want out of you is good hard work and some poontang every day."

I thought for a short while she would go into convulsions but she continued the charade, "My Lor, you mus be sum man, but you ain't neber seen muh boy frien'. He de biggest gol durn Marine you eber seen."

With her crap I wasn't sure what her skills were but soon found a load of files that had been put together and maintained by an expert. The most pressing piece of work was at the top of the stack—offering some insight as to the depth of my new secretary. It was reports that Sam Martin had scheduled to deliver at an Armed Forces Committee hearing. I picked up where Moody had left off after reading his instructions and recommendations. At different times I was conscious of added noise when members of the staff arrived for the day. The report was just finished, except for final typing, when the intercom phone rang. Susan Bonnet asked me to come to her office and without further explanation broke the connection. Sam Martin had a busy staff. I wasn't aware that they had arrived in such force. Sally Gordon grumbled about having too much work on her desk, when I gave her the report to be typed.

Susan was sitting at her desk and motioned for me not too talk. She led, and I followed, in an inane conversation as we inspected her office. She had found three bugs—one in a dried flower arrangement, one in the telephone, and another by the coat rack. During our search a fourth one was found over the door adjoining the Senator's office. Someone was very interested in what went on in Sam Martin's domain. I suggested we go to the lunchroom for a cup of coffee. Susan asked about my plans for a secretary and laughingly approved my decision to keep Sally Gordon. John Moody had tried for two years to clean up the street talk vocabulary—but to no avail. Susan further assured me, I would have the best secretary on the Hill. That was proven somewhat, when I received the typed report, which wasn't due until the following Monday. I tried to find a mistake in the typing—there was none.

We were discussing the office bugs when Susan warned me of an impending visitor. Cliff Grogan joined us, and after a couple of minutes suggested that we needed too talk. I offered to come to his office, but he insisted on joining me and left before any other suggestions could be offered. Without knowledge of Grogan's identity, Susan was concerned about Senator Cotton's staffer talking in front of hidden microphones. I was sure that friend Grogan wanted me too talk in front of the same devices. My office was also bugged, with some effort; I found three microphones, while reviewing the report for Sam's visit before the Armed Services Committee. The idea of a notification to the Senator of the devices caused some amusing thoughts. Someone was in for a rough going. I expected a number of Agency Chiefs would have some uncomfortable moments in the coming days.

My secretary had an excellent product with the completed report. There were no holes in the document, and it sure was smooth reading. I couldn't find a mistake, and it occurred to me that she might have edited some of my work. I stepped to the door of Sally's office to let her know that her morning work was complete. The outside door opened and the "biggest gol durn Marine" that I had ever seen was entering. He was a big man, and the Marine dress uniform gave him monstrous proportions.

She introduced him as Terry Hardison.

Looking him up and down I asked, "Is this the puny ass Marine you have been talking about?"

This gave her an opening, "Yas suh, an I tol him all dem bad things you bin saying tuh me. Honey, yuh gotta perteck me. Dis mean ole man say he gon git in mah britches."

I told Terry that I expected him to keep her line and make her stop begging for something she couldn't have. He went along with the banter and even sided with me—blaming her for all of his problems.

They left laughing when I said, "Get her out of here Sarg, she fouled up this report so badly, I will have to retype the whole thing."

I was exploring my office when Susan Bonnet came in with an inquiring look. I held up two fingers and pointed to the telephone and desk. We found two other devices—one in a lamp by the couch—the other one over the door to the secretarial office. There were three obvious ones in the Senator's office, and I was betting there would be more cleverly hidden. I turned up the radio and moved to the center of the room before whispering that Sam was going to have a stroke when he found about all the bugging. She smiled at the thought. I suggested she call Sam at a pay phone after leaving the office. She started to turn away but I stopped her by taking her in my arms. Her arms came up and locked around my neck. We kissed and before we broke I run my hands down across her buttocks and lifted her skirt. She responded with a harder and deeper kiss before drawing away.

She whispered, "It's not the right time."

After regaining my composure I reminded her in a normal voice that Cliff Grogan would be stopping for a visit. She already knew, but I wanted those listening too know that other people knew of my plans. My door had been left open and promptly at 1600 Cliff Grogan entered the outer office. He acknowledged my wave and a pointed invitation to coffee. We sat for a few seconds, after he was seated, with appraising looks at each other. He broke the silence by asking a number of questions about Senator Martin's plans for handling future trade delegation meeting. I wouldn't comment on any of his suggestions and reminded him that Senator Cotton was the Chairman and would be filing the final report from the meetings in New York. I suggested that any meetings planned would be in the report.

Then he changed subjects—my feeling about the Chinese? I told him that they were just another group of politicians and suggested that he may know more about them than I would. He registered some surprise but didn't pursue my comments.

Instead, he asked, "What about, uh, what's his name? The one who is going to be the next Premier."

"Tsu Dong Ping," I responded.

"Yeah, that's the one. What do you think about him?"

"We don't have much on him. Senator Martin told our staff to concentrate on Chin Hau," I answered.

That stopped him momentarily, and we discussed other things concerning the Senators. Then he abruptly asked if I thought Dong Ping would become Premier of China.

With a shrug, I said, "You probably know more about that than I do."

He was silent for a long moment, then, "You have mentioned a couple things which I might know. What are you talking about?"

I laughed and said, "Hell, Cliff, I've known all along who you are. About three years ago, you were pointed out to me at Penn State. That was the year the CIA sent out field agents for recruiting. Oh, and by the way, you better tell your boss that Sam Martin knows about the bugging of these offices."

He tried to deny his way through, but clammed up when I called the security office and ordered an immediate electronic sweep of the suite. Grogan sat; not saying a thing, while the sweep was in progress. The offices were free except for the devices already found, plus one other in my office. It was a different type than the others and Grogan was very interested in it.

When I called Security I had suggested they send someone out to watch any cars leaving the area. The Security Chief reported that two cars were seen leaving the area—one, a green Chevrolet—the other, a gray Buick.

Grogan denied knowing about any of the devices that had been found—I expected those actions from him. I specifically asked him about the green Chevrolet. He laughed and denied any knowledge of either of the vehicles. We left the building and he warned me to be careful because the "big leagues" played for keeps. He waited while I closed the door.

We paused on the sidewalk and he said, "I don't know anything about anything, but I have never seen that strange looking device before."

He continued, "If I stop by your apartment tomorrow morning, would you take a ride in the Virginia countryside?"

He was surprised when I accepted the invitation for the ride without any questions. I watched, as he turned and walked toward an automobile that was parked across the street.

I left for my apartment wondering who belonged to the strange bug, and what the CIA wanted to talk about. It had been a long time since I had had any involvement with the agency, and they were probably still looking for someone called "Leader." I would have to watch my steps and make sure someone knew my schedule at all times. I stopped long enough for a sandwich before heading home. The doorman told me that a young woman had stopped twice looking for me. When he described her I told him that if she came back—send her up. Upon reaching the apartment I found nothing out of place. The only evidence that others had been here were my traveling bags just inside the front door. No one of consequence knew that I had taken this particular apartment because I had never slept in the rooms. I had signed the lease and left for New York and the trade meeting.

A short time after entering the apartment, the telephone rang and the doorman announced that a visitor was on the way. Doreen O'Halloran introduced herself and her name matched all appearances. The old folks would have said the Map of Ireland was there—framed by red hair, flashing green eyes, and an impish grin. She had the information on the gray Buick. It was registered to Horizon Auto Rentals, and leased to Mr. Chow Ling of the Peoples Republic of China. The Irish grin was very much in evidence when I asked how she had got the lessor's name. With an exaggerated whisper she said that her baby brother was a policeman, and he would do anything she wanted. I told her, if that were the case I would be interested in all Chinese who might lease automobiles. She grabbed the telephone and soon was talking to "Bucky," and told him that WE needed such information. She hung up saying that her baby brother would be calling back, and it would be best if she stayed and took the call. I offered and she accepted sandwiches and milk. Before I could move she was heading for the kitchen to fix sandwiches. Maybe someone did look through the apartment—at least the refrigerator was not empty. Susan must have been the one who ordered the supplies.

I went to change clothes, and when I returned the redhead was sitting at the table eating and grinning around a mouthful, and pointed to a place for me. We sat there and cleaned up her sandwiches. She drank a half-gallon of milk except for the one glass that she had poured for me. Hungry and healthy, and as I got to know her, full of, for the lack of a better word, delightful bullshit. Her brother worked for the traffic division of the District of Columbia Police Force. I was wondering how he could find the information we needed so fast. Baby Brother Bucky must have been a whiz at the computer. The young policeman called and told Doreen that the only people who rented from Horizon Auto Rentals were from the Peoples Republic of China. All of the vehicles were under the name of Mr. Chow Ling. My friend Chow was a very busy driver because eighty-six cars were leased to him. It was a good bet that Horizon Rentals also belonged to the Chinese.

After that information, I asked my visitor if she worked for Senator Martin and was informed that she was senate pool driver. I decided that with a brother in the police force, she might be someone who could be of use for many reasons.

Then I asked, "Can you keep that pretty mouth shut?"

Before she could answer I continued, "Be honest now. I don't want any crap."

She noticed my demeanor and said quietly, "You tell me not to talk and I don't talk."

"Fair enough," I said, "Don't talk about what you have done for me today. Now talk—would you like to be my driver?"

I could not help laughing at her reaction, "Fu-fu-fu, uh, damn right," she sputtered.

I felt that a good day's work had been done: located the bugs, completed the report, and found a path to the District's law enforcement agencies. I instructed Doreen to go about the job changes in a natural way, with notices made and whatever may be needed to leave the transportation pool. Then I asked if she had any attachments that might cause jealousy if she worked strange hours and schedules. She assures me that that there was no one who could exert that type of influence. She told me in no uncertain terms that she was her own boss about when and where she went.

After my new driver had left I called Susan Bonnet, and she confirmed that Sam Martin was steaming about the office bugging. I knew why Sam kept her, when she expressed no surprise or concern as I told her that Cliff Grogan was CIA. The only concern and advice for me was to make sure everyone understood that others knew about the "ride in the Virginia countryside, on Sunday."

# Chapter 7

I had just finished the morning paper, when Cliff Grogan was announced. On the way down on the elevator I was thinking that the CIA must be eager to talk if we were starting this early. During the ride into Virginia the conversation was kept in a mundane vein. I was issued a visitor's pass at the duty office in the CIA building. Grogan led me through a maze of offices and passageways to the covert operations branch of the agency. It was obvious that we were taking the scenic route to confuse my sense of directions

Cliff introduced the Covert Operations Director, Bill Walsh. There were other agents but no further introductions were made. I was offered a chair that sat alone in front of the Director's desk. There were a few smiles when I moved the chair toward the side of the room with my back to the wall. When I sat down, all of the occupants of the room were in view.

Walsh got right to the point, after thanking me for coming, he said, "Tell us what you know about Hsu Dong Ping."

My answer, "I can't tell you any more about him than the media has reported."

The Director of Covert Operations had a low boiling point, his face flushed, and he growled, "We don't want any crap from you. Why is that Chinese gentleman so nervous around you?"

"Hell, ask him," I said, "I had never heard the name Hsu Dong Ping before he was introduced in New York."

Cliff Grogan broke in quietly and asked, "Why don't you answer our questions?

Looking at him I responded, "I have been asked one question and have answered it. If you are looking for gossip—forget it—I don't know any."

Walsh started blustering and I stopped him with, "If you have anything to ask, ask away. If you think I am intimidated by you assholes—forget about it."

Cliff Grogan said, "O.K., O.K., We picked up some tension between you and that particular Chinese Delegate. What is that all about?"

I denied knowing what he was talking about and reminded Grogan that he was there and knew that my separation from Dong Ping was almost a table length. I even mentioned that the delegate used a translator in all his communications. One of the other agents said that they did not believe Ping needed a translator. I just shrugged my shoulders and did not respond to that statement.

Grogan stopped us with a wave of the hand and asked, "What did you say that caused him to drop his earphones?"

I shrugged and reminded him that all I did was read the Senator's statement and thank the Chinese staff for their cooperation. Which I did, after the Senators had requested the action.

One of the other agents said, "That is bullshit. He was scared out of his ass going down the steps."

I answered, "If that is your assessment, fine, but if you saw him going down the steps, you must have seen me with Chow Ling at the top of the steps. Ling, by the way, is Chin Hau's top aide."

The agent started blustering and cursing, and I suggested that if he kept it up I would pinch his pointed head off all the way down to his ass. Grogan stepped in to cool the situation. I told Walsh that it was time for me to leave, and he said that I could leave when it suited him. I stood and told him that there were not enough people in the room to stop me. There were some growls when Walsh was told that at least three people, including Sam Martin, knew that I was at CIA Headquarters.

He tried to talk it down saying, "That is so much trash. You may have told them you were coming, but no one can say you made the trip."

I looked at Grogan and said with a smirk, "Cliff, tell them about the red Mustang."

I pulled that one out of the hat. The Mustang had stayed with us for a while on the way south, But I had no idea who was in it or where it was going. Grogan had seen the car and told his boss that there was such a vehicle out there. He was not sure where it went after we turned off the freeway. For long moments, no one said a word. Then Walsh asked if I would help identify some people.

"I will sure try," I said, with a smirk.

On Walsh's signal, a projector was set up, and I received a sort of jolt. The pictures on the screen showed Dong Ping's flight down the steps. It was the same footage that had played on the newscast. No one said any thing as we watched. While it was being re-wound, Walsh asked if I could identify anyone.

I said, "Sure, Chow Ling and I are at the top of the stairs. And, of course, I recognized Hsu Dong Ping." Then as an after-thought, "Since then I have met the tall woman reporter following him, and we have an appointment for an interview."

One of the agents started to ask; "Did you see…?"

He was stopped in mid sentence by a signal from Walsh and Grogan. I believe the agent was going to ask if I was aware of the gun that she was carrying. Since they didn't want the question asked—I wasn't about to make a comment.

For the next hour, the film was run, rerun, slowed, and stopped. Each time it was stopped, I would deny knowing the person in the frame. I was lucky—John Silvers and Carpenter were caught full face, but there were no questions concerning them. Jacobs and Josephs had been caught in side views and were approaching, when the Chinese entered their vehicle. I was getting bored, or pretended to be bored of answering the same questions over and over again. Some of the agents were becoming exasperated because they didn't believe my story.

Highly trained investigators have a gut feeling about a story, and I could tell that these guys had a crimp in their gut. The questioning changed to another direction. Someone had taken cuts from the action film and enlarged them to still photographs. Each picture had a line of sight marking showing Dong Ping looking toward an individual. As he appeared at the door, the line was on Chow Ling and me. My explanation was that it would be natural for us to be picked up because we were recognizable. His looks toward Silvers and Carpenter could have been directed at other people or just casual observations, as he headed down the steps. The same was true for

Jacobs and Josephs, as they were strolling on the sidewalk near the vehicle. The most dangerous pictures were of Dong Ping, standing by the car, looking back over his shorter comrades. With fore knowledge, there could be no question that he picked up all five of us. But once again, other people were in the same line of sight. I knew that no one was convinced, but there was no way my story could be broken unless I screwed up an answer. I also knew that the longer I stayed, the better the chance for a screw up. I took the offensive by asking for the film to be run again, and would ask for a stop and give my explanation for Dong Ping's line of sight. There were enough Chinese about the area that it was almost impossible for him not to be looking in their direction. The procedure continued and I pointed out that he apparently spoke to an aide who in turn used a hand held radio. When Silvers came into view, another Chinese could be seen talking into his lapel. I talked over Carpenter by pointing out other Chinese converging on the delegate party. No one mentioned Dong Ping's hesitation when Carpenter came into view because I pointed out the "gorgeous reporter" who was pointing a microphone at Ping.

Then with what was meant to be surprise, I exclaimed, "Look, has she got a gun in her off hand?"

Everyone laughed when Walsh observed that a "dumb ass reporter" is a dumb ass reporter, even if she is a beautiful Chinese woman who may be carrying a gun. Some chuckles could be heard as Carpenter moved from the scene. I was relieved because the other friends were a part of the long-range scenery. At the best shot of Jacobs, I drew attention by suggesting the bag lady in the picture was really Cliff Grogan. The room lights were turned up and Bill Walsh was staring at me. I did not waver and held his stare until he shifted his gaze. Long silent moments passed and I realized now that they were trying the silent treatment. An old Detachment X-Ray man did not fall for that kind of crap. Walsh finally broke the silence and told me that he didn't believe anything I had said about not knowing Dong Ping. My shrugging shoulders and grin caused his face to flush.

He finally said that it was too much of a coincidence that Dong Ping was nervous only when I was in the area. He went around my shrug and silence by chewing out his agents for not having picked up the movements of the Chinese, until I pointed out the different individuals. He told the agents that he wanted all Chinese in the pictures identified. That suited me because as long as they were looking at the Chinese, our group would be relatively safe.

Walsh directed his attention back to me, "What about your buddy, Chow Ling?"

I answered with some relief, "Now you have asked me a question I can answer. The first time I met him, he as good as admitted that the Trade Delegation was a cover. He commented that Chin Hau was probably not his boss."

Grogan and I left the Covert Operations Office. There was a moment of shock and concern when we met a group of people entering the building as we were leaving. One of the men marked me to the extent that his head turned as we passed. I did not look back because he may have recognized me from Huntsville, Alabama. He was the one shooting at the plane as we left the ground. That was a troubling situation because it was likely that he would put everything together, especially if he crossed my path again.

The ride back to DC was quiet. Grogan and I passed only a few comments. Most of the past couple of hours had been loaded with tension. He asked with a grin if I had seen the red Mustang on the way north.

When he pulled in front of the apartment, I opened the door and he said, "Watch yourself, friend. You are playing in the big leagues, and everyone you will meet will have a big stick."

I waved and he continued, "One of the bugs did not belong to anyone I know."

He grinned and waved when I said, "Thanks, friend."

# Chapter 8

The succeeding few weeks was busy and interesting. Sam Martin returned, steaming about the bugging of his offices. When I arrived that first Monday, he was already on the telephone. The CIA Director was the first to deny any knowledge of the allegations. The same thing happened when Sam went to the FBI and District Police. He didn't stop there; his last threat of a subpoena went to the National Security Council. When Senator Sam became agitated, things happened. Within two hours, he had issued summons to all the Agency Directors and the DC Chief of Police, to appear before Senator Cotton's Sub-Committee on Intelligence. All this happened over the objections of the President and Senator Cotton.

Susan and I were officially summoned to testify along with Cliff Grogan and the Security Sweeping Team. The sub-committee hearings became a media event, especially after my testimony about the CIA interview, and when the Lieutenant of the sweeping team mentioned the cars leaving the scene. I was in a tough spot because I didn't want any attention, but it kept coming. One of the fleeing automobiles had been identified as belonging to the CIA. Bill Walsh was trying to get the attention off his agency. When he was asked why the CIA was involved with District problems, he said they had become involved when it appeared that someone, or something, frightened Dong Ping, a foreign leader.

The news clip, showing the flight of the Chinese, became news again. On the forth day of the hearing, I arrived with Sam and was surprised by finding Chow Ling and Hsu Pei Li in the audience. They were sitting in the front row of the spectator seats. Both returned my wave, and after getting the material set up for the morning session, I went to greet them.

Chow Ling smiled and said, "Greetings, most famous one. I am envious of all the attention you are receiving."

They both laughed when I leaned over and said, "If Chin Hau will agree, I will exchange jobs with you."

"No way, Jose," was his response, much to the delight of the surrounding people.

I turned to Pei Li and asked if she was covering the proceedings as a reporter.

She laughed and replied, "I wouldn't miss it. We don't have such excitement in the Peoples Republic of China."

I indicated the media section of the room and asked if she would like to be seated there because it would give her better view of the participants. I caught a slight nod from Chow Ling before she answered in the affirmative. I escorted her to the podium and introduced her to Senator Cotton. He was effusive in his greeting and welcome. The southern charm flowed like molasses.

After helping her get settled I went back to Chow Ling and asked, "What the hell are you doing here?"

He responded, "My friend, it seems I know something that you do not."

The gavel fell before he could elaborate, and Sam Martin was waving frantically to me.

He led me out of hearing range and said, "Boy, do we ever have a coup! I just got a call from Chin Hau asking if I wanted Dong Ping to testify. He will be here at 1030. We better tell Jeremiah. He would crap his pants if we don't."

I looked over at Chow; he had a wide grin on his face and returned my thumbs up.

Senator Cotton gaveled the meeting to order and said to the audience, "Ladies and Gentlemen, I have an announcement. I have been notified that we have a special privilege. Mr. Tsu Dong Ping has asked that we hear from him. He will be here in a few minutes, so we will suspend our regular schedule until he arrives.

The media representatives went into frenzied gyrations trying to gain advantageous positions, all the while shouting question which no one would answer. Chow Ling and Pei Li immediately became stars. Watching them, I finally understood the phrase "inscrutable oriental." They would smile, shrug shoulders, and deny knowledge. The reporters were milling about trying to talk to anyone who was involved with the committee. They had smelled a story with Dong Ping's departure from the trade meetings, and no one had been able to break through the silence of many people. Some of them became agitated toward me because I would not cooperate with them. According to them, a senator's aide was expected to answer their questions, even if the subject was off the record. I didn't help them, and told each one that they would be the first one I would call, if I found the truths of their suspicions. They became angrier as they compared stories and found I was making everyone the same promises of cooperation. They tried finding proof of the allegations that Dong Ping felt threatened by something, or someone—especially when I was around. Tsu Dong Ping's arrival at the hearing room caused a further stir. He and his interpreter were escorted to the witness seats where he was met and welcomed by Senator Cotton.

When the Chairman regained control of the proceedings and after welcoming the Peoples Republic of China's "rising star," the audience became expectantly quiet. The interpreter was given lengthy instructions before the visitor commenced speaking in Chinese. We were told that he welcomed the chance to address this "August Body" of United States Senators. The Interpreter told the sub-committee that he was prepared to read a statement from Tsu Dong Ping. After the statement, there would be a chance for questions from the Senators. The proceedings almost immediately become a bust because the junior members of the "August Body" called for the witness to be sworn and put under oath. An argument erupted among the committee members, and the Chinese sat stoically listening to the interpreter's muttering. Sam Martin finally got the Chair's attention and scolded them for this type of display. Sam made a big deal out of the moment and went as far as to advise the "important official of a sovereign nation" to walk out of the hearing room. Senator Martin offered to accompany the official in the walkout.

Without a change of expression, the Chinese delegate bowed to Senator Martin after the interpreter finished speaking. I admired the control. If I had not known he was Long Ball Kwong, I would've sworn that he couldn't understand the English language. Once order was restored, the interpreter read a long statement that, in most part, was the Chinese byline of criticizing the United States for all the world problems. Tsu Dong Ping was inserting himself into world affairs and this appearance before a body of United States Senators gave him a bully pulpit. The statement closed with an emphatic denial that Mr. Dong Ping felt threatened by any person or any group of people. During the statement, he never looked in my direction for which I was relieved. Other than a cursory glance at the beginning of the statement, I remained busy with paper work. I had noticed that a couple of CIA operatives were in the audience. The Chinese agents were liberally spread around the room. I was sure all of them were looking for some sort of by-play between Ping and myself.

After the statement, the Chinese Leader spoke through the interpreter to the Committee, "On the day in question, a great deal of attention, by your media, CIA, FBI, and this body has been made because of my hurry to get to my transportation. I had received word that the Premier of my country was waiting to speak on the telephone."

He paused before continuing with his first smile, "Which of you Senators would not hurry if you knew that your President was waiting to speak to you?"

The room erupted in laughter, and for all intents and purposes, the hearing was over. The decision was to censure anyone who had the audacity to bug a United States Senator's office. The warning was given that if any person or organization were caught in such acts, they could expect the full weight of the United States Senate to fall on them. Sam was burned a little, but there wasn't much he could do, because Senator Cotton refused any further testimony.

I watched as the room began clearing, and the Senators and reporters surrounded Dong Ping. He was very polite and paid attention to all. He even rotated in position and we came face to face, over about twenty feet. Even as he smiled for his audience, his eyes were hard and threatening toward me. He momentarily allowed concern or fear to show, as I pointed a finger at him and dropped the thumb. He knew that I had just threatened him. With as much arrogance as I could show, I turned my back on him, hoping he would take it an insult as it was intended, and a display of disrespect.

# Chapter 9

One afternoon, I was interrupted by a call from Sally Gordon.

She said, "Mistuh Bossman, suh, they is a purtty li'l ole red headed gal waiten to see yuh."

Her giggle came over the intercom as I answered, "Well get off your lazy ass and show her in."

Doreen O'Halloran was smiling as she entered. She told me that her job at the agency pool was terminated, and she was ready to work for me. I warned her again about her time belonging to me, and before making other plans she would have to have it cleared by me. She assured me that no problems would occur and she was looking forward to the job. I instructed her to be ready for work the following Monday.

As an after-thought I asked, "What kind of driver are you? Do you think you could drive while being harassed by dangerous people?"

She thought for a few minutes and then with a grin and flashing eyes, she said, "You ain't seen driving until you ride with me. In dangerous situations, I am the one causing the danger."

"We'll see," I answered with a smile.

I told her to ask Sally for help in the necessary paperwork and pressed the secretary call buttons to introduce them formally. They hit it off immediately, especially when Sally started her crap.

"Law Honey," she said, "Ya sho yuh wanna wuk fer him. He try tuh git in my britches all de time, and ya gon be inna a car wif him by yoself. He cain't keep his hans offen me."

Doreen broke up when I said sternly, "The only hand I am going to put on you is one across the ass."

"See Chile. See Chile," Sally said, as they were leaving. "He a mean ole man. Always wantin' poontang, and here yuh are, a purtty li'l ole redhead is gon be by yoself wif him."

They were both giggling as the door closed.

I came out a few minutes later and they were busy filling out the employment forms.

Sally, in her public manner, said, "Boss, what you require is worth more than the Senate pay scale. The wages can be raised if Doreen works for you personally. That's how we are taking care of it. I have checked with Miss Bonnet, and the Senator will approve whatever you send him."

I said, "O.K., where do I sign?"

"See Doreen, I told you he was a hard man," Sally said with a grin.

A few days later during a meeting of the Armed Forces Committee, I overheard a conversation between two Marine Colonels.

One said, "Carl, your memo about a small arms expert came across my desk this morning. I have a Sergeant Hardison in my outfit. Without exception, he is the best in the Corps."

The Colonel sounded, and looked, familiar but I could only see his profile and couldn't place him. I had seen many Marine Colonels in the last couple of months for it to have any significance. This Sergeant Hardison, mentioned by the Colonel, had to be Terry Hardison, Sally's "big gol durn Marine."

My attention had perked up when that name and capabilities were mentioned, and a few nights later, I called John Silvers and repeated the conversation. He suggested that I try and find this Sergeant Hardison because none of us knew anything about the state-of-the-art weapons. I laughed and told him that we were way ahead because the Sergeant was the boy friend of my secretary. I also mentioned that we might have a driver if needed, but wouldn't know for sure until her capabilities were tested. Silvers ended the conversation by saying he would get in touch with our friends and sound them out about involving others in the plans.

We agreed that I would call him on Saturday at 1100 at his number two phone. He was the only one of the group that I would contact. He had furnished a list of telephone numbers and we worked out a schedule for the calls, unless otherwise noted. We had agreed that because of scrutiny by the CIA, and possibly the Chinese, that our actions had best be guarded.

For instance, this call was being conducted in a booth at a public school in Woodbridge, Maryland, and at a country crossroads somewhere in Iowa. We didn't know, nor would we ask, the exact location of the telephones.

The first trip out with my new driver—and I was convinced that she was indeed, a driver. We had been to Baltimore and on the way home, late at night, there was little traffic. On one stretch, with no lights visible, I abruptly told her to reverse direction of travel. Before I could finish speaking, the speed increased and she steered across the median in a place that I would have sworn couldn't be used for a crossing. For the balance of the night we prowled the Maryland countryside and she proved her abilities. I was a nervous wreck when I told her to take me home.

She smiled and said, "That was fun."

We arrived at the apartment at 0600, and I told her to get some rest and be back at 0930. When I walked down to wait for her, she was pulling up to the loading zone. We drove into Maryland again, and a few minutes before 1100, pulled into a highway rest stop.

On the first ring, Silvers answered and immediately said, "There are a lot of people around me. I wasn't expecting a community yard sale. We have been invited to the mountains for the Thanksgiving holidays. Bring your people and we will take a look."

With those few cryptic words he broke the connection without my acknowledgment. During lunch I told Doreen that she had been invited for the Thanksgiving holidays. She stated that she had no plans that would interfere. There was no surprise noted when I told her to be ready on Tuesday, before the holiday, and be prepared for a week in the mountains.

After returning to my apartment, I called Sally and invited her and Terry for the same vacation. She didn't ask any questions, except I heard her ask the Sergeant if he could take a week's leave. She said that they would go, and then the questions started. I put her off and told her we would discuss the plans at a later date. I also asked Terry to stop by some day soon. He came in the following Friday. This was a huge man; he filled the door and overwhelmed the chair.

After a few minutes of small talk, I asked, "Terry, can you teach a bunch of old men to use some of the new weapons, and not discuss the lessons?"

He looked across the desk for a few moments and answered, "If they could shoot the old weapons, I can teach them the new ones in a very short time."

"Fair enough," I answered.

He didn't ask any questions nor did I elaborate. When Doreen arrived, I closed the office for a conference. They listened intently as they were told that the invitation for the holidays wasn't to be discussed by anyone. They didn't speak after being informed that what may occur could be dangerous, and before they became involved in such situations, all avenues open to them would be discussed. They still did not respond when told not to discuss our conversation except for the people of our party.

I said, "If anyone, can't, or won't join in my endeavors, tell me up front and as long as there is no talk, it will not be mentioned again."

No one moved.

I waited for a few moments and then, "O.K. For the time being we are going to a mountain vacation and you will get to know some very fine people. We will drive—leaving next Tuesday, and will be gone for one week. Terry, I need your help on the return trip—my car is already out there. Doreen, go to a rental agency on Tuesday morning and get us an inconspicuous model for the week."

I paused and then said with a grin, "I know all this crap sounds like cloak and dagger, but very likely this will be the only time we discuss such trash. So enjoy yourselves. I plan to."

During the time since New York, Hsu Pei Li had called a number of times and we met for lunch twice, and neither of us had mentioned the interview. She called on Friday, a week before Thanksgiving and we agreed to meet at my office at 1630. We made small talk and enjoyed each other's company for almost half an hour. When she took out her recorder, I was ready for questions about the United States Senate. That didn't happen and she wasn't interviewing me—she was questioning me—and most of her questions were about the past years. The staff started leaving, and I suggested we finish the interview over dinner. She agreed but insisted that we use her automobile. It was a little uncomfortable, but I agreed to go with her. Many of my thoughts were about this beautiful woman, but other thoughts were about the possible spy equipment installed in the vehicle.

Dinner was a great experience. Pei Li talked about growing up in Mao

Tse Tung's China. Her family was farmers in an eastern province, but she and a brother were brought into the Communist Party's school system at an early age. She was destined to be a teacher or nurse, when she turned twenty-one. After some changes in Party hierarchy, some of the brighter students were allowed to pick their careers. Her brother had gone into government service, and was presently posted in Brazil as an attaché .She had selected the field of journalism and other public services positions.

Her questions were directed at my past and especially my naval experience. I wasn't surprised at the definite interest in the Korean War era, and my feelings toward her country. I was somewhat amused because I was certain of her prime interest. She was looking for a connection between Dong Ping and me. We kept off the land war because of my insistence in discussing my sea duty. That part must have been galling to the Chinese Secret Service because there were no records of my having gone ashore during the war. At no time did she mention Dong Ping. It was also amusing to speculate on him trying to explain my presence in a front line unit of Marines. Even in his position, it must have been uncomfortable for my friend Long Ball Kwong. He knew something that could have personal safety connotations, but there was no background information to back up his knowledge.

We spent a couple of hours after dinner listening to a piano in the restaurant lounge. It became obvious why we used her automobile—her people knew our location. She received a telephone call at 2030. After the call, she appeared distracted and concerned about some situation. Her disclaimers didn't persuade me, and she was abrupt in preparations for leaving because of a busy schedule on Saturday. This was the first time she had mentioned a Saturday schedule.

During our drive back to the city—the first few miles she was quiet and pensive and appeared worried about something. After a few miles, her attitude changed abruptly as if she had made a personal decision. Once again, she became a bright and delightful companion. Upon arriving at the apartment she drove directly to the parking garage and I indicated my space. The engine was switched off, and she stared straight ahead with no conversation for a few moments. She took a deep breath and sighed as she got out of the automobile. I met her at the rear, with a great deal of alacrity, and told her that I had an errand to run and wished her goodnight. I could almost feel her relief, as she ran back to the car door.

She looked back over the car and said in a tremulous voice, "Someday."

I answered, "It will be tough to wait."

In my mind, her telephone call was directions to do whatever was needed get me in a compromising spot. It was a tough call for me, because of her desirability, even though she was an agent for her Government. When I returned to the apartment I was sure that an observation post had been set up next door. One of the television stations had a late news show, and I turned it on at high volume. The next few minutes were spent searching for listening devices. Sure enough, there were two that had been placed near the bed. Someone thought that we would go to bed and was hoping that I would talk about many things.

I looked at myself in the mirror with a sheepish grin and mused, "You probably would have talked about any subject she wanted to discuss."

I did talk, by saying into one of the devices, "I will give you thirty seconds to clear out. I'm beginning the count now."

Just as I got to my door, the door of the next room slammed, and I watched someone beat a hasty retreat for the exit stairs. I call the desk clerk who informed me that the next-door apartment was vacant. No one was allowed in, because the tenant was in Europe and left instructions forbidding anyone to enter. I didn't push it. I didn't push it because I knew how to open locks and this one was simple.

At a casual glance, there was nothing in the rooms except for house furnishings. At a closer look, I found a rumpled place in the carpet under an empty suitcase. Then with a closer search I found a large packet of a white substance that I was betting was heroine. The kitchen was different. Someone had spent a long day and night or was a very hungry individual. The place was littered with debris from a pizza and a chicken takeout meal. The dinner sack gave me pause, because I had seen the Chicken Colonel's containers at the Chinese embassy. That night, Brother Bucky O'Halloran got the tip of his life. He led a search party to the apartment and was the one who noticed the rumpled carpet. The District Police confiscated the drugs and were waiting for the return of the missing tenant. Bucky would not disclose his informant. I liked the O'Hallorans; they wouldn't talk when they were asked not to talk.

Wednesday of the previous week, Susan Bonnet and I had received engraved invitations for the Saturday night dinner at the home of the Ambassador, Peoples Republic of China. There were twenty guests and all were in formal attire. Waiters circulated freely with champagne. When dinner was called the Ambassador and Madam Hau led us into the dining room. The table was immaculate and beautifully laid out in a most formal manner. There were utensils that I could not identify. Crisp white linen napkins were topped with silver, crystal, and china that must have cost a king's ransom. Soup and salad came first, and then very large goblets filled with baby shrimp and a secret dressing of Madam Hau's family.

The waiters served, and took away service with hardly any notice. I was sure that all of us were duly impressed—I was. This was a formal exercise within a formal exercise. The piece-de-resistance came as the main course. The waiters came in formation with linen draped serving trays and placed them in a line down the middle of the dining table. Chin Hau clapped his hands and the covers were whisked away, unveiling five readily identifiable red and white buckets of chicken. Our surprise delighted our hosts. The Ambassador laughed with a low-throated chuckle, while Madam Hau started an infectious belly laugh. It was indeed the most formal fast food dinner we had ever experienced.

Susan was left to her own devices with the other guests because Madam Hau led me into her study after the "finger licking good dinner." All of Alan Drury's books were on the desk with *Advise And Consent* open, with a marker inserted. We spent over two hours discussing writers, philosophers, and sages from Drury to Confucius. Many of the eastern references I had never heard of and never read. We exchanged reference lists, and I admit that the one she gave me was much longer than the one she received. She very graciously apologized to Susan for monopolizing my time. Amends were made when the guest started departing. We were invited to stay for a good night brandy. The four of us spent the next three hours without politics rearing its ugly head. I still wonder sometimes if Madam Hau obtained any needed information from me. If she did, I enjoyed furnishing the secrets.

Some of the questions that had been rising were soon answered. When I returned to my apartment from the Embassy dinner and our visit with Ambassador and His Lady, there was a message from Pei Li. She invited me to her place the following day, if I would bring hamburgers, fries, and milk shakes. The Chinese were becoming fast food junkies, and through the grease she would attempt another interrogation. Upon arrival, I found her among pictures, notes, and other material. She explained that she was behind in her work for the Chinese television audiences. Her word processor carried Chinese symbols, so there was no way for me to see what she was writing. While we were eating she handed me a stack of photographs, and asked if I could identify some of the people. She explained that the pictures were taken in New York during the trade delegation meetings. The first part of the stack was the U.S. Delegates and staff members—most were identified with name and position. I was asked to confirm the information.

She separated this group and asked me to look at others that had not been identified. The first picture was Susan Bonnet with her name and a question mark. Her explanation was that she didn't know Susan's title, and other people wanted to know how I should be introduced. Susan's title satisfied her, but she continued questioning me about my position. I gave her no relief and she soon dropped that line of questions. She asked some penetrating questions about Cliff Grogan, and stated that she had information that he was an agent of the CIA or FBI.

I brushed that aside with a shrug and said, "You never know about people in this town. Even visitors such as you, may or may not be what is claimed."

She looked at me for a long moment. I wasn't exactly thrilled by what I imagined seeing in her eyes. Was she a danger to me? She shrugged her shoulders, laughed, and handed me another envelope. I was glad that my attention had been drawn away from her, when the pictures were removed from the cover.

They were 8X10 enlargements of Silvers, Carpenter, Jacobs, Josephs, and me. All of the photographs were annotated with our names, nicknames, and service information. Attempting to be casual, I shuffled through them a couple of times and offered them back to her.

When she would not take them, I dropped them on the table and asked, "What do you want to know about me?"

I continued, "The information on these guys indicate they were Marines, and they weren't members of our trade delegation."

She said sharply, "Tell me about them."

"What can I tell?" I asked, and then said, "You appear to know something about them, so tell me what is it you are after. It looks as if these pictures were taken recently, in a public place."

"They were taken on the steps of the United Nations Building, and you were there at the same time," she answered.

"None of them were with me. So why are you asking me about them?"

"Our, uh, my information is that you know them very well," she said.

The one short stutter was the only break between us. She sat quietly and wouldn't answer when I asked for her sources.

I believe there were tears in her eyes when I stood and said, "I think we should call this off. Don't expect me to answer any of your questions. I have known for sometime that you are not a reporter."

She didn't move or say anything when I prepared to leave.

At the door I turned and waved, which she returned with a sad smile and said, "I am a reporter, you know."

I answered, "One of these days."

The tears did fall then, she whispered, "I am not sure I can wait much longer."

I waited outside her door for a few moments. Most of my questions and reservations were answered.

I couldn't hear everything she said but did hear, "He knows that I am in intelligence. He would not answer…"

An elevator door interrupted my eavesdropping—most of the occupants were Oriental, who were moving in all directions.

# Chapter 10

    Doreen had been instructed to pick up the car, my bags, and come prepared to leave for the trip. When I arrived at the office, Sally had everything ready that needed my attention, and told me that Terry was waiting at her apartment. She grinned and stuck out her tongue because I asked when Terry had arrived at her apartment. We had just finished the last minute chores when the security office called and notified Sally that our transportation had arrived. In less than a half an hour, we picked up Terry and were on the way out of town. I sat in the back seat so I would not be readily identified.

    I noticed a change in Doreen's attitude as we left a stop light.

    "Got a problem, kid?" I asked.

    She answered, "I think someone has made us. Yep, they are turning back and following us, Boss."

    "Turn north on the belt way, then south and lose them." I said.

    She grinned at me in the mirror, and as she made the approach to the freeway, the car jumped under her foot. We joined the traffic among horns and squealing tires. She took us around the first turn and immediately to an off ramp, under the overpass, back to the south bound lanes before I could get my breath. She moved into a group of fellow travelers and slowed her speed.

    "There they go," she said, "The green Olds."

    From our position on the road, I noticed that the Olds passed the off ramp and continued north at a high rate of speed.

    We turned off the freeway on one of the secondary roads to the west and increased speed. I had instructed Doreen that we needed as much distance from DC as possible in the first two hours. At 1300, we decided it was time for lunch. We turned onto the freeway system to the west and pulled into the first truck stop. During lunch I told them that I would drive in case someone was looking, over to the west, for a woman driver.

I liked these young people, their curiosity must have been aroused by the road action, but none of them had asked a question. They appeared to be excited about the vacation. We got back on the road about 1430 and for an hour, a steady stream of conversation and traveling games kept things moving. Soon, the drone of road noises and lack of radio reception began to control the atmosphere. Doreen turned and leaned back and flashed a drowsy smile when Terry made a comment about being able to relax, since we had a sensible driver behind the wheel. The private conversation between Terry and Sally soon ceased, and I was left watching the mileposts flash by. The early-week traffic was not heavy, and the cruise control kept our speed just below sixty-five miles per hour. I didn't want any notice from a bored highway patrolman, and at our speed, didn't feel any threat. At one time, I became concerned with a helicopter that paced us for a few miles. It probably was a traffic, or news aircraft because it turned away from the highway and did not show again.

We had been on the freeway for almost five hours, and I was beginning to look for a place to stop.

Sally roused, put her hand on my shoulder and said, "Please, Mistuh Bossman, stop; I gotta pee."

We pulled off at the next exit for fuel and food. While we were eating, I told them my plans called for an all night drive and a motel for the following day.

Terry asked his first question, "Are you in trouble?"

I replied, "No one is after me, but a lot of people may be interested in my movements. All this crap is precautions against possible recognition from my recent television exposure. We should be able to relax now, because I told a number of people that we would be heading north for the holiday."

Again, they didn't ask further questions, but I assured them that they would be told everything that might involve a concern for them.

Terry took the wheel for the first part of the night drive. Doreen and I claimed the rear seat, and all were warned not to sleep because of the long day confined in a motel room. For a couple of hours the conversation was steady, but as the time and miles piled up there was nothing to talk about. Sally moved over to Terry, and they were soon involved with each other. It was apparent they enjoyed being together because a giggle would come from Sally and then a low-throated chuckle from the Marine.

I leaned over and asked my driver to tell me about Doreen O'Halloran. She had grown up in a family with six brothers, and all of them were dirt track racecar drivers. Their father had trained the boys and they, in turn, trained their sister. From what I had already seen, she had learned her lessons well. She also told me that her father had taught the family to be automobile mechanics. The five older brothers had doted on her all her life, and she had spoiled, Bucky, the youngest brother. I already knew how efficient he was, as a policeman with a computer. Doreen casually mentioned that all her family would be available if ever I needed help. I hoped that they would not be needed.

We stopped one time to stretch legs, go to the bathroom, and have coffee before continuing the trip west. Doreen claimed the wheel as we left the restaurant. We had moved through Virginia, a part of North Carolina, and now were approaching the Mississippi River through Tennessee. We crossed the Big Muddy into Arkansas and started looking for a place for the day. I didn't want to remain in a large city. We turned off the road and wound down into a small town that advertised a motel and restaurant complex. After we ordered breakfast, I went into the motel and paid cash for two rooms with two beds each. Off-the-road rooms were requested because of highway noises. The clerk was a small, weather-beaten man who was not concerned about my requests. Without a word, he marked the cards with a "do not disturb" note and a wake up call at 1730. He put the cards into a room file and didn't ask for any identification. I returned to the restaurant and dropped the keys on the table.

Sally took one and said, "Dis one is ourn."

After looking at Doreen with a grin continued, "Dat lil ole redhead is yourn.

Doreen didn't appear embarrassed being in the room with me. She took the bathroom first and was asleep when I came out later. She was a beautiful young woman and very desirable, but she was that, "young woman" who trusted her Bossman. I crawled into the sack and the next thing I knew was waking up at 1400. I quietly dressed and went out to the telephone booth in the lobby. The clerk appeared to take no notice of me, but I expect he knew who was in the booth. The telephone rang one time and Lydia Carpenter's voice was a pleasing sound. I told her where we were and she said that it would take at least two hours of driving for the planned rendezvous.

She asked me to hold and I could hear voices in the background

Lydia came back on and said, "Leave at 1530 and take State Road 417 out of town for fifty-seven miles—you will be at Owen Crossing. It is just an intersection with a name. Keep straight on for one mile. Take a left into the woods for about five hundred yards to an open field. Someone will meet you. If you are later than 1730, no one will be there. Can you make it?"

I told her that I was sure we could, but we were getting snow with about one inch on the ground. She told me that if we arrived late—wait until 1830, and if no one showed up we were to start driving to Larkspur and would be met on the road. I was surprised at the strange instructions but didn't ask any questions, and she didn't elaborate. Her only other comment was to express pleasure concerning our visit. I called my friends and soon we were on the road without contact with the local people. The snow was steady as we continued the trip, and when we started moving up the eastern slopes of the Ozark Mountains, the snowfall became heavier. I watched the time and the odometer and at fifty-six miles we started looking for Owen Crossing. The sign was exactly fifty-seven miles from the motel, and we were seven minutes early. Doreen slowed the car to a crawl and we almost missed the turnoff because of visibility.

Sally expressed all our feelings, "My Lor', Bossman, where you taking us?"

I heard the noise before seeing the helicopter that was sitting in the field with rotors lazily beating a heavy white cloud. Charlie Daniels materialized out of the snow with a big grin splitting his face.

With a wave he shouted, "Let's get out of here while we can."

Another figure appeared and Caleb asked for the car keys. Without another word he drove the vehicle out of the field. The pilot got us settled in the helicopter, and the aircraft lifted into the air with zero visibility. The flight to the Carpenter house was an experience I wouldn't be interested in taking again. All that could be seen was blowing snow and every so often we would abruptly bank, and a tall tree or a large boulder formation would ghost past.

Daniels didn't say a word, but every time I looked he was grinning—he was actually enjoying the flight! There were no distractions because his passengers were glued to their seats with fright. Nothing was said until the craft dipped over a ridge and the lights from the ground could be seen.

We sat down, and the engines were cut, and I said, "Sure am glad that's over."

Daniels laughed and retorted, "That was a nice flight. I enjoyed having you as passengers. You were well behaved—best I have seen."

None of us had the strength to respond.

All of my old comrades and their wives were waiting and called greetings from the front porch. They paid lots of attention to the young people that were with me. Sally Gordon was soon the center of attention. She entertained all of us with her descriptions of the helicopter flight. Even the taciturn features of Carpenter would break into a smile at some of the more descriptive phrases. Lydia Carpenter herded us into the kitchen for dinner. I became aware of a real change in Linda Josephs. She appeared to be at ease and no longer reminded me of a bird ready for flight. There was no change in the demeanor of Samantha Silvers and Darlene Jacobs, but Lydia was showing signs of pressure. Her outward appearance was the calm beautiful lady of before, but there was an undercurrent clouding her eyes. She paid attention to all her guests, but her eyes would often swing to her husband. Silvers, Jacobs, and Josephs were relaxed, but Carpenter was definitely on edge. I had never seen the Marine sniper in this state. I had to believe that our hosts were worried about something more than the welfare of their guests.

After dinner I watched them go to the kitchen when the telephone rang. I didn't want to eavesdrop and stood clear until the conversation was completed. When I spoke from the door their private conversation abruptly ceased. We covered the situation by light talk about whether I should drink coffee or the House Stump Juice.

"O.K., friends, what is going on?" I asked quietly.

Their eyes caught briefly and Carpenter simply said, "Mistah Gorman say he's goin' to either run us out, or take us out. He cain't run us out."

They told me they had been considering calling off the holiday, but couldn't contact us because of the travel plans. The only part of Gorman's plan they knew was the threat. There didn't seem to be any question that he would not attempt to carry out his warnings, and he had the support from many of the local law enforcement agencies. Lydia said that the County Sheriff wouldn't be in Gorman's camp but neither would he join this camp. The Carpenters could only count on their closest friends. Most of them were already deployed in, and around the neighborhood to keep an eye on the situation.

I said, "Hell, you have quite a group here that Gorman may not know about. We were a pretty good fire team at one time."

Lydia responded, "We don't want to involve you. It is our problem."

I put my arm around her shoulders, squeezed, and answered, "I don't know about the others, but me, I am involved. That ugly husband of yours has helped me a few times."

Carpenter grumbled, "Watch him afore he starts tellin' war stories."

We talked for a few more minutes. The problem between the two factions had deteriorated from feuding and fussing to feuding and fighting after the manhandling of the Gormans during our last meeting. The fact that the Gorman's' stash houses had been destroyed had not helped the situation. The Gorman operations were large enough and lucrative enough to concern many people. Lydia stated that the others had to be warned, and we decided that I would do the talking because of my three young friends.

When we rejoined the others drinks were refilled and served, I said, "Let me say something to all of you. Our hosts just told me they tried to call off this party because they didn't have enough food. Before they could call, all of us had taken off and couldn't be reached. So we have made the decision that we will eat turkey, and you all can eat all the spam you want."

My audience started laughing and asking how to build a spam turkey. I noticed that John Silvers had not joined in and was watching the three of us.

Nodding to him, I continued, "Seriously, the Carpenters did try to call this off because of a dangerous situation."

All eyes were on me, showing concern.

I turned to Terry, Sally, and Doreen and said, "I promised you three that before you were in danger, I would warn you. But this situation has taken us all by surprise, and we'll get you out of here as soon as possible."

I continued turning to my old friends; "The rest of you, the Carpenters are being threatened. A local stud horse by the name of Gorman says that he is going to rid the neighborhood of the Carpenter family. Charlie Daniels will be here in a few minutes to fly you out—as many as wants to go."

Before I could finish a real surprise occurred, Linda Josephs said, "I think we should stay."

Her husband quickly agreed along with Sarg and Darlene Jacobs. I had not expected anything different.

Samantha Silvers said sternly, "They promised me turkey and I am not leaving until I eat."

She dug John in the ribs and said, "That goes for my husband, too."

I turned to my group and Sally rolled her eyes and said, "Bossman, if ya think ah'm gittin back inna that machine, you is as crazy as the crazy man who fly that thin."

Terry seconded his fiancée's decision by saying that he was considered an expert in all field weapons if and when that expertise may be needed. A thumb's up sign and an Irish grin told the O'Halloran decision. A general hubbub of agreement rose around the room. Lydia Carpenter tried to stay it by pointing to who we were.

She said, "Just look who is here, two college professors and their wives, a state senator and his wife, and half of a United States Senator's staff. If you stay here, your lives could be in danger."

John Silvers made a statement that took us back to Korea.

He said quietly, "You can't live forever."

The statement stopped all arguments and caused us to reflect on what could be our future. Some faces paled as the owners contemplated what had just been decided. I broke the silence by telling them that we had one of the best combat commanders from the Marine Corps in the room. I suggested that John Silvers take command. He waited for a time, squeezed his wife's hand, and stood before us—Captain John Silvers, United States Marine Corps.

He asked Carpenter if we needed sentries and was told that we would have at least an hour, and probably more, if the Gormans started a move. The next few minutes he used for organization. We were split into two teams: Sergeant Jacobs to guard the easterly approaches with Lydia, Linda, Samantha, Doreen, and me. The southerly team was Sergeant Hardison, Darlene, Sally, Josephs, and Carpenter. The Captain would set up between the two teams. Carpenter and I would join the Captain is case of a surprise approach by the enemy.

There were no shortage of weapons and ammunition. We were issued a specific weapon, and after instructions by Terry Hardison, the Captain told us to leave it by the exit doors. The west team would use the back door with the front door for the south. Carpenter also offered me the automatic that I had left with him the last time of a Gorman visit. There was a raised eyebrow from Sally while the automatic was in sight.

It turned into a surprised look when Carpenter said, "Heahs you gun from las time."

It was amazing how fast we were returned to normalcy. The Captain and the Sergeants were huddling, and all of the others went into the kitchen for coffee. Josephs asked if I had been trained for this kind of duty. He made the observation that I appeared more at ease than the others did. He was the second one who had asked that question in the recent past.

# Chapter 11

I didn't have time to answer Josephs about previous training because the Captain and Sergeants returned and we were assigned areas of responsibilities. It wasn't long before normal conversations were being held with an occasional nervous twitch caused by adrenaline flow. Shortly after midnight, Lydia led most of her visitors to bed. John, Samantha, and I were left alone by the fire. Samantha told me that the men had told them what was going on with Long Ball Kwong and warned that the women would be included in the plans or they would report the proposed action against Long Ball. My argument was against the idea of anyone being involved with the Chinese, other than the five Korean War veterans. John shrugged his shoulders and suggested that another conference would be in order for the next day.

The river was becoming a popular place. I had no negative thoughts about helping Carpenter with his problems, but with the women involved I was no longer so sure about going ahead with the assassination of Long Ball Kwong. One of my thoughts was that I would take on the job alone. That was soon discarded because it would be an impossible task. I argued with John and Samantha that if more people were added to the mission—more people would be needed for support. The discussion ended with no results and we went to bed.

My last thought before going to sleep was, *I wonder if anyone of Detachment X-Ray is available.*

The night finally passed with only a few naps for me. When I awoke at 0530, I remembered my thoughts of Detachment X-Ray during the night. This was a surprise because that part of my life was over, but when you start planning to kill a world leader, past training would be remembered. We would have been in our element in Detachment X-Ray, and there would have been no questions about taking on the mission.

"Hell," I mused, "I don't even know the location for any of those people, and there is no way of finding them."

I felt at home in this house, so I had no second thoughts about going to the kitchen and plugging in the coffeepot. It was still dark and snowing heavily when I stepped out to the porch. Thanksgiving Day was going to be white and cold, cold hell, it was already below freezing and cold had been passed at thirty-two degrees. This thought became true when I saw the thermometer registering twenty degrees above zero. The weather wouldn't be conducive for a fight on enemy territory, and I doubted that Gorman would make an attempt.

I returned to the kitchen shivering and found Lydia and Samantha sitting at the table drinking coffee.

Lydia remarked, "I plan to keep you because every time you visit, I find coffee brewing in the kitchen before anyone is out of bed."

She continued in a more serious tone, "Samantha told me of your reservations about us last night. There is one thing you don't have to worry about. Linda had an operation and a growth was removed from her spine that was causing the erratic behavior. She is fine. As a matter of fact, she probably is the meanest one in this whole outfit."

Samantha laughed and added to Linda's new reputation, "Yes, and she would giggle all the way through the fight. Navy, you have to accept us. I won't allow John to do something like this unless I am with him. The guys have told us the whole story and we support your plans. But they can't be put forward without us."

"Don't pressure me, " I said, and then with a laugh, "Or I will get Linda after you."

We all laughed because frankly I didn't know what to do.

After breakfast there was no sign of a let up in the snowfall. We agreed that probably the day would be ours to enjoy. Carpenter suggested we go for a walk, and I shook my head at Terry and he settled back into his chair. This wasn't for him yet, and I hoped all of them could be kept at a safe distance. The weather was so bad we followed the snow guides to the stables. We helped our host with the morning chores without any conversation. After feeding the last horse, Carpenter led us into an adjoining tack room. We sat there, calmly discussing whether or not we would assassinate Long Ball Kwong. It was almost a certainty that he would become the next Premier and we would have to advance our plans before he returned to China. In any case, we could expect to have the full weight of both countries coming down in the investigation because, somewhere along the line, our interest in Long Ball would be aired in public.

An observer watching this scene, without hearing the conversation would have seen five friends passing around a bottle of whiskey while holding a conversation. We discussed my reservations about having the women involved. Their husbands told me that the women would blow the plan by planting rumors of an impending attempt on an important person's life. There was no convincing my friends that I had the most reasons for wanting Long Ball killed. We discussed the possibility of involving more people. All of were certain that we would need Charlie Daniels and his helicopter. There was some discussion about a driver and another shooter, but I did not want the young people to be at risk on all of our projects.

My comrades felt the need for more people, but I was attempting to hold out for no others, except maybe the helicopter pilot. They out-voted me because of their wives. I finally capitulated and we decided that if the plan went further, we might need more people. With the women acting as rear guard and lookout, it was definite that they would need a supporting shooter, and our team would need an accomplished driver.

I told them for the first time about my years as a part of Detachment X-Ray. Josephs said that he had been sure that I was more than a senator's aide.

I said, "No, not anymore, I left those folks a long time ago."

"What am I doing in command?" asked Silvers.

"Because you are the only one with command experience as the leader of this group. It would take some adjustment for them to completely trust me in a firefight. They remember me as the boot of an outfit."

There were some chuckles when Carpenter grunted, "Uh huh."

Sergeant Jacobs took over and said, "Navy is right, Captain, we don't have time to train a new commander. We know we can trust you in a command situation. We can call on Navy for special expertise."

I nodded in agreement and continued, "All this may be a moot point because Long ball is scheduled to leave for China in a few weeks. They are expected too be out of the country before Christmas, and I see no indications when or if he will ever return to this country. I am betting that he will not, under the present circumstances. All bets are off that he will be the new Premier early in the New Year. Do we attempt to take him out before he leaves?"

There was a general consensus that we had to get him before he left the country. Yet, all of us were in agreement that we presently were not capable of taking such actions.

The conversation continued with Silvers saying, "We certainly need some heavy preparation, if we even get close to him."

Joseph said with a chuckle, "Shit, Captain, let's assign the training schedule to Carpenter. He seems to have some things going at this time."

Even Carpenter chuckled as Jacobs said, "If we are going to do it, next year will be too late. I say let's go for it now. We probably — No, we *won't* get another chance if he gets back to China."

Carpenter told us he was expecting arms and ammunition to arrive at anytime. We decided to go ahead, assuming that we could get to the Chinese before he departed the country. To my relief, it was decided that the others would only be used in supportive roles. Their part would only involve planning and acting as rear-guard and they wouldn't participate in the actual hit.

One question arose, which went unanswered, "What would happen to anyone who wouldn't support our actions after being told what we were planning."

I don't think anyone had an answer because we were talking about family and close friends. I was sure that no one wanted an answer to that question.

We stepped out of the tack room and were surprised by the beating sounds of a helicopter rotor. The snow kept the aircraft hidden until it landed in front of the house.

Someone exclaimed, "That is one hell of a pilot or a stupid fool."

We walked around the corner of the house and met Charlie Daniels.

He saluted us with a big grin and said; "Only fools would walk around in this kind of weather."

Joseph's laughed and replied, "We know a fool when we see a fool, and you are a fool because we can see you, fool."

The arms and ammunition that Carpenter was expecting was on the helicopter. One case was ammunition, and the other held ten Israeli machine pistols still packaged as they come off the assembly room floor.

Charlie looked at them in some surprise and asked, "What kind of deer are you people after?"

We left the boxes in the garage and made for the warmth of the house. The comfort of the house was not the only pleasurable sensation. Mixed aromas of Thanksgiving dinner permeated the whole house, causing appetites to soar. The women ran us out of the kitchen and dining room. We received hot mugs of coffee laced with Carpenter's favorite brew. After some persuasion, the helicopter pilot finally agreed to stay for dinner. His protestations diminished somewhat after he was introduced to Doreen O'Halloran. He couldn't keep his eyes off her, and I suspected similar interest because of the blushes and hasty retreat. Daniels brought the news that the Gormans had left home unexpectedly the night before. Rumor had it that someone in the family had died. The news from the sheriff's office told us that the Gormans wouldn't be back for a few days. The pilot also told us that the jail was well covered, and we would probably know, before the Sheriff, when the Gormans were returning.

The cooks told us that snacks were ready for those who could not wait. We were forbidden to eat very much because dinner would be at 1600. All the preparation was complete except for the cooking—a ham was cooling—while venison roast and turkey were occupying the same oven. The women joined us and Samantha Silvers asked pointedly if there was something the group should discuss. A momentary silence occurred, as everyone sat back with an expectant look.

John Silvers spoke up; "The five of us are involved in something, which most of you don't know about. It is a dangerous situation, and we don't want anybody to get hurt, especially without knowing all about the situation."

He looked directly at the four young people and continued, "Our wives know basically what we are planning, but the four of you are not the least bit involved. If you become involved there is a chance that the best thing that can happen would be a long, long term in jail. All of us may get killed because we are planning to kill a man in cold blood. Now is the time for you to tell us to shut up. Only one of you has to speak and say no. If that happens we close this shop, and that will be the end of it as far as you are concerned. Don't hesitate, for any reason, to stop your involvement right now. It may be too late for second thoughts if you don't halt this conversation."

It had been said and silence hung heavily over the entire group. Drinks were refilled and passed around. No one spoke, except to say thank you or excuse me. The five of us exchanged inquiring looks without speaking.

Terry Hardison broke the silence, "If we go along with this, what will be our involvement?"

Jacobs answered, "You will be asked to support us. We will pull all the triggers, unless you have to bail us out. That will not be defense, if you are caught."

Josephs spoke up, "If we get caught and you get away—you must stay away. Only jeopardize yourselves if needed, and confessing your part isn't needed."

There was another period of silence, finally broken by Charlie Daniels, "Shoot," he said, "I knew I should have left. Turkey dinners never come free, but hell, Miz Lydia's cooking is worth it. Whatever it is, count me in."

Sally asked, "Boss, can the three of us talk?"

"I hope you do," and after my answer, they went into another room.

When Daniels turned back after watching Doreen disappear, I said, "That redhead is something, isn't she Charlie?"

He looked at me with an embarrassed grin and answered, "You bet your bottom dollar."

Then in a more serious tone, he asked, "Who does she belong to?"

Amid laughs, I said, "I don't believe anyone has the nerve for claiming her."

You could tell that Charlie Daniels was delighted at that information.

Terry led the two girls in and said, "Tell us what you need."

I spoke up, "I feel responsible for you three. Are you…?"

Before I could finish Doreen spoke up and said that she had made up her own mind and that I shouldn't feel responsible.

Sally said, "Yeah, Bossman, shut ya mout. All you is looking fer is poontang, and we ain't giving ya enny."

The laughter stopped when Silvers started telling them the whole story, and a couple of gasps were released when he mentioned the target's name.

"OOOEEE," Linda Josephs exclaimed, "I thought you guys were after some waiter in Chinatown."

"The big he coon himself," Daniels muttered.

The silence deepened and we did not relieve any pressure by speaking. Silvers actually held up his hand when Jacobs started to speak—but then relief. A timer went off, and Lydia led the women into the kitchen. In a few moments, we heard the first nervous laugh, which finally turned into an indication that they were enjoying themselves. We were soon called to a feast, and I marveled how light-hearted and enjoyable a meal we had served to us. The conversation of the afternoon hadn't dampened any spirits, but it was close to the surface because every so often, an eye would wander to the distance—trying to see the unknown—but the unknown offered no answer.

During dinner someone asked a question I had pondered many times. John was asked how Long Ball Kwong got the name. We were told that Kwong had been a student athlete at the University of Chicago and was a star baseball player. He was the home run king; therefore the name. All the team members took the name "Long." It followed that John Silvers would become Long John Silvers from the Stevenson story *Treasure Island*. According to Silvers, none of it made any sense, but in those days most things were fun.

It was a magnificent meal with great friends. The conversation covered many things, but Long Ball's name wasn't mentioned again. A casual observer would have never guessed that we had come together to plan a murder, and in the short time had agreed to involve ourselves in an unrelated situation. The Gormans were in for a rude awakening, or least those who were to survive. The coming weekend would probably be discussed for years in this beautiful and peaceful mountain community. The feud between the two factions had been going on for generations. If things went well, we would probably end the feuding during a snowstorm that was whipping this section of the country. The weather was a plus for us because we could use it for cover, and still demonstrate abilities needed to carry out an assassination. In effect, we would be rehearsing our plans for Long Ball Kwong.

Thanksgiving dinner was finished and all turned to for the mess cooking duties and other chores that had to be completed before nightfall. The men were just getting back to the house, when the telephone rang. It was Caleb with the information that the Gorman family would be returning to their home on Saturday. We began making plans for the confrontation to be made somewhere near Owen Crossing. The helicopter would be used for insertion and a fast escape. On this mission, only Terry Hardison, from our support group, would be involved in the ambush. Doreen paled when she heard our plan, but smiled bravely when Charlie squeezed her hand. Sally grabbed Terry's hand and led him out of the room.

# Chapter 12

Thanksgiving night was a restless time for all of us. I finally got up at 0330 and found Silvers and Carpenter already in the kitchen. It wasn't long before all of our party was up and about. We were still making plans, and after breakfast Lydia Carpenter again tried to get us to stay out of the Gorman problem.

Charlie Daniels stopped her saying, "Miz Lydia, your other friends may agree, but your local friends wouldn't last long, if we had to face Mr. Gorman alone."

I tried to lighten the prevailing mood; "You aren't getting me back in that chopper with Daniels while it is snowing—especially if he is on a joy run."

"My Lor, yes," Sally exclaimed, "He still ain't got a chance at that lil ole red head, and that would make 'em nervous and mad. I don wanna fly enny mo with that crazy flyin man."

The short exchange was enough to relieve the building tension. The men headed for the barn for the morning chores. Our storm conference was in the tack room. We asked Carpenter for his best guess on what we would be facing on Saturday. He said the Gormans generally traveled in a three-car convoy with the family in the middle vehicle.

I mused, "Shucks I have already been there and done that."

Carpenter's guesses about the Gorman travel arrangements were on target. A call came in the next morning at 0700 with the news that the Gormans were on their way home. The first car had two men and the driver; the third car was full with four men and the driver. A surprise passenger was in the family car. A woman was riding with the three Gormans and a driver. The woman became a concern for Josephs, but Lydia warned that the female was probably Christine Gorman, who was a grand-daughter. Lydia also stated that she was more dangerous than anyone in the convoy. She had already killed her husband and a boy friend—the community was suspicious about the boy friend's wife.

We deferred to Carpenter to make assignments for the ambush. He and I would take the family car, Josephs and Jacobs the first vehicle, and Silvers and Hardison would take the third car and be alert for any further reinforcements. Charlie Daniels would stay with the helicopter and would back any party needing assistance. There was a radio conference between Carpenter, Daniels, and Caleb, who was leading the local Carpenter force. They decided that the ambush would occur as the convoy cleared Owen Crossing. Caleb and his crew would block the north/south highway routes. That would make sure vehicles were forced to the west, passing the turnoff at Daniels' landing site. Caleb reported that the convoy would be tailed just long enough for an intelligent estimate of time of arrival at the target area. The snowfall would be to our benefit, as long as we didn't get short of time. We would head for the target zone, as soon as we received the word that Gorman was an hour from Owen Crossing.

The women were briefed on the mission, and under strong objections they were excluded from the ambush. Linda Josephs cut all arguments when she stated that someone had best be near a radio in case the enemy came scouting. She took command and organized the women for a possible firefight at the house. Then Linda wanted to know what was funny, when I laughed with Lydia and Samantha.

There came a wide grin when I said, "Nothing is funny around old "blood and guts" before a fight."

The balance of the morning was taken up in weapon familiarization for those who hadn't been shooting for the past few years; therefore Terry Hardison was busy with all of us.

Josephs suggested that I discuss ways to accomplish the mission. It was amazing how fast we went from ambush to mission.

My first words were, "If you have any hesitation or thoughts that you cannot kill in cold blood—don't come. If we go in with a single mind we should be able to carry it off, with no casualties. On the other hand, if anyone hesitates—just momentarily—it is likely that some will get killed."

It was silence for all of us for a few minutes. We were preparing to murder, and we were basically law-abiding citizens, and didn't believe in murder.

I shook it off by saying, "On a mission such as this, if we get complete surprise, we will be finished in about fifteen minutes."

I asked Carpenter if there was any doubt that Gorman would carry out his threats to do away with the Carpenter family.

His response was "Nope."

Charlie Daniels said, "If Mr. Gorman has his way, there will be another thirty or forty of us wiped out. He has the support of the State Police Barracks out on the highway and the police forces of Gorman and Maple Grove. We probably can depend on Sheriff Dickerson and a couple of deputies and maybe the Constable in Larkspur, but the Sheriff is one of our problems—if he catches us—we go to jail."

Jacobs spoke up, "Let's do a good job and not get killed or caught."

John Silvers looked up and grinned, then said, "You can't live forever, but I don't see any reason to die out here in the Ozarks."

I waited a few minutes and no one spoke further, "O.K. The way we did it in Detachment X-Ray was to hit fast and hit hard. We have to get them stopped, and that can be done by blocking the road as they enter the curve by the landing field."

My mind wandered back to a crossing south of Huntsville, Alabama. My instructions came directly out of my memory of that mission. The two missions were similar, except for the snow.

I continued, "When they get stopped, Captain, you and Sergeant Hardison hit the last car with explosives and gunfire from the rear and the driver's side. Sergeant Jacobs, when the explosions go, you and Josephs hit the front car from both sides of the road. Carpenter and I should be able to get the Gorman car between us and throw explosives under the body and open it up for all to see. I am betting that it is reinforced and underneath is the target. Remember, anyone who lives will be a threat, either with a weapon on the spot, or testimony somewhere down the line. And for cripes sake let's not shoot each other."

I turned to Charlie Daniels and continued, "Charlie, have the bird in the air and hovering over the Gorman car as soon as the convoy is stopped. If no one calls for help, or you hear us break off, get that chopper to the field and get us out of there."

I continued for all, "If we miss, we will have to make a run for it. Carpenter, do you have a hidey hole up here in these mountains?"

He looked at Lydia and when she nodded he answered, "Yeah, there is a nice lil huntin' shack up by the river on Black Bear Ridge."

Jacobs spoke up, "Well, that must be all the answers, the only question left is when do we go."

The scouts called and warned that the Gorman convoy was running without problems and would be at Owen Crossing at 1500. We were getting cut short on time because of the darkening atmosphere. We had decided that the ambush wouldn't be feasible after 1600. The women were still trying to talk themselves into the action.

Carpenter stood up and, "Nope."

That ended the conversation and we continued preparation for the mission—clothes and food was packed in case we had to run to the hidey-hole. At 1300, Charlie proceeded to start his aircraft. In about thirty minutes he had it warmed and the rotors were turning. Good byes were said and a few hands clutched at sleeves but there was no hesitation in loading the chopper.

If they were all like me, all hearts were beating at fast rates. The wind had increased and was blowing drifts—while fresh snow continued to fall.

Terry Hardison spoke, "Don't worry, Old Folks. If you need help just call for me."

Someone grumbled that kids were all the same. Give them a chance to be a man, they would probably crap their pants. From then on the flight was easy, and my friends were relaxed. They did not seem to understand! Flying in a helicopter during a snowstorm was dangerous! It had only been a short time since I had made the first flight with Daniels. I am still amazed that we made the first flight without crashing. He landed in the field—how did he do it? I had zero visibility. Before departing for our stations, we spent a few minutes in the cabin of the aircraft making sure we knew what was going to happen. They asked me to go over the ambush plan again.

After a few minutes of discussion Silvers said, "O.K. then that is it. We best get set up and get ready. No matter how easy the stop will be, we are getting short on time with early nightfall."

The snow was still falling heavily when the helicopter had taken to the air. I don't know about the others, but it was white-knuckle time for me. Charlie grinned, as he straightened out from the takeoff, and headed into the blinding snow at a fast rate of speed. The trees and boulders were still there and he missed them again. I had no idea where we were until he set us down in the open field near Owen Crossing. We unloaded the equipment and started for the road. The helicopter went into idle. We had discussed this and decided that it would likely be to our benefit to have the engine warm.

We were in place by 1430, and Carpenter received word that we could expect the convoy a few minutes after 1500. We were spreading the word, when a tree fell across the road at the curve about three hundred yards from the crossroads. I admit that I hadn't heard, nor did I know that Caleb's crew was in the area, and remember thinking that I had to be more observant if I was going to play with the big boys. I groused to Carpenter about not hearing the other men in the area.

Carpenter grinned and said, "Just a bunch of hillbillies helping their neighbor."

Right on time, a few minutes after 1500, we heard the report that the convoy was passing through the intersection.

We heard the growl of four-wheel drive vehicles. Even then I was startled when the first car came around the curve in the driving snow. Brake lights came on and the car went into a skid when the driver caught sight of the fallen tree. Carpenter and I were already up and moving as we heard the explosions at the following automobile, and then at the lead vehicle. He made a run up the right side and I took the left. I threw a cluster of grenades under the front tires and opened fire as I traversed the length of the car. The machine pistols were hammering all around us. I stopped in a blind spot and reloaded the weapon. Then I threw a cluster of grenades at the rear window and watched them bounce off the bulletproof window. I had time to hit the deck before the grenades went off harmlessly. I rolled in front of the car, and Carpenter was throwing more grenades underneath the body. I did the same on my side and could see the results of the explosions through the windows. No one could live in that vehicle.

To my surprise two figures came out the left side, I opened up with the machine pistol, and the largest figure fell immediately. The smaller one disappeared into the trees.

Carpenter opened up and I heard Gorman yell, "Wait boy, wait! I'm coming out with no weapon. Hear me now. Hear me now. I'm not armed."

I stepped back and said, "Carpenter, one of them got away. It must have been the girl."

Gorman brayed, "You got problems boy, 'cause she is the best fighter in the family. You best turn me loose, and I will get her and we will make our way home."

The other men came up and I started to explain the problem. Suddenly, an automatic weapon opened at close range. Had it not been snowing, she probably would have gotten John Silvers and me. I saw her just in time to knock him aside and felt the bullets tug at my sleeve. She tried to change position but was caught in the legs with shrapnel from a grenade thrown by Josephs. She went down cussing and firing, and Gorman must have thought he had a chance. He moved on Carpenter and we caught him from both sides with .45 slugs. When he fell, I stopped shooting but the Sniper finished his magazine—reloaded and fired another fifteen rounds at his antagonist.

In the meantime Jacobs and Josephs captured the girl. She came stumbling in and we relaxed. Only her neighbor watched her. She grabbed one of the captured guns, and Carpenter hit her with an empty weapon. I had seen many dead people fall and she was dead. The radio crackled and the scouts warned us of approaching vehicles. We threw all the unused explosives into the wrecked automobiles and broke for the landing field. The grenades started going off, and we heard the helicopter go out of neutral. We hit it on the run, and some legs were still dangling, as the pilot jerked it into the air.

We took off in the direction of the ambush and could see that the approaching vehicles were under flashing lights. We could not tell if they were state or sheriff and really didn't care. Charlie took the aircraft up on a steep climb and broke out of the snow at seven thousand feet. The heading was changed and the throttle was at full power as we made for the Carpenter place. We soon heard from the scouts that the escorts were from the State Police.

Daniels stated, "Sure glad it isn't the Sheriff. He is going to be tough, but we will have time to get settled before he takes over the investigation."

Carpenter called Lydia and told her we were coming in and no one was hurt. He also asked for the table to be set, so we could have dinner or at least be eating, if someone came calling.

We landed in the yard, and the first thing Daniels did was open the engine compartment and started shoveling in snow. Jacobs and I caught his reasoning and soon had the helicopter covered with the white stuff. Then before we went inside, Charlie started his heating system, as if he was preparing to start a cold bird. That also would furnish a reason for melting snow. The young man knew his stuff. We were sitting at the table when the word came that the police cars were on the road. Our pilot jumped up and we soon heard the engine revolutions increase and then reduce to idle. He came back and took his place at the table.

Carpenter went to greet his new guests. A captain, a sergeant, and two patrolmen came in after being invited. The Captain looked us over with a sneer and asked Carpenter to account for the day. The Hill Billie drawl was almost suffocating, as our host told the policeman we had consumed too much corn liquor to account for the day. I didn't know the sniper had such a sense of humor.

The patrolmen weren't amused and Carpenter finally said, "Well Cap'n, take a look. We are tryin' to eat supper, and all the chores are done. Charlie is cleaning snow off the chopper. Show me sum tracks off the place. Matter of fact; tell me why you are here. I ain't got time, or wan to take time, to answer dum questions."

Lydia smiled and asked the cops to have something to eat. She was not doing it out of friendship, but to make them feel more uncomfortable. The Captain tried to regain control of the situation by demanding Carpenter to identify us.

"These are my friens," snarled Carpenter.

The Sergeant was experienced and knew that they weren't getting anywhere and suggested leaving.

The Captain wasn't finished and blustered, "Well, I am not satisfied. None of you are to leave without my permission."

Josephs spoke up, "You better clear it before Monday morning because that is when I am leaving."

I kept the pressure on, "Best clear it by Sunday, Cap'n, that is when I am leaving."

John Silvers asked, "Just why are you so interested in us?"

The question went unanswered and the Captain stormed out with his patrol following. Carpenter and Daniels escorted the lawmen to their vehicles, and from the kitchen we heard them start the engines.

Daniels shut down the helicopter engine, and when they returned to the table there was no demand to recount the actions at Owen Crossing. We had discussed this and agreed all knowledge would be limited to the actual ambush.

John Silvers said, "Too much has gone on for many people to know the details. We trust you, but someone could make a mistake. You will be getting news accounts shortly, and we expect to see the Sheriff soon."

Lydia spoke up calmly, "If you are expecting the Sheriff, you must have been successful in the operation."

"Are you satisfied?" she asked her husband.

He answered, "Yes'um, Mistah Gorman cain't hurt us no more."

Then Lydia told us what we hadn't heard before. The Gormans had rode rough shod over the entire county until her family, the Carpenters, and the Daniels had decided that enough was enough. The first confrontation was an ambush set for Lydia's brother and sister-in-law. Then two of Carpenter's uncles had been killed. The Daniels family led the first raid on the Gorman stronghold. Mister Gorman, as we knew him, lost a son, a brother, and an uncle. The feud had escalated from there to the point of our mission at Owen Crossing.

The young people were so silent I was becoming concerned.

Lydia spoke to Terry, "We are so sorry that you and your friends became involved in our problems."

Sergeant Hardison looked around with a faint grin and replied, "I have heard about you old guys and didn't believe any of it. Now I am a believer."

The pallor he had been wearing disappeared with a blush, when he made that statement. That broke the tension and soon everyone was together again and hands were reaching for other hands. I winked at Daniels as a pretty redhead took his hand.

The demeanor among us had changed by a dramatic degree. There was no talk except for polite murmurs. The men were sitting in a room full of people in the grips of a hundred meter stare. During the war I had seen men sitting in the same fashion—alone, among many—their eyes focused on a distance with nothing in sight. I do not remember any thoughts I might have had or any action I may have taken. There was no feeling of fear—just the shock of combat. Combat, that's how it felt, and the mission had been completed. During the action there were no thoughts other than carrying out the mission. I can only speak for myself, but my mind had blanked out the people involved. In combat, you should never visualize a face. The Gormans and Kwong were nothing but targets. Targets take on human characteristics, when you are fearful of the consequences of the action. I was surprised, after all the intervening years; Detachment X-Ray was not far away.

Sometime around 2000, I became aware of my real surroundings. The shock of combat had passed, and as I looked around, it was evident that Carpenter was back also. He motioned toward the kitchen, and we left the others with their own thoughts. We could hear the murmur of the women's voices from the family room. We had just poured coffee when Charlie Daniels joined us. We were discussing the likelihood of a visit from Sheriff Dickerson. Daniels predicted he would show up by 0800, and we would be in for some tough questions. It was the consensus in the conversation that Carpenter and John Silvers would be our official spokesmen. Silvers stepped in at that moment and asked what our story would be.

We mulled over a few things and Carpenter said, "Shucks, we went huntin' up on Black Bear Ridge."

Daniels grinned, "Yeah, the Ridge is a long ways from Owen Crossing, but did we get anything?"

"Shore we did," Carpenter retorted with almost a smile and continued, "Don yo member that ole black bear what's hanging in the wood yard?"

None of us remembered him but all of us claimed the kill.

"'Fraid not old timers," Terry Hardison said from the door, "It takes the eye sight of a young man to kill a bear in a snow storm. As a matter of fact, visitors always take the first shot. I am proud of myself, but I want to see my trophy."

We all went out to the wood shed, no one questioned the fact, but we wanted to make sure we had seen the kill.

Daniels' prediction that the Sheriff would be in by 0800 was correct. Lydia took the call from Caleb at 0730, warning that local lawman had turned up the road with two cars. Carpenter stood and told his wife to send the lawmen to the barn. We all took our coats, felt for the handguns, and left the house for the outbuildings. When the posse appeared, we were just finishing the chores. This was not a rag tag outfit. We were artfully surrounded and each deputy had a clear firing line. Someone had trained them well. There was no evidence of the state patrol bluster we had seen the day before.

Sheriff Dickerson got right to the point and asked how we had spent the previous day. Carpenter told him about the bear hunt and offered to show the kill. The lawman said it wasn't necessary because the offer wouldn't have been made without a carcass available.

One of the deputies asked who had made the shot.

Terry Hardison spoke, "I made the shot. These old guys can't shoot on a bright day much less in a snow storm, and helicopter pilots aren't fast enough."

There were chuckles, but Dickerson was having none of it. He was there to question people not listen to bright talk. Carpenter suggested we go into the tack room to get out of the cold.

We got settled in the tack room.

Sheriff Dickerson looked at Terry and said, "I don't know you, son. Why did you shoot the bear? I know who can shoot in a snow storm."

He indicated Carpenter because the local people knew of the skills of this particular neighbor.

Terry chuckled and held his own, "I know, Sheriff, these old guys can shoot. They let me have the first shot because I am a visitor. I was lucky enough to make the kill, and I am a Marine from DC.

The lawman appeared satisfied and turned to Carpenter, "Son, you know why I am here. I sure do hope you can tell where you have been the last couple of days."

"Been right here, Sheriff," Carpenter answered, "Cept fo yesterday, when we went up on the ridge fo a deer, but that ole black bear come walkin' through. We gon dress him out in a while. Yuh fellers wan a mess a meat?"

The Sheriff didn't answer, instead he turned to me and said, "I don't know you, where are you from?"

"I am from DC also, Sheriff. I knew these guys back in Korea during the war. I came through this way a few weeks ago and ran into Carpenter. He and his wife invited me back for Thanksgiving, and I couldn't turn that down. They also invited some of my friends. The bear shooter is one of them," I answered, along with some laughs when I indicated Terry as the bear shooter.

Our plans for Carpenter and Silvers to do the talking didn't even get off to a start. This wily country sheriff knew all the tricks. He would be talking directly to one person, and ask a question before turning to another person for an answer.

He was talking to Silvers and asked, "Where did you go hunting?"

He had abruptly turned and pointed to Josephs for an answer.

Josephs stuttered and said; "I didn't go hunting."

Then he covered, "What I mean is, I didn't get to hunt because the Marine shot the bear before I even loaded my rifle."

The Sheriff looked at him for long time—long enough to make all of us nervous.

Evidently, Dickerson realized the questioning was not changing our story and said, "I probably will want to talk to you again, so stay handy."

I decided it was time to question his resolve and said, "Sheriff, I will be glad to talk with you at any time, But I'm leaving on Sunday. I will leave a number to call if I am needed."

The lawman started to object and Carpenter broke in, "Sheriff Dickerson, he wuks fo a Senatuh in Washington. This other guy," pointing to Josephs, "Is a Senatuh from Okalahoma.

"O.K., O.K.," the Sheriff gruffly said, and it was evident he didn't like what was happening, but he didn't have the authority to hold anyone unless he would bring charges. His problem was that he thought he knew what had happened, but there was no way for him to prove his suspicions. The wall phone rang.

Carpenter listened for a few moments and said, "Send em down."

He continued after hanging up the telephone, "Sheriff, Cap'n Jordan of the State Police is comin'."

For the first time, the Sheriff showed a sense of humor. He turned to his Sergeant with a side-glance and a grin for us, "See what that dumb bastard wants."

The State Cop tried to assert his authority, and the Sheriff wouldn't put up with the idea. He finally told the Captain that the incident happened in the county and county officers had jurisdiction.

The cop sputtered, "The hell, our cars were in escort."

Dickerson said quickly, "If you observed the ambush, why didn't you arrest the perpetrators on the scene."

One of the deputies snickered and whispered loudly, "That wasn't an escort. They were following too far away to catch anyone."

We all laughed when the State Cops stormed out telling us not to leave the county.

Dickerson said, "Now Captain, you tell the Colonel that I told these boys it was all right if they left, as long as I know how to get in touch with them."

The Sheriff turned back to us and said, "They are jerks, and I will not have them messing around in my cases. This is my case, and you boys know something about it. You can leave but you better keep in touch with my department, and I know people from all over the country. They are from all kinds of law enforcement agencies, so you can't hide. When I say keep in touch, I mean keep in touch Monday, Wednesday, and Friday. If you don't like those conditions you can complain about your civil rights in my jail."

Jacobs started arguing and Dickerson listened for a few minutes and responded, "Son, it is simple. If you can't do it my way, you will be invited to take a ride down to the County Seat today."

Jacobs looked at him and grinned, "Nope Sheriff, I bet I can find a way to make those calls."

We went back toward the house, and Carpenter led us into the wood shed. He was making sure the Sheriff got a look at the bear. It was a big black animal and the locals stood around trying to guess how it would dress out.

"Les see," said Carpenter, as he unsheathed a skinning knife that was hanging from a peg. Someone had prepared a good alibi. The Sniper was good with a knife too. In just a few minutes, the hide dropped from the carcass

Then with a faint grin he handed me a butcher knife for the disemboweling. My other friends laughed, and I closed down the mirth because it only took a couple of minutes to open down to the ribcage.

Carpenter grinned and asked, "Wheah did yuh learn that?"

I retorted, "You guys thought I was a city boy. I have butchered more hogs than any of you have ever seen—including you hog country professors."

Laughs followed when I indicated Silvers and Jacobs as the hog country professors.

One of the deputies spoke, "Shoot, I thought that I remembered you," he said to Jacobs. "You were my ROTC instructor at Iowa State."

Some of his friends started ribbing him about the ROTC and the atmosphere eased a bit. I glanced at the Sheriff. He was trying to appraise us, but he also seemed to be more at ease.

Lydia and Samantha came out with steaming coffee, and of course, there was a bottle of whiskey for lacing the brew. The Sheriff smiled faintly as he held the bottle up against the light. He watched a perfect bead form when the bottle became horizontal. All of us knew that the Lawman was testing a great mixture of mountain-brewed corn whiskey.

One of the deputies said, "Shoot, now is the time to find out where this pure brew is made, but Sheriff we have to taste it and make sure it is pure."

Dickerson responded, "Oh, you can bet I will ask, if there is some left when we finished the coffee, we will take it as evidence."

The last time the lawman held out his cup, Jacobs made a show of squeezing the last drop in to the mug.

Dickerson finished his drink and said, "Drink up boys, we have to go. The snow had started again. I had not noticed but there was another heavy-fall starting." The lawmen refused an offer of food from the kitchen and/or a cut of the bear.

# Chapter 13

The media was having a field day with the story being reported, repeated, and reported again. The reporters were becoming frazzled because no one would talk. On camera, one said that someone had to know something, because the Gormans were one of the foremost families of the region. Sheriff Dickerson had his deputies walking a straight line, with no talking. Later in the afternoon, one of the reporters made contact with the State Police and learned that the Gorman convoy was being escorted when the ambush occurred. The information really made a splash, and the State was embarrassed by the news. First, the media was asking why the State Police were escorting private citizens. Second, why, if they were escorting the convoy, did the private citizens lose their lives?

The Commander of the Police Barracks was soon cornered. He tried to use the weather to explain all the unexplainable information. When those excuses didn't wash, the Commander said that the suspects had been identified by his department, and reported to the Sheriff. Dickerson denied this report and went on camera, much to the discomfort of the State. He suggested that if the Police had suspects, they should have been arrested or at least brought in for questioning. It wasn't long before the speculation began to focus on the Carpenter and Daniels family. The media also suggested that if the families weren't involved, they would know who were in the ambush party. Caleb called almost immediately, after the report, with information that Carpenter Road was closed because of a snow slide.

I said among laughs, "Shucks, jest good ole country folks warnin' neighbors of a danger."

Carpenter grinned when I asked, "Wonder how that slide occurred?"

We were up on Sunday morning and found a dazzling sunrise. The coffee was just beginning to perk when Caleb called and said that the slide had been cleared. The State Police was reporting that all roads were clear to the Interstate.

I said, "Folks, I think we should leave before the media finds the road cleared."

It was hustle and bustle getting breakfast, getting the cars packed, and warmed. We decided that it probably would be best if all the visitors left—the Carpenters were relieved. We said our good byes without delay. Terry and Sally were in the rental. Doreen and I took my car that had been left from the trip "jest a little piece down the road."

Charlie Daniels waved to Doreen, and before he could get to the helicopter, she was in his arms for a fast kiss. She ran back with a flaming face as all of us started whistling and applauding. We were on the road toward town within forty-five minutes of the report that the road had been cleared of the snow slide. Daniels escorted us out with the helicopter, and one of Caleb's scouts was waiting to run ahead of us to the freeway. It didn't take long to cover the "little piece," and the escort honked as we turned east and the Silvers group continued to the northwest. Daniels buzzed us as we gained speed. Doreen waved and the helicopter hovered in front of the car. She squealed with delight as we read the sign in the pilot's hands, "I LOVE YOU."

She giggled with a red face when I said, "Shucks, I didn't think that Charlie had noticed you."

The road was clear and dry, and I was willing to test fate. So as they say, I put the pedal to the metal. After three hours of travel, we crossed a county line, and I slowed to the posted speed. The radio reporters were still speculating and rehashing the ambush story. An excited report came in that the river road had been cleared of the snow slide. The next report wasn't so exciting because the reporters rushed out and found the Carpenters alone, with the information that all visitors had left early in the morning. One of the reporters told of an incident, when he insisted that our names and locations be released.

He exclaimed, "Mr. Carpenter is a dangerous man. He threatened to shoot me if I didn't get off his place. I think he would have shot me."

According to other reports, this particular news hawk was trying to hide in the garage when Carpenter found him. He was lucky that the Sniper only threatened him.

I kept a steady pace for the run to the Mississippi River. We were in touch by radio and Terry assured me that he had enough fuel for the trip. Someone had filled both automobiles with gasoline. We crossed the bridge into Tennessee about 1500. After regaining the freeway, we pulled into a service center for fuel and food. Doreen had been silent for the entire trip, and I hadn't disturbed her thoughts.

As we walked to the restaurant, I put my arm around her and asked, "Any problems, kiddo?"

She looked up with a weak smile and said, "I am worried about Charlie."

Terry and Sally were walking behind us and the Marine spoke, "No need to worry about that helicopter pilot. He can take care of himself."

A morning newspaper was at the table we selected, and after a careful perusal I found the story of the Ozark ambush buried in page seven. That didn't bother me in the least, because we did not need to catch national attention. My young friends wanted to talk about the mission.

I explained, "You generally know what happened. We ambushed people who were threatening to kill the Carpenters and many of their neighbors. The best way to handle this is not to dwell on it—don't talk too much between each other. I don't think we will have any problems because Carpenter apparently carries some weight in the community. Sheriff Dickerson may ask us to talk to him again, but we will face that when it happens. I will try to cover you, if anything unexpectedly comes our way. The story appears to be important only in the local area. That is good and frankly the less you know the better it will be for all of us."

There was a motel in the complex, and we decided to check in until the next morning. The desk clerk had no trouble with the request for adjoining rooms. She also honored our request to be placed away from the main traffic area. Once we got settled, Terry and Sally joined Doreen and me.

I said, "Sally, we haven't heard much from you in the past couple of days. Are you O.K?"

I knew she was all right as soon as she started talking, "Bossman, I bin scared tuh say enny thin, an dis ole big Marine has kep me in da bed, mos time. Maybe it's the mountain air. He is rabbity all de time."

# Chapter 14

We spent an uneventful afternoon and evening in the motel suite—instead of going out, we ordered in for dinner. I was sure that we would be completely clear of any media attention by noon. The story wasn't getting much play east of the Mississippi River. The plans were to leave early and drive straight through. I called Susan Bonnet and reported that we were on the way home and asked if any problems had arisen. She said the only thing out of the ordinary was the number of people who were trying to locate me. Many wouldn't leave an identity or message.

She broke off the conversation with, "Hurry home. I have something for you."

She laughed and wouldn't tell me what I would be getting. She didn't have to tell me because each occasion brought complete satisfaction, I told her that we would be in on Tuesday morning and that I was eager to get there.

The trip back to Washington was tiring but uneventful. I entered the office at 0630 and Susan Bonnet was waiting.

She gave me a long, lingering kiss before saying, "Buddy Boy, you sure are important to some people. Your friend from the CIA has been looking for you on a daily basis. Your Chinese friend has been looking for you almost as often, and I am jealous because you didn't take me to wherever you went."

"You didn't want to be there because it snowed the entire time we were there," I responded.

She arched her brows and asked, "We? We who?"

She stepped to the door, flipped her skirt at me and blew me a kiss when I whistled. I went into the office after getting a cup of coffee and my telephone was ringing. I allowed the intercept to answer, and it was Cliff Grogan wanting me to call. I listened to the other messages and Grogan was on a number of times. Chow Ling closely followed him. There was also a message from Madam Hau.

I called the Ambassador's residence and was surprised when Madam Hau answered. After the greeting and apologies for calling so early, she invited me to a reception for Mr. Dong Ping. She also asked me to bring Susan and volunteered the information that the reception was being held because of the imminent departure of Dong Ping. I held off, with some effort, asking when the Delegate would be leaving. She broke the connection after telling me she was starting the third Drury book, and rewarded me with her delightful laugh, when I remarked at the speed she was reading.

The imminent departure of Hsu Dong Ping was information I was interested in but didn't want to hear. His leaving early would reduce our chance at Long Ball Kwong. I was still considering this new twist to our problem when Cliff Grogan called and chided me for being away from the office so long. He must have called from the hall because in just a few minutes he stepped into my office.

"Where have you been?" he asked.

"If you work at an honest trade you will receive invitations for Thanksgiving holidays. I had a great holiday but don't ask me where I have been," I said in a whisper.

He tried to pin me down as to the exact location while trying to make it sound like innocent interest. The CIA Operative was especially interested in who my friends were and what we did over the holiday.

"Just ate turkey and dressing," was all the answer I offered.

His questions were beginning to have an edge, as if he knew little but suspected much. All I could do was hope he hadn't come across Silvers and the others. If they were fully identified, our plans would have to be put on hold. It was a known fact in the nether world of Washington, D. C., many times the CIA and other intelligence agencies took action before really being asked or directed. If they had an inkling of a plan, which crossed their interest, the planners would be at risk.

At the door Grogan turned and asked if it would be possible for us to meet later in the day. I agreed, until he suggested another trip into the Virginia countryside. There was no way that he could get me back to CIA headquarters without someone of trust to go with me.

I asked, "Cliff, if I go there with you, is it all right for me to bring a friend?"

He hesitated a few moments and then said, "Sure that would be O.K., but your friend may have to stay in the waiting room."

"Senator Martin probably wouldn't agree to stay in the waiting room," I answered with a grin.

He matched the grin and said, "Maybe we shouldn't bother the Senator. He is probably too busy for such trivial pursuits."

We haggled a while and finally agreed to meet in the lounge of a downtown hotel. He laughed when I asked if the hotel had been debugged. While we were sparring, I heard Sally enter her office. Grogan heard her too, and made his departure.

I made a short call, and she came in after I had hung up the telephone. It was obvious she was upset. The Capitol police had met her and Terry when they arrived from the holiday trip and took them to police headquarters. They were questioned for most of the night and no one would tell them why they were detained. I called Terry and he related basically the same information, and it didn't take an expert in human relations to know that we had one irate Marine in town. He didn't mention it but my first thoughts were that Sally's apartment had been staked out because she worked for me. After settling the secretary and Marine down by suggesting they stay out of a possible fray with the police, I would determine why they had become targets. My next move was to call a friend at the District Police Station, and asked what was happening between my staff and the district police. He told me that he had no knowledge of the situation but would ask around and return the call. I called the Marine Barracks and asked to speak to the Commanding Officer—a Major Johnson came on line and introduced himself as the Executive Officer, Marine Barracks.

I asked if the Marines had been notified of the questioning of Sergeant Hardison. The Major said that the note had just been delivered to his desk.

I said, "Major, Sergeant Hardison was with me and some friends for the entire holiday weekend. I will vouch for his actions during the leave period.

I have already called the police. You can bet I am not going to put up with my staff and friends being harassed. In case you don't recognize me, I work for Senator Sam Martin, and he will be advised of the entire situation."

Major Johnson was evidently a man of action; He called the police before I received an answer from my contact on the force.

The policeman called and said, "Hey, lighten up, the Marines are on our butts too. The Marine and his girlfriend were questioned because of a request from the CIA. What the hell are you getting me into?"

I answered, "Nothing pal, but you can bet that someone from the CIA will get an ear full when I report this to the Senator. He will probably call you folks, too."

The officer chuckled, "I think it is time for a few days off."

I inquired and he denied knowing why the CIA was interested in the couple nor did he know what questions they were asked.

Cliff Grogan was waiting when I reached the hotel. He offered a drink and dinner. I asked the waitress for a cup of coffee. We sat for long moments and I waited him out.

Finally, he shrugged his shoulders, as if to loosen the muscles, and asked, "How about telling me about your vacation?"

"There is nothing to tell that would be an interest to you. Except for the kids who work for me, you would not know any of my friends."

He almost caught me when he replied, "I think I have seen them, and you guys did a great job at Owen Crossing."

It was all I could do, not to react to that statement.

I looked across the table and said, "Thanks, but we didn't do anything at Owen Crossing, except, we were picked up near that crossing. We rode with a helicopter pilot who must have had an eye on every knot on his head. He flew through a snowstorm, in and out between boulders and trees. He didn't blink an eye, but neither did I, because mine were closed in absolute terror. As a matter of fact, I still pucker when thinking about that ride."

Grogan looked at me for a couple of seconds and replied, "You know that I am talking about the ambush a day or two after Thanksgiving."

I shook my head and said, "You are talking about some other folks. The people I was with went deer hunting, and killed a black bear instead of a deer. He was a big sucker and dressed out close to four hundred pounds. We heard about the ambush when we returned from the hunt."

He grinned and said, "O.K., O.K., I know all about that bear. Ben Dickerson said it was a big one, but so was the convoy you hit."

"Sorry Cliff, I do not know what you are talking about, and I do not like the implications you are making. What do you care about a feud in the Ozarks? Don't ask too many question and be careful."

I stood up and continued, "If your Ben Dickerson is Sheriff Dickerson, you also know that he questioned us and left us butchering the bear. So if this story continues to play, you might warn your friend Ben Dickerson to be careful also."

He asked quietly, "Am I hearing threats?"

Just as quiet I replied, "No threats—just facts."

He tried to stop me, but I walked out of the restaurant without looking back. Sheriff Dickerson had warned us that he had some long lines that could be pulled. If the CIA knew something, we were in definite trouble. If they only suspected, we had problems—problems could be solved—troubles had to be faced. My immediate concern was to get in touch with John Silvers. At the first telephone booth, I made a direct call to his home.

When the intercept answered, I said, "I will meet you at number two at 0600."

It was a code that he and I had agreed to use. In effect, he was told to be at his number three telephone at 0900. It was a simple number transposition, but we wouldn't use it enough for anyone to break it, even if they heard the message.

Later that evening, Terry Hardison called and said that he had been asked to introduce me to the Colonel of Marine Barracks. Major Johnson had reported our conversation and the Colonel wanted to follow up on that report. Terry could offer no further explanation as to why the officer wanted to meet with me.

Then he gave me a start, he said, "Colonel Tolliver probably wants to talk about the police questioning that Sally and I went through."

He continued, "Mr. Green, I believe they knew something about our vacation. They were more interested in you and your friends than Sally and me. Most of their questions were about how you may have been involved in the ambush. One asked me if I was involved. We denied any knowledge."

I stopped him with, " Sergeant we will get together in a day or so, and ask your Colonel to call me."

"And you," I continued, "Do not let this crap disrupt your and Sally's, life or plans."

I didn't want him saying much about the vacation in case someone was listening. I had looked a couple of times without finding any devices, but that didn't prove anything. The conversation with the Sergeant resurrected a name I hadn't heard in many years. Tolliver? It couldn't be the same Tolliver I had known years ago in Detachment X-Ray! It was an intriguing idea because there had been a saying in the services.

"If you stay around long enough you will see everyone twice."

I wondered if I was going to see an old comrade for the second time. The Tolliver I knew was a Marine Sergeant, and this one, a Colonel in the Marines I didn't know—yet.

Things were beginning to back up. Other people were getting too near, and this had heightened when the CIA used Sheriff Dickerson's name in a familiar manner. I called Doreen and instructed her to pick me up at 0430. It would take us some time to get to one of the safe telephones, and I wanted plenty of time to lose any followers who wished to know about my movements. I had already picked up a tail that appeared shortly after we had returned from the Thanksgiving holiday. I was ignoring them at the present because I wanted them to become comfortable about their duties.

Susan Bonnet called and invited me to dinner and a "special" dessert that couldn't be described by unsatisfied people. I had experienced her desserts and was always more than satisfied. Her low, husky laugh came over the receiver when I suggested that she slip off something that was comfortable when I arrived.

She ended the conversation whispering, "I slipped that off before calling you."

I didn't waste any time heading for her place. What an offer!

# Chapter 15

Doreen rang my doorbell at 0430 and readily accepted the offer for breakfast. She asked where we were going and I put off telling her.

Her freckled face broke with her infectious grin and she whispered, "I do believe, we are going for a ride in the country side."

My only answer was a wink and a shrug. I was becoming more aware of the attention of my, if not enemies, competitors. It was a great concern that I seemed to be drawing attention rather than residing in the shadows. I began to think more and more about my "house down by the river" in Venture. There were a few years that I wanted to get back to—no one thought anything about Jake Green moving around the neighborhood. If I was stopped, it started a conversation about the last fish I had caught or the one I was going to catch. Now I was beginning to feel as if I was the fish nearing the baited hook. My redhead had parked in front of the apartment house. After breakfast we went down, and I made a big deal out of checking tires and the spare in the trunk. This was cover for me to inspect the neighborhood. While I was looking into the trunk I spotted a silver and black Chevrolet station wagon parked at the corner. It might be a family going on an outing, but I was betting the children were covers—if they were children.

Doreen looked at me in surprise when I opened the door for her.

Her surprise turned into a grin when I whispered, "The Chevy wagon at the corner, watch it as we leave.

She caught me by surprise when she turned away from the curb and accelerated into a U-turn. The car skidded as we took the first left and she immediately pulled into the curb. I looked over my shoulder and the Chevy was turning into the street. It started to speed up as it passed us. There was some hesitation at the first intersection, but then the vehicle took off at high speed without changing directions.

Doreen had kept the engine running, and at the last sight of the station wagon, she took off and turned at the first intersection. She evidently had practiced her moves because after a few minutes of turning and back tracking, we saw the sign to the beltway.

My only instruction was, "North."

We entered the freeway at the speed limit, and she expertly moved to the left lane. I told her to observe the posted speed and settled down for the ride.

Doreen broke me out of a doze, "Boss, I think we have company again. There is a maroon Plymouth, two cars back, marking us. Every time I make a move with speed or lane change, he matches it."

I turned, looked back, and found the Plymouth and told her to increase speed. She did and in a few minutes the following automobile was marking us again, this time, three cars behind.

The cat and mouse game kept up for a few miles, and we were getting near to the exit into the Maryland countryside.

The Irish grin blossomed when I said, "Lose them."

It was pedal to metal through traffic, down an off ramp, and back on at the next entrance to the freeway—with tires squealing all the way. The tailing car didn't have a chance. It stayed with us through the first off and on movement, but at the second off ramp he couldn't make it. Doreen had out-driven them and had brass enough to come back on the freeway, pull up and wave as we passed in the opposite direction. They were startled but there was nothing for them to do. We left the freeway at the next off ramp. After a leisurely approach to the beltway, she moved over to the right and drove at a sedate speed until we came to the correct off ramp. I enjoyed her skills, but it sure was "white knuckle time" when those skills were demonstrated.

We moved into Maryland and kept our route at random. She drove on almost all the roads in the area, and we even rode across a city park to a bank of telephones. I dialed the number, and John Silvers answered on the first ring. He listened without interruption as I told him what had transpired with the CIA and that Long Ball had decided to return to China. He questioned me about the CIA and we agreed on common reasoning that if the CIA knew facts, we had problems, but if they were speculating then that was their problem. We also speculated that it wouldn't be long before we would be under the scrutiny of the FBI, that is, if they were not already in the picture. It did seem strange that the CIA was moving ahead of the FBI in a domestic situation.

John was somewhat concerned to find that the CIA had talked to Sheriff Dickerson.

I said, "John, I am not sure the CIA called Dickerson. That old buzzard probably called them. If you remember, he said something about being able to reach long distances in the law enforcement community. He is too much of a professional to be just an Ozark Mountain Sheriff. John agreed with me, and after discussing the situation decided that he would contact Carpenter about the Sheriff, along with a call to Jacobs and Josephs. This was cautionary. We didn't want them surprised by anyone asking unpleasant questions. He also suggested that we hold onto the story about the bear hunt during the Gorman ambush. We also set a date for the next contact, and I suggested, except for emergencies, I would initiate all calls between us on a schedule that he would provide. We decided that would be enough to discourage any ideas about breaking our communications network. He gave me the list of numbers for the telephones I should call, and each call would initiate a schedule for the next call.

Silvers asked, "What about Long ball?"

"That is tough," I replied, "But I am planning to confront him before he leaves or we take him. The Chinese Ambassador has invited me to a going away party."

There was a long pause and I continued with a question, "Want to go to a party with me?"

He chuckled and said, "Now wouldn't that be a surprise for my old school chum. If you can swing that invitation, you bet, I would like to see that bastard and let him speculate about any possible future plans."

I laughed and said; "Now you are talking like a Jarhead. I am sure that Madam Hua will extend the invitation to a famous Professor and his Lady."

I returned to the car and Doreen asked, "Boss, what have you got going now?"

I answered, "Nothing to worry your pretty head about. We have done this before. I just enjoy riding with you and watching every traffic law on the books being violated."

"Yeah, and look what I got into by driving for you, "she quipped, "Your friends are nice, but they are dangerous. They remind me of Daddy and his brothers."

Then with faked scorn she said, "Sure did enjoy being with Daddy and my uncles."

I retorted, "I bet you did, and you scare the hell out of me. Let's get out of here but don't run back across the park. Someone may arrest you. If they do—I don't know you."

She giggled and asked, "How fast?"

We stopped for lunch at one of my favorite small towns—Woodbridge, Maryland—which was over twenty miles from the telephone I had used to call Silvers. Surprise! We were ordering, when two CIA Agents walked by the booth. One of them had been at the agency when Cliff Grogan invited me to take a ride into the Virginia countryside. He acknowledged my salute with a tight grin, and they took a table next to us. I could only conjecture why they were in the area, but I fully expected to be questioned before we left. *Surprise and shock!* The waitress was serving us, when Chow Ling and an associate came into the restaurant. I couldn't believe we had been followed, so it was a guess that both organizations were covering the area around the Capitol. Chow Ling looked around, spotted me, and turned toward our booth. With a satisfied smile he took a seat next to Doreen. The associate waited for an invitation before taking a seat on my side of the table.

I had been surprised enough. After long moments of observing each other, I decided it was time for me to do the surprising.

I said to Doreen, "Watch yourself Babe, there are two CIA agents behind you, and Chinese intelligence agents sitting alongside and across the table from you."

The two Chinese were taken aback and become tense because they weren't aware of the proximity of agents from the competition. The two local spies tensed and appeared to be upset at having their cover blown.

Doreen lightened the atmosphere when she started laughing and said, "Boss, we are the only ones who knows everyone."

Chow Ling was the first to recover and joined us, at the discomfort of the three other spies. Doreen may have taken all of us out of a dangerous situation with her laughing at that situation.

I was really enjoying myself because Doreen and I were the only ones comfortable with the situation. Chow Ling appeared to appreciate the setting, but he was uneasy with enemies sitting behind him. His associate had his hand buried in a coat pocket probably clutching a weapon. To keep them on edge I questioned them about being in Maryland at the same time and same place. There was some stuttering that was unconvincing, when they tried to tell why they were in the neighborhood.

I didn't let the Chinese off the hook, either.

"Friend Chow," I asked, "Now just what are you doing out here in the countryside? Are you spying on someone?"

He had no easier time than did the Agency people. Doreen and I finished lunch and left them in a more-tense situation—now they were alone together and I had suggested they were in Woodbridge for a meeting. It was clear to me that all hands had apparently found my general area of operations—be careful, Buddy—be careful—was the silent advice to myself.

A message from Madam Hau was on the telephone answering service when we arrived back into town. It was the only recording on the device, but I noticed at least three calls that triggered the answering message. None of these calls were completed because the caller hung up rather than leaving a message. I called the Chinese Embassy and while waiting for Madam Hau, I found myself wondering how the intelligence communities were reacting to all my calls to the Embassy. That thought alone was enough to cause a smile.

She came on line and apologized for having to postpone the party for Dong Ping. He had unexpectedly decided to stay in the United States for another two weeks. I tried not to allow my enthusiasm for his change of plans to show through during the balance of our conversation. As a matter of fact, I was careful to acknowledge the postponement without mentioning the future Premier of the Peoples Republic of China. This was my chance to arrange an invitation for John and Samantha Silvers.

I said to Madam Hau, "I'm afraid that I can't make the new date for the reception because I have some old friends coming to visit. Please accept my apologies, because I was looking forward to seeing you again."

Without hesitation she replied, "What are their names? By all means, they are invited. Where can I send the invitations?"

She hushed all my protestations.

I finished the conversation, "You are very kind, and I think you will enjoy them. Their names are John and Samantha Silvers. John is a department head for one of our mid-western universities, and Samantha is one of our great ladies. You can send the invitations to me."

I called the Silver's home from a street telephone booth, and Samantha answered.

Before she could call any names, I said, "There is some bad news for your husband but good news for you. The good news is that you are invited to a party. The bad news for your husband is that he has to buy you a very expensive gown for a formal affair."

Without calling my name she laughed and said, "I will be glad to tell him the bad news, and we are looking forward to the party. Let us know when you expect us."

I promised that I would and gave her a message for John—I would call him on Saturday at 0930 this time on telephone number four. She apparently knew the code because she had no problem with the message.

On Friday morning, I have just removed my coat when Cliff Grogan called for a meeting. He refused to come to my office, and I refused to leave because of the workload. We were expecting Senator Martin back before Christmas, and we knew that he would be keeping the entire staff busy. This gave me a valid reason for not meeting with anyone, especially Cliff Grogan and others from the intelligence community. The fact that I was under scrutiny from so many agencies was beginning to offer a special challenge to me. With so many digging into my personal affairs, I couldn't expect my friends to continue in the Long Ball Kwong chase. The information that Long Ball had delayed leaving DC certainly offered an exciting prospect for all of us. I decided the next call to Silvers would be an attempt to separate my friends from my personal endeavors.

The telephones were busy. Terry Hardison called and asked if I would meet with his Colonel—Colonel Tolliver. I agreed if we could meet across the Potomac River near the Marine Barracks. There was no need for people on my side of the river to see me with a Marine Colonel, and it would give me a chance to take a hard look at this particular Colonel. The way things were going for me, he probably wouldn't be my old comrade from Detachment X-Ray days. In a way I hoped he was, because Tolliver had been a good friend for a number of years, but that would give the intelligence people something to chew on, if they could put me with military people.

If it were the same Tolliver, he would have to explain his re-entry into the Marine Corps. The Navy had emphatically discharged me with a medal and all sorts of commendations from commanders I could not remember serving. The Colonel came on the line and after introductions by Sergeant Hardison, Tolliver invited me to lunch the following day at the Navy Base Officer's Club. I tried to match the voice with the two men in mind, but it was no deal. Sergeant Tolliver had been a younger man than Colonel Tolliver and I couldn't distinguish any remembered similarities. I worked through the afternoon and into the early evening. Cliff Grogan called and I was so busy, I couldn't meet with him. Chow Ling called and I used the same excuse with him. There was one call that was disturbing. It was from the FBI District's Special Agent. I had expected the call but it was a shock and worry when it came through. The Special Agent wanted me to drop by for a chat, and I promised I would, when I could shake loose from my work. Senator Martin's busy schedule became my excuse for another time.

The calls continued the next morning, and I continued refusing all meetings. I finally asked Sally to hold my calls because I was going to be on the phone for some time—then the telephone was left off the hook. Sally was suspicious and came in and rolled her eyes at me with a grimace that turned into a smile. At noon I replaced the instrument and she brought in a stack of calls for me to answer. I asked if there were any messages that concerned the Senator and she shook her head.

She said, "My Lor' Bossman, whut yuh doin?" and giggled when I dropped the calls into the trash.

# Chapter 16

Since it was Friday afternoon, I decided to make myself scarce. I asked Susan if she knew where I could hide for the rest of the day. She smiled and handed me her keys. When I left, Doreen was sent home with instructions to pick me up at 0600 for a short ride. Then I took a tortuous route to Susan's place. A couple of people had tried to tail, but I was sure all had been eluded after an hour of walking. It was an exciting trip, but what was coming made it all worthwhile.

She came in at 1700 and when I opened the door she asked, "Why are you still dressed?"

It did not take long for both of us to rectify that situation. We stayed in that fashion until I left for my place at 0430.

Doreen was early and I answered the door in a towel.

She grinned and said; "The "old Tom" has been courting. What time did you get home?"

"None of your business, nasty minded girl," I answered with a snarl.

She was laughing when I turned back to the bedroom.

Before I closed the door, she called, "Want me to fix some breakfast."

I waved at her and, and when I returned breakfast smells were floating all around the apartment. She was almost as good a cook as a driver. I attacked the food like a starving man. I was qualified because with the business of the night before I didn't have any dinner.

When I finally looked up from the attack on the food, the green-eyed imp asked, "My goodness, when was the last time you have had food? Other activities sure make you hungry."

She was grinning broader when I offered to slap her.

We left at 0730 for the Saturday telephone call to John Silvers. As expected, we had company and they followed us unto the beltway. Doreen kept glancing at me waiting for the word to lose our followers. We were in the left lane and she had set the speed at eighty miles per hour.

The sign showing the Richmond exit at a half mile flashed by and I said, "Take us toward Richmond."

I was always astonished how fast she could react. We went across three lanes of traffic so fast that no one had time to blow their horns. As we took the exit, I watched the tail go by and could see the surprised features of the passenger. I was sure that Cliff Grogan was the one with an open mouth and wondered if he had come for the ride to teach others how too run a tail.

"Sorry I'm late," I said, when Silvers answered on the first ring. We made plans for attending the party for Dong Ping, or, as we knew him, Long Ball Kwong. A house was available in Georgetown and arrangements had been made for the keys to be sent to his home address. We had a long discussion about the possibilities for the others of our team to make the trip. John commented that if Kwong left for China, our chances of seeing him again were very slim. I agreed with him and we reluctantly offered the possibility that the hit would never go as planned.

I wanted the entire team to meet so I could talk them out of participating in my plans. The situation was changing faster than we could keep track. And I knew we shouldn't expose any others in the eventual plan. It had been a terrible idea to involve them in the first place. Terry Hardison had already participated in an ambush and had been grilled by the police on related items involving the entire group. We were extremely lucky that he couldn't be tied to the Gorman affair. Sheriff Dickerson had left a soft spot; he had been introduced to the Sergeant, but the situation of other involvement had to be settled before we could advance other plans. We were very aware that time was running out for such an endeavor. I told John that I was more worried about the FBI than about the CIA because the FBI worked directly for the Justice Department, and in effect, in this type of case, the CIA worked only for the CIA.

On the way back to the apartment Doreen had tried to question me, but left it alone when I told her that she didn't need to know and probably shouldn't know my plans.

As we turned off the beltway she said, "They are back."

She parked in front of the apartment, and we sat talking for a few minutes.

She smiled broadly, when I told her to take the weekend off, and said, "I thank you, and the helicopter pilot thanks you."

This was the first time she had mentioned a visitor and shrugged it off when I suggested she should have informed me.

"Not that I would have given you any time off, you understand," I said, "But maybe I could have taken Charlie to dinner and let him enjoy D.C."

"Huh," she grunted, "I make sure he enjoys himself."

I raised my eyebrows, and she suddenly realized what she had said. I laughed at her flaming red face.

I got out of the car and spied the tail a couple of spots down. I started walking toward them, and they immediately attempted to move away. Before they could leave, I stepped in front of the automobile and wouldn't be bluffed when the bumper brushed my legs.

I did not recognize either of the agents and told them, "You better get your ass off my street or I will call the cops."

They tried to bluster about the rights of any citizen being on any street in the country.

I retorted, "Stay here or come back here, and I will throw so many charges at you, the cops will be all over your ass. Tell Cliff Grogan that I am tired of it. If he doesn't pull off the tails I will set a senator on to the CIA."

As the Agency car pulled away the Chinese parked a few spaces down the street. I went to their car and told them about the same thing, and they pretended that they didn't understand. One of them was smiling as I shrugged my shoulders and turned toward the entrance to the apartment building. A look back confirmed the actions that they were settling into a set routine. They didn't move even after I looked in their direction. As I walked across the foyer, I asked the doorman to call his boss.

When the Manager came out, I said, "Herb, there are two Orientals in a black Ford sedan just past the front door. They are planning something against someone. I saw them checking and loading weapons."

That was untrue but it would get immediate attention. On arriving at my apartment I went to the window, and the District cops had the Chinese up against the car.

I checked messages before leaving for the meeting with Colonel Tolliver. There was only one message, and it was ignored because it was an invitation for Senator Martin to speak. He wasn't accepting any invitations and wouldn't fill any dates until after the Christmas and New Year's holidays. I didn't see any tails but to make sure I walked away from the apartment and caught the first bus that come along. It was going in the wrong direction, and as we joined heavy traffic I started looking for a way out. I spied a bus a few blocks ahead heading in the opposite direction and caught it by darting through traffic. If there had been any tails I was sure they were caught in traffic. The bus stopped at Arlington National Cemetery, and I left it among a tour group.

At the cemetery I tried to make sure no one was following by staying with the tour group for a block or two and then breaking off and waiting for a possible tail. There was no one following, so I hailed a cab for the Navy Base. The taxi had base privileges and it took me directly to the Officers Club. I planned to get there early so I would be able to observe the Colonel when he arrived. He apparently had the same idea because upon mentioning his name I was escorted immediately to his table. I took a long hard look as we were introducing ourselves, and I was not sure that this was the Tolliver I once knew. He was studying me with the same intensity, with an appraising look that offered no signs of recognition. In Detachment X-Ray, I knew the Sergeant much better as Tolliver than he knew me as Green.

We spent a while in small talk as lunch was served. Then he led the conversation to Terry Hardison. I assured him that Sergeant Hardison shouldn't be in any trouble.

I said, "Colonel, he was with me on the holiday because he is a friend of Sally Gordon, my secretary. I think the hassle came because Sally works for me, and you may have heard the commotion we caused when Senator Martin's offices were bugged. On top of all that, Sally Gordon doesn't take much crap from anyone. As a matter of fact, she probably gave out more crap than any of them, or all of them put together."

The Colonel had acknowledged hearing about the bugging, and said with some appreciation that he had met Miss Gordon and would never forget the experience. She evidently didn't like a statement made by a general, and she told the flag officer where he could go and what to do after reaching his destination.

"That sounds like my girl, Sally," I said and continued, "Whatever you do, don't tell her that I had called her my girl."

He laughed at that and smiling, he said he understood. He thanked me for coming to the Sergeant's aid with the police. We had a pleasant time for a couple of hours. I still hadn't made up my mind about Tolliver until we prepared to leave.

When I started to depart he stood up and offered his hand. I looked into the eyes and saw the crooked grin of my old friend Sergeant Tolliver, United States Marine Corps. After shaking hands I laid the knuckled knife on the table. He immediately created a match. We stood staring at each other with bemused grins for long moments and returned to our chairs.

He broke the tension with a grin, and asked, "When does the tobacco market open?"

We retrieved our weapons and tried to catch up on a lot of years in a very short time. He also said that when he heard my name for the first time, he wondered if old ghosts were rising.

He walked me to the door and said, "That was a long time ago, but I would like to rehash some of the old days with someone who has been through the old days."

I told him that thoughts of the old days seldom came to mind, but rehashing them would be interesting. When we were in Detachment X-Ray we had orders not to talk about, and warned not to discuss the Detachment after separation—but that was a long time ago—and we weren't in Detachment X-Ray now. We shook hands and promised to get together in the near future. I didn't understand his grin but then he dropped a bomb.

"Green," he said, "The General is in town, and we have wondered about you. Before you ask, he helped me to get back into the Corps. He said something about Huntsville when I asked about your departure, and he has questioned me about the possibility of making contacts from the old days. He also ordered that if anyone ever showed, he wanted to be informed."

I was smiling and asked, "I wonder what that old buzzard wants? Is he getting lonely in his old days or is he making sure we remain in Detachment X-Ray?" Remember he told us that once in, never out?"

I continued, "Let him know that I am in town. I would very much like to see him."

I mused after getting into a taxi, *Wonder where and what General Sheffield has been doing since we were together for the last time at Sand Key.*

# Chapter 17

After the meeting with Colonel Tolliver, I caught a taxi back to my apartment. On the way I tried to reconstruct the meeting with my old friend—now Colonel Tolliver, U. S. Marine Corps. I knew that Terry would have to be warned not to try pulling the wool on the Colonel. He was no fool, and the man I knew always did the pulling or was a great assistant. It was comforting that the Commander, Marine Barracks was an old friend especially with the involvement of Terry Hardison. It was understood that friendship did not allow me to jeopardize his career, and I wondered what the Corps knew of his background. That was one subject he hesitated over, other than mentioning that the General had helped him re-enter the Marines. General Sheffield was an enigma. What was he doing back on the scene? Tolliver and I had agreed to stay in touch and have lunch from time to time. There was too much in the past for us to be completely at ease. We were friends, but we knew too much about each other

When the cab pulled to the curb all sorts of people were waiting. My previous warning had not been too impressive with those guys. The Chinese were in a green Plymouth. The CIA was using a blue Ford, and the Senator's chauffeur was waiting with a Lincoln Continental. I waved to the Ford and Plymouth as we pulled away from the curb.

I spoke to the driver, "Bill, keep watch behind and see if a green Plymouth and a blue Ford are following."

He smiled as we exchanged looks in the mirror and answered, "Yes sir, they are back there. They pulled in behind as we turned the corner. The Plymouth is leading the Ford, and I have just finished a defensive driving course, want me to lose them?"

He was eager and I said, "Just for a couple of minutes. Take two or three fast turns to get their blood flowing and then slow down."

He laughed and said, "You are a mean man."

He took two fast turns and then double-parked forcing both cars to pass. Then he pulled in behind them.

Through chuckles I said, "Speaking of being a mean man, you out stretch me. Get ahead of them so they can tail us like good kids."

He honked the horn as he passed both vehicles, and I waved at two drivers who were staring ahead with no notice of other automobiles

The chauffeur drove to the Senate Office Building, and I received frowns after waving at the two tails. The drivers of those cars would probably get the same reaming in two different languages for allowing a chauffeur to take them with a limousine. Sam Martin was in my office, which took me by surprise. I sat down and waited for him to speak. It was evident that my old friend was uncomfortable. He hadn't spoken after our greeting.

He leaned forward and asked, "Whut you got y'self into, old buddy? I have strange people in my office waiten to talk to you."

He paused a second and continued, "The CIA is callin' fer your scalp, and the FBI wants to talk to you real bad."

I lied to my friend, as much as I hated doing that. I didn't feel that a United State Senator should be involved in our plans for Mr. Dong Ping.

I said, "Sam, those jerks have been after me for some perceived plot or other since we left New York. I don't think I told you that the CIA invited me in for conversation, not too long ago. Even with all that, I think it's time for me to move along because I certainly don't want you to become involved with anything, even if it is just speculation or misguided perception."

"O.K.," he said, "I have been asked to look at some pictures."

I retorted, "A dollar to a doughnut—they are pictures of the Chinese going down the steps of the United Nations Building. Every person in this nation and much of the world has had chances to see those pictures on public and private television numerous times."

We stepped into Sam's office and were greeted by Cliff Grogan and his supervisor, the District Special Agent of the FBI, and the District of Columbia Police Chief.

I looked around and said, "Well now, everyone would be present if Chow Ling was here. Is he going to be late?"

Sam asked, "Who in hell is Chow Ling?'

I turned and told him that the CIA and FBI had tailed our staff, along with the Chinese Secret Service, in which Chow Ling is a well-placed official. "You know Sam, he was Chin Hau's aide during the trade talks."

They all sputtered and tried to deny tailing, but I had taken the initiative away from them because they weren't sure if the other agencies were involved in the surveillance. Then I scratched them a little bit, and much to their discomfort told how a young, red-haired driver had out-driven them in all occasions.

"Gen'ulmen, You best have some good pitchers to show me because if you ain't, sumbudy is goin to be in a heap of trouble," Sam said quietly to the discomfort of the supervisory personnel.

The CIA had set up a projector and Cliff Grogan said, "Senator, we would like for you to see these pictures and listen to our questions for Mr. Green, and his answers."

Sam answered, "O.K., if they ain't the ones on the Chinee runnin down the steps at the UN. If thet is whut you got, Son, don't even turn 'em on."

Three or four people tried to talk to Sam, about new things that should be discussed about the pictures. He shushed them and stood indicating the meeting was over. I looked over at Grogan as he started securing his equipment, and winked at him. He smiled faintly and shrugged his shoulders.

He stopped by my office before leaving and said, "Be careful Buddy, you are walking in dangerous territory, and we think we know where to find the piece of ground you are exploring."

Without saying more he left.

Before closing my office I stopped in with Sam, and suggested it might be better if I resigned from his staff. He asked if the government or his office would be in jeopardy. I assured him that the only problem would be the fact that I was associated with the office.

He said solemnly, "Yes, it is my office, and I say who will be associated, but you remember it's my office."

The warning was made with a slight grin, but my old friend wasn't making small talk. I knew that when he spoke with absolutely none of the "good old boy" idiom. It was a relief that I had his support, but in all good conscience, I couldn't stay. He had not been taken into my confidence because, had he known what was going on, he would've tried to put an end to it. Just moments after the last visitors had left, Sam called on the intercom phone and told me he was going on a fishing holiday with the President and Senate Majority Leader and I was invited. It was hard to do, but he accepted the refusal without further discussion.

He ended the conversation with, "Ole buddy, do whut you gonna, but do it before I get back."

I was startled—did Senator Sam Martin know what was coming down the pike? I was relieved that he and the President would be out of town for a few days. Maybe we could get the job done before they returned to the Capitol. Even though the plans didn't directly include them—it would be an embarrassment if a Senator's employee got caught in a plot to kill a world leader. Other things had to be done; one of them was to cut Terry and Sally out of the action. Doreen was going to be a problem because of a certain helicopter pilot. Charlie Daniels was already in town, but I figured a redhead and a freckled face was his major draw. I was trying to figure a way to take them out of the action before resigning from Sam Martin's staff.

Sally put up an argument when I told her to take a couple of weeks off during the holidays. She settled down when I suggested she take Terry along. Terry put up a longer argument because he had already helped on one of our missions. I told him I was sorry for allowing him to become involved in such an undertaking. I assured him, that if needed, I wouldn't hesitate to call his Colonel to keep him away from our actions.

I said in a friendlier tone, "Colonel Tolliver and I are old friends, and he is no man to try to snow. If he asks a question answer it truthfully. Do not try to give him a line because he has already used it. I doubt if he questions you further, if he does, be truthful but don't volunteer any information."

The red-haired Irish lady would have none of it.

She flatly said, "Bossman, I go where Charlie goes, and there ain't a thing you can do about it."

She softened the statement with a dazzling smile when I said she was foolish to hook up with an old reprobate and a run down pilot like Charlie

Daniels. I also called Silvers and told him to expect the key for a house in Georgetown in the mail.

There was a message to call Madam Hua on my answering machine.

"Wonder how she found my number?" I mused.

The number to call was her personal line and she answered immediately. We got into a deep conversation about the Drury books. She questioned me closely as to how I personally felt about the news media. She laughed softly, when I told her even beautiful Chinese reporters were sneaky and all reporters should be watched.

"I hear there is one Chinese reporter that you like to watch," she chortled.

A full belly laugh came when I retorted, "I can't bear to watch her because I always lose my breath."

After sometime she said, "You can count this as my personal invitation to our reception for Mr. Dong Ping. He has decided to remain in your country until after January first. You, your lady, and friends are most cordially invited, and the formal invitations will be delivered tomorrow. In that, you will find the reception scheduled for the Friday before your Christmas Day."

When she broke the connection, I immediately checked the calendar. We had almost two weeks before the party, and a little over three weeks to take any action against our old friend, Long Ball Kwong. I wondered how he would react to John Silvers. Saturday morning the telephone rang, and it was Silvers letting me know that he and Samantha had arrived. He made a comment that the house was more than they expected for a rental.

He laughed when I said, "That's no rental, my friend. It belongs to a gorgeous flight attendant who is vacationing in Switzerland without me."

I broke the conversation and told him that I would call back. We weren't too concerned about someone listening but I didn't want much information passed on an open line.

I went to a street phone booth and called Georgetown. They were expecting the call, and John answered on the first ring. He immediately accepted my invitation to go to Maryland for crab cakes. Samantha came on the line and said she had been in touch with Sarg and Darlene Jacobs. They would be arriving sometime later in the afternoon, and I assured Samantha that it would be fine with the owner if they shared the house. None of us had heard from Josephs. He and Linda had disappeared. We all had a chuckle later when we heard that they were in Alexandria, Virginia, with a cousin of Linda's. The information was on my message center after returning from the street booth. I returned the call and Linda accepted the invitation for dinner.

I called Susan and she accepted the invitation, after my apology for asking so late. She accepted my explanation that the crab cake dinner was unexpected because my guests had just arrived. We traveled to Maryland in Josephs' travel van and all of us had a great time, with special friends, during the drive into the countryside. Susan fitted in with the others, and they accepted her from the start. She complained cheerfully about my not having introduced them before, and wouldn't accept my answer because Sally had told her about the Thanksgiving trip.

There was a momentary lull in the men's conversations. It was a disquieting statement because we didn't know how much Sally had talked about the holidays in the Ozarks. It was Susan's question, which got an answer to one of mine. Where were the Carpenters? Samantha said that they would be in on the following Tuesday. She also said, for my benefit, the situation for the Carpenters had changed for the better since Caleb had been appointed sheriff. That was a surprise, but the strong, unobtrusive man would probably make a good lawman. What had happened to Sheriff Dickerson? He had appeared to be well-entrenched as sheriff of the county. I would feel more at ease when we found him.

There was a general laugh when Darlene Jacobs remarked, "Well maybe, just maybe, we can get Carpenter to discuss the changing of the county lawmen."

During the discussion of the Carpenters, Susan said that Sally and Terry were delighted with the demeanor of Carpenter and thought his wife was terrific. Samantha described the missing friends for Susan's benefit, especially the differences in attitude. Carpenter was silent almost to the point of being morose, and Lydia was vivacious and one of the beautiful women that other beautiful women agreed was beautiful. We pulled into a seafood restaurant in Woodbridge, Maryland. I didn't expect to see anyone from the city.

The first person I saw was Cliff Grogan when Susan said, "Oh look, there is Cliff and Molly Grogan."

I didn't want to look, but what was the CIA doing in Woodbridge? The last time we were here I met CIA agents along with the Chinese. Maybe I would stop coming to this out-of-the way village on the Eastern Shore.

The Grogans had been seated by the time we arrived at the desk. It was a very large establishment with a number of different rooms. I knew that Cliff was smoker so I asked for a non-smoking room. The women headed for the bathroom before taking their seats.

When they left the table Jacobs asked, "Navy, is there something we should know?"

I told them that the man Susan had pointed out was a CIA Agent who was especially interested in my movements.

I explained, "This is one of the ones putting on pressure because of the Chinese news tape. He has seen all of us on the video, and I have been questioned about the people on the tape. This is a huge place so chances are we won't see him, but if we do, maybe he won't be able to put us together on the newsreel.

Silvers said, "Well, let's hope he doesn't see us."

That hope was dashed when the women returned.

Susan exclaimed, "We saw Cliff and Molly and invited them to have dinner with us."

The men exchanged shrugs and faint smiles. The Grogans approached and I introduced everyone while we were moving around to make room for them at the table. It became apparent that Cliff was searching his memory for the identification of the three men. He was closest to Josephs and tried to strike up a conversation. Linda may have felt the tension because she captured the conversation, and after a few minutes, Grogan began to relax. The balance of the evening was very enjoyable. On a number of occasions, I noticed Cliff studying his new acquaintances.

The memory searches didn't pay off that night but bright and early on Monday morning he called, and said, "I have looked at some video this morning, and I saw your friends."

The telephone went dead before I could respond.

What to do? That was a problem that couldn't be put off. I left the office and in a roundabout route made my way to the Georgetown house. I knew that no one could have tailed me, but I parked on a side street four blocks from the house. From past visits I knew that an alley abutted the property's back yard, and that is the way I approached. Darlene Jacobs was surprised to find me on the back porch when she answered my knock. I told them the problem that faced us and this caused a serious discussion. We understood that no decision could be made without Carpenter and Josephs.

"Do not move from this house," I cautioned and continued, "You go outside and someone will make you in short order. Friend Grogan has probably already staked out all of the surrounding areas. Do you have enough food for a couple of days?" I inquired.

They assured me that it would be no problem to stay out of the public eye. We decided that Josephs should be warned not to move around Alexandria, and John Silvers suggested I put in a call to Carpenter. There wasn't much more we could do, and it was imperative that I stay visible to all interested parties. We made up a cover for them not being visible. They were on vacation and on the move throughout the Chesapeake Bay region; therefore, they couldn't have been seen in the local area many times. I would make sure that Cliff Grogan heard that my friends were traveling. No one had missed me and no one noted my arrival to the office. I sat waiting for the expected call. It was not a long wait because the call came through at 0845. It was Grogan and he tried to put me on the defensive, but I wouldn't play his game.

After the greeting, he abruptly asked, "What do you have to say?"

"Nothing," I retorted.

Then it became a waiting game. It was the old silent treatment used by sales representatives in their closing techniques. The premise is that the first one who speaks, loses. Sometimes, it takes nerves of steel to withstand the pressure.

After holding the telephone for two minutes by my watch, I broke the silence; "It was good hearing from you, Cliff. Bye."

I heard him shout something before the connection was broken. I immediately called out to Sally and told her that I was unavailable for the morning.

I instructed, "Don't lie to anyone. Tell them I'm not taking any calls until after noon."

She didn't allow anyone to speak to me, but ever so often she would bring in my messages. Grogan called a number of times, and according to her, he was steaming because I wouldn't take his calls. A number of messages came from unknown callers. I suspected that some were operatives working for Grogan.

Sally came in at 1100, and said that visitors were waiting, and I said with a leer, "I am too busy to see anyone, my little sweet patootie, but you can sit on my lap—just lock the door."

"Sho you are. Yuh jus wanna play wit me, and I ain't gonna let you play, and I ain't gonna give you enny either."

She went out with a grin and a flip of her skirt. I wasn't lying about being busy because the Senator had some important committee business coming up in his home state while on vacation. He asked me to stay until that business was complete, before making my resignation official. At 1130, I put in an appearance, by going out through Sam's anteroom and back in my door. I was not surprised to find a very agitated CIA Operative waiting for me.

I said "Hello, Cliff, come on in and have a seat."

He followed me and waited while I looked through the call slips.

I smiled and said, "That was a strange call this morning, Cliff. I just noticed a number of calls from you in this stack. How can I help?"

He actually snarled, "You know what I want. Those people Saturday night were on the tape during Dong Ping's panic. You didn't say anything about knowing them when we were asking about the video."

"Now Cliff," I said, soothing enough to really get up his ire, "No one asked me if I recognized anyone, except for the Chinese. Those guys just happened to be there and Saturday night was a date made at that time. We were in the military. Just a reunion."

He raged, "Reunion hell. You guys were in Korea together and this all has something to do with Dong Ping."

I laughed at him and said, "Cliff, you are imagining things. I was in the Navy and all those guys were Marines. We were in the Yokosuka Navy Hospital at the same time."

He sputtered for a few minutes and said I was going to be called to his headquarters. I really upset him then by asking who had the authority to call me to the local spy shop.

"Tell Walsh that he doesn't have enough weight in his fat ass to summon me."

Grogan sat glaring across the desk, finally shrugged and said, "O.K.,

Buddy, I have warned you over and over again. I am sure I will be seeing you in the future."

"Let's hope not, friend," I said coldly.

We stared at each other for a couple of minutes without a word between us. Finally, he saluted me and walked out smiling. He was in good humor because I heard Sally laughing at something he said. Me? I wasn't in such good humor. Circumstances without controls were beginning to pile up, and as they began to pile up, the idea of taking out Long Ball Kwong began to be daunting. It was bad enough to have the Chinese interested in my personal movements, let alone the CIA. I was now hearing about FBI questions to some of my friends and acquaintances.

Tuesday morning I called the Georgetown house from a street pay phone booth. Silvers answered and agreed we should have a meeting as soon as possible. He said that the Carpenters would be on a United Flight at 1130. We discussed meeting them and decided not because we would have one person not identified with the others. Carpenter hadn't been seen with any of us by the local authorities. Silvers suggested calling the plane before landing time and at least leave them a message. I moved to another station and called the aircraft and got through a number of operators with minimum information changing hands.

When the flight attendant answered, I said, "I have a message for some friends in seats twenty-one and twenty-two. Tell them that the Navy is underway but the Marines will land without support. Tell them to spread the word all along the line." I continued, "I will hold until you deliver the message."

She was back in a few minutes and told me that the Marines would take good care of the Navy. I hung up and checked the time. We had been on the line one minute and fifteen seconds. The call was completed, probably without notice, unless the flight attendants happen to remember the message for some reason. I took a long and careful way to the airport and left a message for Mr. Carpenter. I asked the clerk to see that it was delivered before the passengers left the plane. The message was the telephone number of the Georgetown house, and with it being delivered before the passengers disembarked, there would be minimum attention drawn to the Carpenters.

Upon returning to the office, I found a United States Marshall waiting to escort me to FBI headquarters. He wouldn't answer any questions, and I wouldn't leave without some suggested authority.

Sam Martin came to my aid, he asked, "Son, do you know who I am?'

The young lawman said that of course he knew Senator Sam Martin.

Sam then said, "Well son, you go back to the ones who sent you, and tell them that they need an official summons to take any of my people out of this office."

The officer nodded and left the office. In just a few minutes, the Senator received a call from the United States Attorney's office requesting that I volunteer to meet with the FBI. The folks must have heard the Senator talking without the down home twang.

I shrugged and told him that a request was different than an order, and I was curious why the FBI wanted to see me. Sam grinned and gave me thumbs up; when I asked Sally to make an appointment with the federal people the following day at 1700. I listened in on the conversation and there were some grumps and complaints. I heard a background voice that sounded like Walsh from the CIA. In a few minutes they called back and wanted to change the time and location for the meeting. I refused both counts, and told Sally to inform them, that 1700 at the FBI Headquarters would be suitable for me. I wasn't ready to allow any of the agencies to dictate my actions.

Doreen was in the office and I asked if she was ready for some highway chases. She said that she was always ready to go chasing anything.

With a smile she said, "I was beginning to think you had abandoned me. You have been running here and there without my protection."

She left and in a few minutes called with the information that the automobile was ready, and that we might have to lose three cars. She was parked in a loading zone in front of the office building and I spotted her three vehicles, plus one sitting further down a side street. Someone was ready in case we turned back on the trailing vehicles.

While I was getting into the car, I pointed out the fourth car, and told her to lose them in the shortest possible time. She pulled away from the curb slowly and suddenly gave full throttle and turned back through traffic, but before reaching the fourth tail she made a fast turn into an alley. Doreen made a number of spurious turns and reversals until we were satisfied that the tails had fallen on hard times.

I gave her the Georgetown address and with giggles she said, "Horny, horny, horny," when she recognized the address.

We turned into the alley behind the house, and Doreen was surprised when I closed the garage door with a remote.

She asked, "You sure you want me to come in?"

She actually blushed and took a step back when I retorted, "Sure. Come on in and watch. You may learn something."

Her surprise heightened when she heard Darlene Jacobs laughing from the back door. She gave me a pop on the shoulder when she recognized the mid-westerners. When Lydia and Carpenter came to greet us, Doreen hugged them, and then casually looked around the room.

Lydia let her go for a few moments before saying, "No, he isn't with us now, but he is upstairs."

Even Carpenter laughed when she hit the stairs three at a time. Samantha and Darlene had set the table with coffee and sandwich makings.

We took seats and I asked, "Carpenter, where did you put up?"

"We got a room down at the airport, since we not good enough fer these folks," he drawled.

Linda Josephs said in grand style, "Well it's time we got rid of you, Hill Billy, but you can let your raggedy wife spend some time with us."

"Huh, no siree, city folks stinks worse 'n country folks."

Silvers looked at me with a grin. It wasn't often that one heard a word of humor from the Sniper. Josephs told me that he and Linda had moved to Georgetown the previous night. We sat around the table and Samantha served coffee while we made our own sandwiches.

She called up to the young folks but there was no answer.

Carpenter did it again, "Maybe they asleep."

Silvers asked Lydia if she had been training him in social graces.

The Sniper almost brought the house down with, "Huh, I was saying social graces wen you punks wus still shittin' yeller."

The small talk went on for a few minutes until John Silvers said, "We may have a problem with our plans. Navy, tell them what has been going on around here."

I responded, "The CIA became suspicious when Long Ball panicked and ran down the stairs at the United Nations after seeing all of us in one setting. The spooks became suspicious because of a reaction from Long Ball while I was speaking in the Trade Delegation meeting room. That was when our friend realized that ghosts of the past had come to the present."

I continued, "I was questioned by the CIA spooks before going to Carpenter's place for the Thanksgiving holiday. I still didn't think much about it, until the tails showed up and the Senator's offices were bugged. There is one agent, Cliff Grogan, who has been pressing me for information. He became suspicious after Long Ball reacted to me upon recognition. Everything was going great, and I was staying ahead of the CIA and the Chinese; oh yes, the Chinese are also suspicious. Their lead agent is a smoothie by the name of Chow Ling, and I am pretty sure that Long Ball has told him about a possible problem with us. Then the unexpected happened last Saturday when we went out to dinner, and who, but Cliff Grogan joined us for dinner in a small town on the Eastern Shore. The next morning he called and said, 'I have just watched a video, and I recognized your friends at the United Nations.'

I added, "Since then, of course, Sheriff Dickerson has suddenly come into the picture from this end. He is well known at the Agency."

After a moment of silences Silvers said, "That is where we stand. Except for Carpenter, we have all been tied together. It appears that the Chinese and our own CIA is suspicious of our intent."

Before anyone could answer, I interrupted, "Include the FBI and the Attorney General. I have an appointment with those folks tomorrow afternoon."

Josephs spoke up, "Do we still have a chance at Long Ball?"

"Probably not, unless we tweak him a little," Silvers continued, "Navy and I are going to a party in his honor, and he might be stubborn enough to at least give us time. At the present he is scheduled to leave on the First of January, but if he is the Long Ball of old, he may stay over a day or two, just to watch our plans unfold."

Jacobs spoke for the first time, "Well, if he accommodates us, let's not disappoint him."

"One more thing," I said, "Dickerson evidently has related what he knows about Owen Crossing to the CIA and I don't know about others."

That caused some silent speculation, because each of us knew that we were sinking deeper and deeper in a morass of unknown proportions. The law enforcement and intelligence agencies were drawing a pretty tight noose. We still had a couple of cards to play, because no one had identified our plans and Carpenter also was unknown to our enemies.

"O.K., " I said, "I have cut Terry Hardison and Sally Gordon out of all these plans. I am afraid the little redhead is in if we hold on to Charlie."

All of them agreed that Terry and Sally should not be involved. We were discussing how to get along without the helicopter.

Charlie Daniels said from the stairs, "I stay."

Doreen repeated, "I stay."

"That settles it then," Silvers said, "We continue with our planning until we meet Long Ball eye to eye. That happens next Friday evening at the Chinese Embassy."

He looked at me for confirmation and I answered by nodding.

After the business, the balance of the evening was taken up with visiting and teasing Doreen and Charlie. Carpenter told us that Caleb had been elected in a special election, after being appointed, when Sheriff Dickerson had taken a high paying job with the federal government. Darlene Jacobs posed the question whether or not Dickerson had been assigned to investigate our possible plans. That had to be something else to think about, because he knew of Carpenter's involvement. I left at 0100 and was guaranteed safety. My driver was one of the best and there was a volunteer guard—Charlie Daniels. I didn't ask about their plans when I was dropped at the apartment.

The next morning I told Senator Martin about the scheduled meeting with the FBI and the Attorney General.

I said, "Sam, I should tell you what I know about all this. It started with Dong Ping's so-called flight down the steps at the UN. That, coupled with him dropping the equipment while I was talking, has led the CIA to believe that there is some great plot to harm the Chinese delegate. You know about the questioning at CIA Headquarters. They have been following me like a pack of hounds, and now the Chinese are following them, following me. You remember the office bugging; there was one device that could not be identified. Cliff Grogan thinks it belongs to the Chinese."

Sam started to interrupt at Grogan's name, but I held up my hand and continued, "Oh yeah, Grogan is CIA, and he is the one who took me to see Walsh. I believe Walsh was in the background yesterday when we were talking to the FBI."

"Now to top all this, I took some old friends to Maryland for dinner, and who did we run into? Yes, friend Grogan. He now suggests my friends are on the Dong Ping video, and he is correct, they were visiting for a few days. I made contact with one of them on the way back from Kansas City—the first time I have seen any of them since the Korean War."

Sam was silent for a few minutes, and said, "Boy, you know how to draw attention. Yuh want to go fishin' this afternoon? Before yuh tell me of the meetin' with the FBI, the FBI is goin' fishin' with us today. Call 'em up and tell 'em you cain't go to see 'em cause you are goin' fishin' with the directors of all of them. Oh yeah, the Attorney Gen'l is gonna be aboard too. Tell 'em you will talk to the bosses, if they want to hear yuh.

There was a lot of cussing and sputtering when the FBI was told that I would be unable to make the appointment. In a few minutes, the Federal Attorney's office called and it was the same. This time though, veiled threats, of a possible charge of obstruction of justice, were made between the cussing and threatening. The cussing really got loud when I asked on whose authority would I be charged with such a ridiculous idea. I kept them going until the smoke could almost be seen coming from the telephone. Both offices were on the line yelling and threatening to send the U.S. Marshall to apprehend and bring me to headquarters.

The silence was deafening when I stopped talking. Finally, I let them off the hook saying, "Wait, wait a minute, you folks don't understand I am going fishing with the Directors of the CIA, FBI, and the Attorney General. Now I will be glad to talk to those people about anything they wish to discuss. Or, maybe, you can get invited to the President's yacht. That is how we are going fishing, the 'Big Man' himself will be with us."

They knew when they were beat and started trying to reschedule the conference.

I stalled with; "You call me when I'm near my desk calendar."

I was a long ways away from the calendar—all the way across the room.

The fishing trip was great. It was a beautiful day, and the three bureaucrats were completely out of their heads. The CIA Director went to the President and was rebuffed. The FBI and Attorney general grabbed Senator Martin and he laughed at them. Walsh was aboard and he tried haranguing all of them, and then ordered me to the cabin for questioning, and I suggested he jump over the side.

The President came over to where I was fishing and said, "I don't know what you have done, but those three Civil Servants are really upset."

I answered with a smile, "Mr. President, they have no cause to be suspicious of me. I believe Mr. Walsh is the one pushing and promoting the conspiracy idea."

He chuckled, walked away and sat down with the Senator. It was a great day, not only were the agency heads completely frustrated because I was aboard and not paying any attention to them, they were skunked fishing, also. I caught the only fish of the day, and I thought I would never board that Croaker. He was at least six ounces and every bit of four inches long. I let him off the hook but kept burying the hook in the bureaucrats.

# Chapter 18

I left the apartment Friday morning, and I could identify two tails and there were two other suspicious vehicles. The night before, Doreen was instructed to pick me up at the restaurant where I normally had breakfast. A number of engines were started as I moved away from the apartment building. I walked about six blocks and figured all the tails would be in line and reversed my direction of travel. Sure enough two cars passed and two others pulled into the curb. I wave at all of them and they pretended not to see the wave. When everyone was turned around I reversed again and proceeded to the restaurant. I wanted all hands to understand that I knew them and they were getting edgy, because they couldn't hold the tail without my acknowledgment. While being seated I spied Cliff Grogan and asked the waitress to invite him to my booth. He was approaching, when FBI Agent Warren Smith came into the establishment. He looked my way and I waved for him to join us. I moved to the outside seat and forced them to sit shoulder to shoulder. I wanted to be facing them and not allow easy eye contact between them.

The two agents were sheepish when they took their seats, and I asked, "How did we all wind up at this particular café at this particular time? When are you folks going to stop tailing me? Just call if you want to meet but not when I am with the President."

Smith said with a smile, "Screw you."

The waitress came and we had an enjoyable breakfast with no shoptalk.

When we sat back over coffee, I said, "O.K., guys set the time for a meeting in any public place—not your headquarters--and I will be there. I'll quit screwing around, if you will. Get those tails off me."

We had just finished breakfast when Doreen stopped to picked me up. She had a frightened look. Charlie Daniels had been rousted out of her apartment, and the metropolitan police had locked her in the bathroom. The police had moved on the apartment about 0430, and it had taken Doreen that long to get out of the bathroom.

"Don't worry about it, Sweetheart. Take me to the police station," I said.

She parked the car in an official spot and followed me into the station.

I walked up to the desk sergeant and demanded, "I want to see Charlie Daniels, and I want to see him now. Sergeant, you better hope that he is in good shape."

The cop started to deny knowing what I was talking about, and I said, "Don't give me any crap. Call your Commander."

A lieutenant came out and before he could say anything, "I didn't ask to see a lieutenant, but Lieutenant I am not going to waste time in here. If Mr. Daniels isn't out, in good shape, in fifteen minutes, you, your commander, and your chief, and your Mayor will be brought before the Senate Sub-Committee, which controls the money to operate this crap hole."

He started sputtering about police procedures; I looked at my watch and told him that a minute and a half had been wasted. He turned back into the inner offices and we took a seat in the waiting room. A few minutes later, a superintendent came out and wanted to know my problem.

I pointedly looked at my watch and said, "Ten and one half minutes."

The officer turned and left, causing a few smirks from the desk cops when it became clear that Charlie Daniels wouldn't be delivered on my schedule.

I went to the desk and said, "Sergeant, I have to make an official call to the Senate Office Building. Which telephone?"

He brusquely told me that I wasn't authorized to use a police department telephone.

I just looked at him and asked again, "Which telephone?"

He shoved an instrument over to the edge of the desk, and his eyes widened when I ordered subpoenas up to and including the mayor. The sergeant hustled into the inner office and we walked out of the police station. Before the door closed behind us, I heard the lieutenant and superintendent calling to me. I looked at them and pointed to my watch.

Charlie Daniels walked into Doreen's arms about fifteen minutes after we arrived at the office. He was a little worse for wear but assured us that he was O.K. I took him in to see the Senator and asked him to tell his story. After Charlie had explained what had happened, Sam Martin was quiet for a while. I could tell that my old friend wasn't going to be overly friendly toward other persons in this town.

He leaned back in his chair and drawled, "Well now, I want to do this jest right."

He looked at me and continued, "Issue a formal summons to this young man. I want him to be the firs' witness. Son, set down and tell me again whut happened while yuh was visitin' the local constabulary."

Sam called Susan and asked her to arrange coffee service from the Senate dining room, "and then serve the summons fer a guy, which calls hisself Charlie Daniels, cause he cain't fiddle a lick."

Sam, of course, was referring to his favorite fiddler with the same name. Charlie told us the cops started pounding on Doreen's door, and ordering it to be opened or it would be broken down. They did not offer warrants or identification. He was manhandled and hit a number of times around the kidney area. He had bruises to prove it, along with a black eye, and a split lip. Sam called the senate physician to examine the kidney bruising. When the telephones started ringing, the Senator was primed and ready. The Police Commander and the Assistant mayor's calls weren't accepted. They tried a number of times, and the Senator finally answered them with, "Shet up and listen and don't call again. I want to talk to the Chief of Police and the Mayor—no one else.

The doctor reported that the kidney bruises were cause by a number of blows by soft, blunt instruments. He said that Charlie should be examined again in a few days for x-ray comparisons. The facial damage appeared to be from a blow by a fist. This followed Charlie's story. He said the beating was done with a wet rolled towel, and the fist came because they weren't satisfied with his answers about why he was in DC. He also remembered that a FBI agent was with the police and cautioned them a number of times about their methods. He didn't know the agent's name. It took a call to Special Agent Smith to find that the agent in question was none other than Walter T. Swackhammer, Agent in Charge of the District of Columbia FBI office. Swackhammer was surprised by a summons also. Then the roof fell in on all those concerned.

Doreen came in and said to Charlie, "I'm going to tell them."

What she wanted to tell was that when the police came into her apartment, she was in bed under the covers. The cops threw the covers off and forced her to crawl across the bed, and then submit to a full body search by three of the policemen. The same actions were taken against Charlie. The redhead was steaming with anger and her pilot friend was dangerously quiet through the report.

They were angry, but I had never seen Sam Martin so furious. He was trembling with rage when the Mayor called, and Sam refused to take the call. The same thing happened to the Chief of Police. Each of the officials called a number of times. The Mayor's secretary called and told Susan that the Mayor was scheduled to be out of town for the following week and wouldn't be able to attend the sub-committee meetings. Susan grinned at me when she received a message that if the summons were not answered, "His Honor, the Mayor, would find his ass in the hoosegow."

When I was leaving Sam's office he said, "You call those clowns and explain to them that if they aren't in the committee room by 0900, a contempt of Congress warrant would be served before 1000."

I passed Susan's desk, and said, "If those jerks call again, transfer them to me."

She answered in a stage whisper, "Can I listen?"

"Put it on the intercom, if you want," I whispered back with a grin.

"Yes, yes, yes," came from a group of staffers along with a lot of giggling.

Susan was too much of a professional to do something like that, and I knew it would be safe to say what I wanted to say. As a group, the Martin employees were probably the most closely-knit office staff in town. The "yes, yes, yes" was a good-natured attempt to show their approval of the actions being taken. They were ready to take on all of the Capitol, when one of their own was threatened. Doreen was considered one of their own.

The Chief of Police was the first one to call and was insulted to be shifted to a staffer.

I listened to his complaints for a few minutes and broke in, "Do you want to talk to me?"

As he said, "No, I do…"

I hung up the instrument.

He called back and angrily asked, "What kind of people do you have there? I was cut off."

I retorted, "Chief, you weren't cut off, I hung up when you said that you didn't want to talk to me.

He said in a more level tone, "I can't come to the hill on Monday. I have to go out of town to a meeting."

I broke in and said, "Wait, Chief, you don't seem to understand. If you don't get your ass, and your assholes up here, you will be in contempt."

The Mayor was on the telephone as the Chief hung up.

"Mr. Mayor," I asked, "What can I do for you?"

He said with a forced laugh, "You can get Sam Martin to see me. He and I go back a long way."

"Can't do that Mr. Mayor. Right now, your old friend probably wants to skin you. He is adamant that you be at the committee meeting, and he says that you will be held in contempt of Congress if you are not there by 1000."

The Mayor tried to explain about the Conference of Mayors he was scheduled to attend and how important that would be for the city. I told him that there was nothing I could do, nor did I want to do anything.

I broke off the conversation, "Mr. Mayor, you evidently don't know why Sam is so angry. I would suggest you talk to your police chief before showing up on Monday. Also, you can tell them for me, a few of them will have to answer for what occurred."

A few minutes after the calls from the city, Sally announced Charlie Daniels. I met him at the door, and we discussed the raid for a few minutes. It was no secret that this was one angry young man.

I called for coffee and after it was served asked, "What do you need, Charlie?"

He did not speak for a few moments and then asked, "Do you remember the Gormans?"

Before he could say anything further, I held my finger to my lips for silence. Too many people were watching me and might have outsmarted the senate electronic sweeping team.

"Oh yeah," I then answered, "If you have a few minutes let's take a walk."

He understood and we left the office. We walked over to the Washington Monument and stood at the reflection pool, before either of us said anything. We were far enough away from the crowd to be relaxed, but I still kept my voice down.

"What about the Gormans?" I asked.

He hesitated for a passing tourist to clear and said in a menacing voice, "I aim to kill some of those bastards, especially the Commander and his team leader."

I said quietly, "Charlie, I know how you must feel because I have had some of the same thoughts, but this would be taking on a big city police force. I'm not sure we have the wherewithal, or the time, to take on an effort such as you are suggesting."

"I know," he said gruffly, "But I am going to talk with Mr. and Miz Carpenter. They will understand."

I answered him, "Believe me Charlie, I understand, and with some misgivings, I will ask John to get everyone together and see if we can come up with some ideas and plans. Is that enough for the present?"

The mountain man gave a quick, back-home answer, "Yep."

We stopped at a public telephone and called Georgetown.

John Silvers answered and I said, "Charlie wants a meet."

We were beginning to sound like mountain men because his answer was, "Tonight at 1900."

I repeated the phrase and Daniels nodded and left.

Doreen was waiting at the office to take me to a meeting at Mount Vernon with the Senate Monument Committee. She was very quiet and almost non-committal. My comments were met with hardly any conversation. We pulled into the parking lot at George Washington's home.

I put my hand on her knee and said, "I know Sweetie, I know, but you can't allow those boorish pigs to ruin your life. They will pay in full, one of these days. Generally what goes around comes around."

She said forcefully, "I am going to sue the city, and if you want, I will leave."

I squeezed her knee and said, "Don't do anything hasty, especially quitting. Who would drive for a decrepit old man like me?"

That brought a faint smile to that beautiful freckled face and she said, "I need a hug."

I pulled her into my arms and held her tightly and quietly. We stayed in that position for sometime, and then she reached up and kissed me and pushed away. She appeared to be more relaxed because the smile was back.

On the way to the meeting room I leaned over and whispered, "Charlie has asked us to have a meeting. We need to be in Georgetown by 1900."

I had not considered her not being at the meeting.

It was still a cat and mouse game. A number of cars would try to tail, and Doreen would lose them. It must have been embarrassing for a so-called professional to be out-smarted and out-driven by a twenty-three-year-old girl. Her father and brothers had taught her well. We pulled into the Georgetown house through the back alley. It was still surprising to me that no one had identified our safe house. John and Samantha had assembled everyone, and there were a number of smiles, when Doreen almost ran to Charlie. When we laughed, the youngsters showed some embarrassment but soon ignored us as they hugged and held each other.

Samantha had a spread for us and it was just visiting while we ate. You could almost feel the tension emanating from Carpenter, and Lydia was staying close to him. Neither of them had said a word, and I become concerned that something other than Charlie and Doreen's problem was on their minds. Josephs was the one who broke the mood.

He pushed back from the table and thanked Samantha for her hospitality and said, "Well now, it seems as if we have a problem with the local cops. Carpenter showed us how to handle locals in his town, but this is different. According to Charlie and a friend of mine on the force, the FBI and CIA were involved and apparently a driving power behind the raid."

Jacobs raised an eyebrow and asked, "Since when do you know a DC cop?"

Josephs quipped, "Heck Sarg, I know more people than a few old soldiers like you guys. His name is Frank Cox and he was in the outfit I was ordered to, after our vacation with Long Ball Kwong."

I suddenly remembered Bucky O' Halloran and asked, "Doreen is Bucky still around?"

She said that her brother was still in the traffic division and would support her actions. He was also threatening to take actions against the police involved. He had already called the O'Halloran family and they would soon be in town.

"Well, now, this is getting interesting. We have insiders in all the local agencies, but we have to get serious now," I was as surprised as anyone when Linda spoke.

The most surprising thing of all was that Carpenter took the lead in the conversation.

The Sniper started the discussion with, "Ah know we come to git Long Ball, but Charlie ast for my help an he gits it,"

John Silvers interrupted by questioning whether or not we could help Charlie and still go for Long Ball.

He said, "We have already taken some drastic steps and are planning more of the same, but we should remember those plans were, and are, against individuals. What we are talking about now includes a police force, and we know that cops stick together, no matter what the circumstances."

Lydia spoke and we all listened, "Maybe you should leave this to us. We are going after them, even if we go alone."

Carpenter spoke again and said, "Yeah, this is a hillbilly fight. Let us do it."

Linda Josephs quipped, "O.K., Hillbilly, you've had your say. Let the real people talk."

There was some laughter—even Carpenter had a faint grin when he answered, "Yes'um."

I let the conversation swirl around me without input.

Jacobs noticed and asked, "Navy, you are not saying anything. Are you holding out for Long Ball?"

There was silence until I answered, "Yeah, I am holding out for Long Ball, but on the other hand I would have called this meeting if Charlie hadn't come to see me. The big question is how we do both jobs. I agree with John, this involves a police force and that puts us into harm's way for a long time. We kill these assholes, and other assholes will always be looking for us. Just think if we complete both jobs, all sorts of people would want to interview the whole group."

I hesitated, looked at Silvers and said, "But you can't live forever. Who can do this job?"

Lydia Carpenter responded, "You know who can do this job—the five of you can."

She took her husbands hand and continued, "Can we find if those bastards will be in public together?"

Doreen spoke, "Bucky says that most of them will be in the motorcade for Mr. Dong Ping when he starts home after the New Year."

The silence was almost deafening, with only a squeak of furniture or a clink of silverware. Jacobs reflected my thoughts when he questioned how secure the motorcade route would be.

He said, "We would have to spread out, and it would be every man for himself with no outside transportation or other support."

Carpenter said menacingly, "Nah, les stay together and each take a target. Then if needed, we kin fight our way out, but no matter what we do, if we take the police we lose Long Ball."

The Sniper knew how to simplify problems. Silvers turned to Doreen and asked her to get a route map of the motorcade. She indicated that Bucky would probably be able to get one. There could be no planning until the route was available. We spent the balance of the evening discussing withdrawal plans. The general consensus was that Charlie's helicopter would be our best bet.

Charlie protested until Carpenter said, "Charlie, you kin fly that bird like an expert, but you cain't shoot fer a hill of beans."

There was a shrug from the pilots' shoulders, with a sheepish grin.

# Chapter 19

Sam Martin was at his best Monday morning, when the Committee on the Operations of the Capitol City convened. He had called an emergency meeting for special investigative actions of the metropolitan police department. The Chief of Police and Mayor had begged all weekend not to be called. They made apologies a number of times and admitted that the policemen in question had acted outside the purview of the law. The Senator ignored them as they sat, uncomfortable behind the witness table. They knew that there was a blistering coming on national television. After the amenities of opening the agenda, Sam demonstrated he was a master at displaying gut wrenching emotions such as displeasure, anger and shame for what he had to do. After this display for the sake of the audience, he opened his statement, with a direct charge against the police force, their Commanders, their Chief, and their Mayor.

He opened, "My fellow Senators, it is with pain that I make these charges, because you know, and I know that most of the boys on the police force are as good as they can be. It is too bad that they can't be serving under better leadership."

The opposition party tried to interrupt him, but when he had ignored their fourth call, they sat back in their seats. He read a list of policemen who raided Doreen's apartment illegally, and then harassed, and mistreated the two young people. He had been speaking in a serious manner, with no hint of an accent.

Then he lapsed into his down-home idiom and many in the audience nudged each other, because they knew he would be at his best.

He said, "Why shucks, if I was that little ole girl, I prolly couldn't stand to be here. But folks, there she is, settin' at the witness table. The young man settin' side her is her feller and they is in love."

He sat forward and continued in a more direct manner, "Yet, the police in this here city busted into her apartment without a warrant. Then they done sum terrible thins without even a trumped up charge to cover why they were there. Why wus they there, Mistuh Mayor? Why did you let this happen, Chief of Police of this here Cap'tol City? The world is watchin' and waitin' with a whole bunch of disgust I s'pect. Ah know ah'm disgusted."

He glared for at least five minutes at the two city officials. There was not a sound until the audience was on edge enough to be shifting in their seats and coughing nervously. The tension had built to a fever pitch, and Sam let it build. Finally, he turned to the opposition leader and asked if he had a statement.

The Senator broke the tension by leaning forward whispering in the microphone, "Are you kidding?"

The first witness was Charlie Daniels, and the helicopter pilot answered all the questions with single direct quotes. He didn't allow his temper to get in the way of his testimony. Some of the minority senators attempted to emphasize the fact that he was in a young woman's apartment before daybreak.

Charlie closed that down when he said, "I was in her bedroom by invitation. By that invitation she gave me the right to be there. Your city police weren't invited. Your city police didn't have warrants. Your city police did not have the right to be there."

Those were cold forceful statements from an angry young man. His anger broke the surface when he was asked to describe the actions of the police.

"I don't think I can," he snarled, "Because those bastards are in this room, and I might gut one or two of them. Back home that would be a given, but our police are good people, doing a bad job. The people in this city have a bunch of hoodlums doing a great job being hoodlums."

There were many objections and cries from the opposition party, but Sam winked at Charlie and pounded the gavel

He said, "No more, no more, we will adjourn fer today."

There were indignant calls from the attorneys for the Mayor and Chief of Police. They wanted to have their clients in the audience, only on the day of their testimony. They had assumed that they would testify on the first day.

Sam said, "No sir, I want 'em here to hear first hand how their police force is misusin' the public's money and breaking the laws of the land."

The media discovered a good subject with Charlie Daniels. His demeanor made it plain that he was covering a controlled but very angry attitude. He wouldn't say very much but everyone could see that this was a furious young man. The public was on his side and couldn't wait to hear Doreen's story. She had left the room at the start of the testimony, but the file photographs did a great job of putting her and Charlie in the public eyes.

Sam Martin kept everyone on edge because when asked if Doreen would be in attendance the next day, he responded, "Mos likely, but I ain't sure if we kin git to her part of the testimony. That pore young girl is sufferin' because of whut so-called public servants has done to her."

He said that as the Mayor came down the steps and made a run for his transportation and would not answer any questions.

Sam got in a real lick. "See, that is the attitude of some of the so-called public servants. They run and hide when they should be shovelin' the manure outtin the stables."

The next day when the committee convened, the audience was expecting to hear from Doreen. She was in the front row seats with Charlie and her brother, Bucky. An interesting thing had occurred; interspersed throughout the crowd, were a number of red-haired men, and there was no doubt that Clan O'Halloran was watching over a member of the family. There were some very uncomfortable policemen seated in the room, because behind each one was one, of the big redheads. Before the gavel, I went over to Doreen, and she motioned her father to join us. Seamus O'Halloran shook hands and thanked me for taking care of his daughter.

There were some general smiles when I said, "Mr. O'Halloran, it's more like she has been taking care of me. Since she became my driver, my eyes have been closed over half the time."

Sam Martin walked in and O'Halloran took me aside and said with a faint grin, "Call me mister again and I'll whup you. It's Seamus."

Then in a more serious vein he continued, "My boys are ready to take on the entire Washington, DC, police force. Bucky is resigning today."

I responded, "Seamus, tell the boys to hold off for a few days, and we need Bucky on the police force."

He looked at me for a long moment, and quietly said, "If you need help, call."

The gavel sounded, I slapped the big Irishman on the shoulder and returned to my seat behind Sam. There was an expectant hush throughout the room.

Sam was being cute.

He looked over the room and said, "Ladies and Gentlemen of the Committee, my 'pologies, but we has to change the order of witnesses. The Chair now calls Mr. Walter T. Swackhammer of the FBI."

A surprised hush came over the room. The audience was waiting to hear Doreen. The visitors wanted to hear the nitty-gritty of the police treatment during the raid. At the same time, they were curious why an FBI Agent would be testifying.

The agent was sworn and Sam began, "Agent Swackhammer, I know you have to catch a plane, but we also need you here. I will be brief. Were you in the company with the District Columbia police, on the night in question?"

The affirmative answer brought the following, "Agent Swackhammer, did you agree with the police action against these young folks?"

Sam was talking without the good ole boy phrasing and the audience was leaning forward with interest. The agent squirmed a bit, but he was honest, "No Sir, Senator, I didn't agree and tried to talk the Commander out of his plans because there were no warrants. As the raid proceeded, I continued to object, and when the young couple was forced to subject themselves to the indignities, I was ashamed to be involved. I told the Commander as much, and he told me to leave if I didn't want some redheaded fun."

All eyes were turned toward the redhead in question, and you could see other redheads become red-faced with eyes that foretold the possibility of danger for certain people.

Swackhammer continued, "I left and reported the incident to my superior, and he called the Chief of Police. The Chief told him that things were under control and should be of no interest to the FBI."

After the Agent had told his story, no one on the committee had any questions, and Sam turned the query over to the committee counsel.

She asked, "Agent Swackhammer, do you see the Police Commander to whom you referred, and if you do, identify him to the committee."

The FBI Agent turned to his left and pointed out and identified Police Commander George Starkey.

Before the counsel could give up the witness, I slipped her a note and she said, "One more question Mr. Swackhammer, why did you accompany the police on a raid such as this?"

Some of the Senators objected to the question, and Swackhammer suggested privilege of law enforcement.

Sam looked around at me and with my affirmative nod said, "Answer the question Mr. FBI Agent."

The witness was squirming, and finally said, "Senator Martin, with all respects, I cannot answer that question because I am under orders to specifically not discuss why the FBI went along on the raid."

Sam looked at the agent and said very quietly, "Agent Swackhammer, you know that I can hold you in contempt, but I am not going to do that—not yet. I have one other question, who gave you orders not to discuss this travesty of justice? If you answer that, you are excused, because I know you have other duties for the FBI."

The agent finally said, "FBI Director Troy Sloan and CIA Director John Marshburn."

Sam turned to the attorney and said, "Madam Counsel, issue a summons for the two directors mentioned, to appear before this Committee when it convenes again."

Walter Swackhammer looked at me with a faint grin and almost sprinted out the door. He didn't want to chance being called back by the Committee. The next witness was Police Commander George Starkey. He was nervous and it is well that he should have been. Sam could hardly get him sworn before he came under the auspices of the Committee Counsel.

The lawyer slipped forward in the chair and asked, "Commander

Starkey, you heard the testimony of FBI Agent Walter T. Swackhammer, do you agree with what he testified about this raid which you commanded?"

The officer looked at his attorney and after a whispered conference, the policeman asserted his rights under the Fifth Amendment to the Constitution. The Counsel, Senator Martin, and the ranking Minority Member held a conference and to everyone's surprise agreed that the witness was within his constitutional rights. The Commander smiled and the Counsel continued, "Commander Starkey, do you deny body searching Mr. Charlie Daniels and Miss Doreen O'Halloran?"

The policeman claimed his rights again. Before the questioning could continue, the Commander's lawyer asked if the Committee would grant full immunity for answers to the questions.

After another conference with the Counsel, Sam leaned forward and said, "No sir, we will not grant immunity in this case, so I will end the questioning of this witness. Commander Starkey, without such immunity, will you continue claiming Fifth Amendment rights?"

With a big smile the Commander said that he would continue not answering the questions.

Sam leaned closer to the microphone and slowly said, "Son, since we have granted all your constitutional rights, I suggest you get some good lawyering, because we have evidence that I believe will convict you in Superior Court. The information will be sent to the Prosecutor. Now, get out of my sight."

Sam Martin was a smart man. He went through all of the witnesses except for Doreen and got what he wanted, without embarrassing the young couple any further. The Chief of Police said in the witness chair that all the cops involved in that particular raid would be suspended and the information turned over to the Federal Magistrate. The Mayor followed and said that he was going to fire the Chief of Police.

Sam retorted sharply, "That is fine Mr. Mayor, but who is going to fire you?"

The Senators took turns taking the Mayor apart, and before he was excused, he was in shock. He had had enough, because by the end of the questioning he promised not only to fire the Chief of Police but he would also resign his office. No one believed him, but the members of the Committee agreed that his leaving office was called for, because of the general conduct of the bureaucracy under his leadership. It soon became apparent that the Senators were using the incident as an excuse to get at the officials of the Capitol City. The members of both parties began presenting evidence that would bury the top management of Washington, D. C.

The last witness of the day was a surprise. It was a secret service agent who had gone undercover, and had worked in the police department supervising the younger officers. The agent was never identified and was allowed to testify under cover. He swore to all the information that had been prepared to turn over to the Federal Prosecutor. The Chief of Police and the officers involved were arrested as they left the building. The Mayor was given an order to turn himself in by 1000 the next day.

This would give him time to gracefully resign and turn over the mayoral duties to his deputy. The Senators took turns apologizing to Doreen and Charlie for what had happened. The next day, editorials were in the same vein, and a recall petition was circulating, calling for the impeachment of all the elected and some of the appointed positions.

# Chapter 20

I left the hearing room before adjournment, and to my surprise found Carpenter waiting. He followed me outside to evade the cameras and we stood far enough apart to give the appearance that we just happened to be there.

He said, "Cap'n say we help Charlie. He wants to know if you kin git Doreen's fam'ly outtin the way on Saturday night."

"I can keep them out of the way, if I know where we are going," I responded with some heat.

He nodded and said; "Told 'em you would go, too. The cops is havin' a party at Rock Fish Lake."

Bucky O'Halloran had furnished the information just as a mad, insulted brother would be expected to do. He was upset because the cops were thumbing their noses and celebrating. They were partying, even after what had been said in the committee room. The Chief of Police had reinstated them before they were ever suspended. He had left the hearing and went directly to the station and took the action after testifying they would be fired. The arrest orders for the Chief of Police and Mayor had also been lifted by one of their friends in the Magistrate's office. The O'Hallorans were planning to take on the District of Columbia police force. Carpenter and I had moved away from each other, without any apparent notice, and I watched him casually strolling down the street and thought to myself, *Now that looks like a hillbilly.* I called a friend in Alexandria, Virginia, from a street booth, and reserved a room for the entire O'Halloran family.

When Doreen came out, we went to the car and after joining traffic I squeezed her shoulder and said, "Tell your father that the family has a room reserved at the Alexandria House, Saturday evening. Make sure you take Bucky and Charlie with you."

She looked into the mirror, and before she could say anything, I continued, "Make sure that the entire family is in that room by 1800 and keep them there until after 2200. Give your dad these instructions, because no one would be willing to go against that old man. Watch the road young'un!"

The last was because she was in the mirror again with a worried look. I knew, though, that I could depend on her.

Saturday afternoon, I dodged the tails and went to Georgetown and found all hands in attendance.

I asked, "O.K., what do we do?"

Before anyone could answer, the women left the room to prepare an early snack. It was a ploy to make sure that they didn't become involved or know the details of our plans.

Silvers took the lead and answered, "Those thugs who hurt Charlie and Doreen are celebrating tonight. They will be arriving at Rock Fish Lake over in Maryland after 1700, when the park is closed to the public. I figure we can get in before then and find a secure position until after the rangers leave for the night."

He looked at me and asked about the O'Hallorans. There were nods of agreement when I told them about the dinner plans.

I said, "Also, without his knowledge, I took Charlie out of the loop. Doreen will take him to dinner with the family. I sent word to Seamus to make sure that no one leaves before 2200."

We all agreed that Charlie would be one of the first people questioned if we ran a successful mission. That is why we wanted all the family to be highly visible, in a public place, when the action occurred. We discussed our first tentative plan to include the cops in the ambush of Long Ball Kwong. It was agreed that it was best to separate the two incidents because we couldn't afford to leave tracks for the police at either place. The party also put all the cops in one spot rather than being separated.

We went to Rock Fish Park in two rental cars that had been lifted off the streets by Josephs and Jacobs. I kidded them about lying about their careers, because they had proven that they were skillful car thieves. We separated and entered the park from different directions, and Carpenter's scouting had been complete. The automobiles were parked in a grove of trees, which had three sides covered by flowering shrubs. The uncovered side would be our escape route. Josephs and Jacobs had come in one of the vehicles and joined us after parking. Then there was nothing to do but wait for the park to close.

Carpenter briefed us on the coming operation. Since he was unknown to the local police, he had been able to move freely around the area. Bucky O'Halloran had good information because the party location was readily identified. He even found the park employees setting up the picnic area. The ranger had agreed that their comrades-in-arms could hold private functions after the public had left the area. We watched as the people were being asked to leave at 1700. Our location wasn't spotted. Carpenter told us that the first cops would arrive about 1900 to ice down the beer and light fires. The others could be expected anytime after that. He also had the information that the guests wouldn't be family members, but ladies the cops often joined for partying. That would make the execution of the mission much easier. We didn't want to hurt any guests, especially, if they were members of a policeman's family.

At 1830, we took up positions that had been selected by Carpenter. Our lines of fire covered much of the picnic area, and we could see each other in case of needed assistance, or communications. Carpenter would give the attack signal when all the partygoers settled down with their third or fourth drink. One of our concerns had been about the late arrivals, but that was answered when our five targets arrived together. According to the loud talk, no one else would be coming to the party and that was O.K. with them. They did not want any "chicken shits" at the party. The commander also answered another question, when he loudly said that the whores would come in about 2200. They popped their first top, as they finished spreading out the equipment that included sleeping bags. They settled down after a couple of beers and were talking about the day in the committee room. We could hear the lies, as they told each other about giving the politicians "what for" during the hearing.

We heard one of them say, "Man, I wish that little red-headed whore was here tonight."

All of them laughed when he said; "I will never forget that sight. She was something, crawling across that bed."

Another quipped, "She wasn't bad to search either. That little old thing was all slicked up."

That acted as a signal, Carpenter, pulled down his mask and raised his hand in the pumping motion to advance. We stood and walked slowly into the campsite without notice, until we stepped into the lighted area.

"What the hell..." was as far as the Commander got in his surprise.

The five of us cut them apart with silenced weapons. We made certain they were dead before leaving the area and took the cars out of the park gate without lights and raced away to the east. After about two hours of driving, we ditched one of the vehicles by running it off the rim of a gravel pit that Carpenter had located during the day. He estimated that there would be at least fifty feet of water in the depression. The women met us at a fishhouse on the Eastern Shore, and they had already ordered for us. We went directly to the table from the porch, rather than through the dining room; therefore, not coming under notice of very many people. The second car had been left in a busy parking lot, and we were sure that no personal tracks had been made during the evening.

The story broke Sunday morning, before I had finished the newspaper. According to the television reporter, some women had come upon the scene of the executions and in a panic fled the area. One of them thought better the next morning, and called the DC police, who in turn called the Maryland authorities.

The TV reporter was making a weather report when the news anchor stopped him and said, "We have a breaking story. It appears that five men were gunned down at a picnic area in Rock Fish Park off Maryland Highway 130. We have a crew heading to the site and will bring you more information as we receive it."

A few minutes later, he came back on with the follow-up report. This time he told the audience some exciting but tragic news. A park ranger had come in with the word that a party of policemen had been allowed to stay in the park for a late picnic. The practice had been going on for years, as one law enforcement agency supported the wishes of their brothers-in-arms.

The reporter said, "We aren't sure, but the dead people could be policemen who were at the night picnic."

He said the first report had come to the police from a woman who would not identify herself. She had been in a panic because she had observed the killing field. Later in the morning, the victims were identified as District of Columbia policemen, and the media frenzy started soon thereafter.

The anchorman said with excitement, "We have just learned the identity of the five men at Rock Fish Park, Maryland. Many of you probably watched them the past week. They are the five policemen who had been questioned by Senator Sam Martin's Committee. They were suspended and then reinstated by the Chief of Police."

The reporter held up his hand and listened intently to his earphones, and said, "We have also learned that the police are trying to locate the O'Halloran family. The family members are incensed for the way their daughter and sister were treated by the five policemen during the raid on her apartment. It was alleged that the officers had no authority nor would they explain why they were at the apartment of Miss O'Halloran. The police are also looking for Mr. Charlie Daniels who had been with Miss O'Halloran on the morning of the raid. He is reported to be her fiancée."

The Chief of Police was interviewed, and he stuttered often, when questioned about reinstating the suspended members of his force. In a very pious manner he said the poor murdered policemen had not been convicted of any criminal activity.

Then he said, with finality, "We are sure that the poor murdered officers were executed by the family and friends of a young couple who were shacking up without being married."

The Mayor was subdued during the interview and denied knowing about the ambush or whether or not the policemen had been reinstated after he had ordered them to be suspended.

Both officials said they were shocked but not surprised that the O'Halloran family would take it on themselves to be judge, jury, and executioner. The Mayor made a statement that he tried to tie the O'Halloran family, through Doreen, to the staff of Senator Martin.

One of the reporters really got on them, she asked, "Chief, do you think that Miss O'Halloran's and Mr. Daniels' rights had been violated by the policemen during the raid? And Mr. Mayor, are you implying that there is a connection between Senator Sam Martin and the deaths of these five policemen?"

The questions weren't answered, because the officials suddenly had duties in other areas. They mumbled something about a far-reaching investigation to be started immediately.

The media frenzy went up a couple of notches when the Alexandria police reported that the O'Hallorans and Mr. Daniels had called and offered a hard and fast alibi. They were at a family dinner in Alexandria, Virginia, that was more than one hundred miles from Rock Fish Park, Maryland. The staff at the restaurant corroborated the alibi. The Maitre'd explained that the room had been reserved on Thursday evening for the Saturday night dinner. The family had arrived together in two automobiles and two vans. Dinner was served about 1830 and was over about 2130. They ordered drinks and coffee and left the establishment at midnight. The staff was questioned about the possibility that some of the family could have left the restaurant. It was obvious that no one had left, because the vehicles were in valet parking.

The DC officials went into deep cover because none of them could be found for the balance of the day. Senator Martin was interviewed and in his best style was "deeply and profoundly" shocked that the Mayor and Chief of Police would point an accusing finger before an investigation had been completed.

He continued, "Why, if I was Mr. Seamus O'Halloran I would be calling some attention to those statements. The city owes abject apologies to this good family."

Again, when Sam wanted to get the message across, the country idiom completely disappeared. That statement ignited the public. The city telephone lines were over-loaded and tied up for more than twenty-four hours, with the people calling for the heads of all city officials.

The FBI wasn't leaving anything to chance. There were two agents waiting when I arrived at the office on Monday morning. They told me to pick the place for a meeting, as long as we met immediately. I had already met Walter Swackhammer and he was the senior man.

He offered a dry chuckle when I said, "Heck, let's go to your field agent's office. I will meet you there."

"Ha! No way," the agent replied, "You drive, I will ride."

When we got into traffic, I eased the tension by telling Swackhammer that I wanted to drive because I needed the car after the meeting—to meet with my fellow spies.

Swackhammer grinned and said, "O.K., O.K."

I watched the young agent who was following, and he made at least two telephone calls and a radio transmission. When we reached the FBI office, the CIA and District Police were very much in evidence. Introductions were made, coffee was served, and Swackhammer started the session.

I held up my hand and said, "Walter, just so everyone understands. I'm here to be interviewed, not grilled. Ask any question you want, but don't try to threaten me or expect me to take any crap."

One of the CIA agents snorted and started to say something, when the FBI Agent held up a hand and stated that I would be treated with every courtesy.

Swackhammer started the session by stating a number of law enforcement and intelligence agencies would like to hear me talk about Mr. Dong Ping of China. I nodded and started leading them through the meetings at the United Nations.

Cliff Grogan had arrived late and was still standing, when he laughed and said, "Cut it out, Jake, you know what we are after. What is your past association with the prospective Chairman of the Peoples Republic of China?"

I answered with a chuckle, "Cliff, you people hang in there. I have told you time and time again that I had never heard of the name Dong Ping until he was introduced at the UN meeting."

That was the absolute truth, and I was almost sure that none of them had heard of Long Ball Kwong.

I saw the case Grogan was holding and uttered a long drawn out exaggerated groan and pleaded, "Oh, no. Not again. Not the video again, Cliff. Dong Ping has already explained why he was running down the stairs."

Grogan laughed, along with the other agents and replied, "Yes, he did explain it, but I want to talk to you about some other people. You, and I know that there are people on this video that you know on a personal basis, and you have never mentioned them."

"Why should I have said anything about them? They are old friends who were vacationing in New York. You people were busy with the Chinese had showed no interest in the tourists who were walking about the area, sightseeing."

While we were talking, another agent loaded the video the projector started flashing the pictures as Dong Ping came through the door at the UN building.

Before anyone spoke, I turned to Swackhammer and said, "Walter, I will give you thirty minutes with this crap. I have been through this story so many times that I thought the video had worn out. According to our friends here from the "Spy Factory" many, many bits of information are happening all on this piece of crap. At first, I was in some conspiracy with the Chinese—then against the Chinese—now these clowns want me to talk about some friends who happened to be near the UN Building at the time Dong Ping says he was rushing to take a call from his Premier."

The projector had been stopped and I looked at my watch and quipped, "Starting now. Ask away Cliff."

The tape ran by Carpenter and stopped on John Silvers.

Before any question I said, "John Silvers, a Captain in the Marine Corps during the Korean War. He was my immediate supervisor for a short time. He is now a Department head at the University of Iowa."

The next stop was on Jacobs and Josephs and I continued, "The bald headed guy is Jacobs and was the Sergeant in our outfit. He is now the Senior Military Advisor for the ROTC program at Iowa State University. Joseph is the other guy. He was a grunt like me and is now a State Senator in Oklahoma. We spent some time at the Navy Hospital, Yokosuka, Japan. That is how we become acquainted. So you see gentlemen, I associate with some very weird characters." No one asked any questions and Walter Swackhammer shrugged his shoulders.

I stood up and said, "Gentlemen, I am a busy man."

Cliff Grogan called over the hustle and bustle, "Jake, where were you on Saturday night?"

There was an instant hush because all of these people would be concerned with incidents on Saturday, because of the Rock Fish Park story.

I did not hesitate, "It is none of your business, Cliff. Why is the CIA mixing in so many local questions? I thought you people were foreign spooks."

Continuing I said, "But Cliff, if Swackhammer is interested, I was at your favorite crab cake house. Check it out."

I left the FBI Office somewhat concerned, because I had let it slip that I had known and worked with the others in the Far East. That is why I mentioned the stay in the hospital at Yokosuka. My cover still would be that I was in the Navy and they were Marines.

# Chapter 21

When I returned to the office after meeting with Walter Swackhammer, I found a message from Commanding Officer, Marine Barracks, Patuxent River.

"The General is visiting Marine Air Station, Cherry Point, North Carolina, and is expecting to receive guests 1930 Tuesday, at visiting Flag Officer's Quarters, Camp Lejuene, North Carolina. Call Commander Marine Barracks for immediate plans."

I put in a call to Colonel Tolliver and the conversation was cryptic but straightforward. General Sheffield was in fact ordering us to proceed to a meeting in North Carolina. The Colonel suggested I meet him at Naval Air Station, Patuxent River, no later than 1100. I looked at my watch and only had an hour and a half to make the trip. I didn't question the General's authority, but it left me in a quandary as to how I could keep the appointment.

That problem was solved by a call from Sam Martin to meet him in the Senate lunchroom.

He was sitting alone when I joined him. He looked over with a quizzical grin and asked, "Ole Buddy, whut you into? Agent Swackhammer called and wants us to meet with the Director tomorrow morning."

I replied, "I can't make it, Sam. I was on my way to exercise the resignation when you called. You and your office shouldn't be associated with me for a while. In the not-too-distant future, you probably will understand. Now, neither Swackhammer nor Grogan have anything against me except for their speculations. What I would like to do is leave immediately and you can tell them I will be back in Washington over the weekend."

"O.K., Ole Buddy, but what you got into?"

I stood up, grinned and offered my hand. When he took it, I said, "Sam, my friend, you don't want to know."

With that, I left and stopped by Susan's office and told her the resignation was finalized and I would be leaving immediately.

Her response was with tearful eyes; "I still live at the same place when you get back to town."

I walked into Sally's office and told her that I was leaving.

She came around the desk and hugged me and said, "You are the best. When you have a chance, stop in and see us."

She giggled when I raised my brow and said, "He is too big for me to refuse."

I gave her a letter of recommendation to "Whom It May Concern" extolling all her virtues as an employee.

Doreen was waiting with the car and smiled faintly when I said, "This is our last trip, kid. Tell that broken-down pilot to be good to you or he will answer to me. You are going back to the mountains with him, aren't you?"

She nodded her head in the affirmative, as she started the evasion tactics only she could do. We were at the Naval Air Terminal in plenty of time, but I would not allow her to wait with me. She came for a hug and maintained the clasp until I pushed her back and kissed the tears rolling down her cheek.

She stood back and in a low voice that trembled, she said, "Bye, Bossman, you be careful."

"You can bet on it, and I will see you, probably some time this weekend. Sam says you have a job, as long as you want it," I replied.

She waved and turned for the car, and I mused as she pulled away, *There goes a driver. I hope the ones she drives for in the future have nerves of steel.* I also thought, *Charlie Daniel, you are one lucky son-of-a-bitch.*

John Silvers answered when I called from a booth near the flight line and told him that I would be out of town for a few days. We discussed the situation and decided to bring everyone out of hiding and have them do some high profile shopping and visiting. We speculated that it would be only a short time before the spies spied them. Our plan was for each couple to make solitary forays into the community and at pre-set times, all would meet in a public place. On these occasions, an appearance of tense discussions would be offered to any one observing. They were to take it to the point that all conversation would cease, when people walked by their table. Our ideas for this were to stretch the resources against us. All of this would be done with no public contact with the Carpenters. Their identity was still not known as our associates. Silvers and I also discussed the real possibility that our plans for Long Ball Kwong would have to be put aside because of his imminent travel date. According to the present plans, he was scheduled to depart for China on January the Second. One thing still in our favor was that the going away party had been postponed from Friday until Tuesday.

I went into the terminal after making the call, and Tolliver was waiting at the information desk having me paged.

"Shucks, Colonel, I am right here beside you. Going blind in your old age?"

"Nah," he responded, "I learned all these strange habits at the North Carolina tobacco markets and we are heading that way again."

He picked up some papers and a briefcase," Let's go visit the Tar Heels."

A Navy jet trainer was sitting in front of the terminal with engines turning up. We made a run for the door, keeping low, and avoiding the jet stream. An air crewman was holding the door open of the six-passenger plane for us to board. When the door slammed the engines engaged and the pilot started his run, off the taxi apron. The plane did not hesitate; the engines were run to takeoff speed as the plane turned into the runway. We just had time to finish buckling our seat belts when the plane rotated and we were in the air.

Tolliver grinned and nodded when I said, "This has to be the General's airplane because every time I flew with Detachment X-Ray, the pilots were always in a hurry to get airborne."

I continue with a question, "Have you got any idea why he's calling for us?"

Tolliver shrugged and said, "Not a clue. This the first time he has made contact since the attack on the Marine Barracks in Lebanon. That day he was threatening sedition, because the administration wouldn't allow anyone to take on the perpetrators."

The Colonel laughed again when I retorted, "I will bet you that the Old Buzzard is activating us again. If you remember, he told us a number of times that once in X-Ray always in X-Ray. By the way, why did he keep you in the Corps?"

Another shrug of the shoulders was all the answer I received.

After a few moments, I said, "I agree with him on actions like the Marine Barracks overseas, when I heard about it my thoughts were—that wouldn't happen so often, if someone would send in Detachment X-Ray."

Tolliver silently agreed with a nod.

The aircraft flew east for about fifty miles before turning south. We were warned to stay buckled up and knew why, when the after-burners were lit off. I could not imagine what they had under the hood of this vehicle, because we were breaking the sound barrier in a trainer, almost as soon as the speed was cranked up. It didn't take us long to get to Cherry Point, North Carolina. The people along the Cape Fear River must have been shaking their heads and "cussing" the Navy for disturbing their afternoon activities. We rolled to a stop at 1800, and there was an automobile waiting alongside the plane as we walked down the ramp steps. We were back in Detachment X-Ray, because the vehicle started rolling as the doors slammed. Tolliver had said that the General was on Base, but the automobile was waved through the gate and turned on Highway 17 toward New Bern. We entered this old, historic town, and in a short time pulled into an open triple-car garage, and the door closed as the vehicle came to a stop.

There is nothing like cloak and dagger—no matter how innocent—one always looks forward to the next event. In the past few years, I had not used any ability in observing my surroundings until Long Ball Kwong made an appearance. Now though, I had inventoried the garage as we were walking through. Detachment X-Ray had returned—I would be able to come to the garage at night, with no light, go to the object needed such as the small harpoon on the rear wall just above the Naval Officer's saber. I spied the observation camera about the same instant, as did Tolliver. He just shrugged his shoulder, and grinned.

The driver let us into the house through a rear door, and then a woman took the lead through a maze of offices and office machines. She knocked on a door and opened it after we heard "enter." General Sheffield was seated at a very large desk and waved to us with a satisfied smile.

He shook hands with us and said, "Everything is under control. The tobacco market bandits are here."

There were a number of chuckles. I looked around and recognized the Coast Guard Chief from Detachment X-Ray, but had forgotten his name. As I was shaking hands with the Chief, another man stood up—the Army Tech Sergeant. I could remember those men vividly, but could not bring up their names. A good job had been done on us by discouraging the use of personal names. The two old comrades said they suffered from the same malady. They couldn't remember any of the names and a few call signs.

A female voice from the corner of the room called out, "Why that is Leader. I would know him anywhere."

I turned slowly and watched George walk across the office. She was a gorgeous woman, and there were some catcalls when we kissed.

She was embarrassed, until another female voice sang out, "You better watch him or he will make you undress in the sand."

Laughter erupted around the room when I said, "Not another female. What have I done to deserve this? George is enough but here comes Seaman Coppage."

I turned with a grin and there she was, a tall, lean, lanky lady almost as pretty as George. I was the envy of the night because two beautiful women come to me for a hug and kiss.

The General called for attention by saying, "O.K., O.K., No more hanky panky. From now on, it is all business."

He still offered a weak smile when George whispered to Seaman, "You are hanky and I am panky."

We settled in and waited for him to start. It took a while, because he observed each of us for long intervals. He was trying to assess the damage to our abilities from the years of inactivity, and wondering if we could be trusted to carry out dangerous missions once more. I glanced around the room and decided that we were still in trim, because each in turn was holding the general's eye contact, without an apparent drop in comfort levels. It was tough, because each of us received at least five minutes of silent interrogation. After over a half an hour he relaxed and started asking us questions about our life after Detachment X-Ray. He paid a lot of attention to me for my life after Sand Key. In an almost casual fashion, he asked if any of the intelligence agencies had contacted anyone concerning Detachment X-Ray. His attention was on me as the others denied being approach by any government agency.

"General," I said, "I have been under the scrutiny for the past few weeks from every intelligence agency in the world. None of the attention has anything to do with Detachment X-Ray."

Apparently satisfied with our answers, he settled back into his chair and said with a smile, "I know none of you are wondering why you have been asked to visit with me."

The others laughed and relaxed when I retorted, "Hell no, General, we are not wondering because we believe you wanted to show off the famous southern hospitality to old comrades."

He allowed the laughter for a few moments, then held up his hand and with a serious look said quietly, "I need help in carrying out a mission, in which none of you should be involved. Over the years, I have been silently heading up the President's Commission on Organized Crime. Detachment X-Ray was abolished shortly after the Vietnam fracas, because we were 'unfairly carrying out missions against the wrong enemy.'"

He continued, "You can imagine who the 'right enemy' was in those days. Many of our good citizens treated the military as the enemy. On occasions, we have formed strike teams for specific missions. Most of these exercises were carried out by law enforcement agents against 'in country' drug operations. Now we have a problem which local agencies can't be trusted to carry because of the possibility of leaks. We want this mission to be carried out silently and completely."

After a long pause, he looked at each of us and said, "We aren't interested in protecting constitutional rights. There is no time for training or getting in shape before we go. If any of you think you would be a hazard to the mission, I want you to face up to it and leave this room. One weak link or a moment of hesitation, could get us all killed and our country embarrassed."

After a long silence he told us that the lack of training time was the reason this particular group had been formed. He did not go any further but later it was apparent why most of us were the chosen few.

There was another long silence and I expect all of us were trying to assess our abilities for carrying out a Detachment X-Ray type of exercise with no conditioning or training. One of my problems would be the coming visit with Long Ball Kwong and his planned demise.

I broke the silence and asked, "General, how long will this mission last? I have some commitments to others, which must be carried out this next week."

He smiled and answered, "This mission has to be completed before 0400 tomorrow morning. We only have one chance at it. It is dangerous, and a new type of operation for some of you. I have faith in everyone, but you must be truthful in your decisions."

For emphasis, he said quietly, "Don't come, I say again, don't come, if you have any doubts about anything."

He stood up and said, "Let's take a ten-minute break and those of you who return from the break will be briefed further. This is the only chance you will get to back away from this operation. When you come back after the break, you are committed to the mission."

The housekeeper invited us into the kitchen for coffee and snacks. Tolliver and I moved away from the group discussing the situation and wondering what the mission would be. He appeared not to have reservations about the situation, and I had none, since the General stated we would be gone only one night. I was sort of thrilled to have the adrenaline flowing, just by being associated with old comrades. The two women approached with bright, unconcerned smiles.

I said, "Seaman Coppage, how in hell did you get caught up in this outfit? The last time I saw you, you were bravely teaching the troops how to survive in the California dessert."

She punched me on the shoulder and quipped, "You taught me well at Dam Neck. I was in California for only five months, before they asked me to talk to General Sheffield. He is a dude and I follow dudes, dude," she said with a smile.

I turned to George and ask basically for the same information, "George, I thought when we last saw each other that you were going into deep cover to never see the light of day again."

She laughed and said, "For years and years I thought I was hidden, but one night I had a call from the General, and he is a dude, you know. I was getting tired of the good life, teaching high school English, and all the young studs thought I should lift my skirts for them, and the older studs were afraid to ask."

I said, "Well now, I can't say that I blame the young dudes because my memory of you has always included the last scene when you flipped your skirt at the General and me. Now I think I know why that old buzzard, I mean dude, kept track of you."

She slapped me on the shoulder but before anything else could occur between the four of us, General Sheffield came in and sat at his desk.

He looked around the room and said with some satisfaction showing, "I see all of you stayed. I bet that you would. Got some good tobacco market odds, too."

He looked over in our direction with a grin, but then the face of General Sheffied showed for the first time. None of us had seen that since our last briefing from him. When General Sheffield was in charge, you could bet that something heavy would be in front of you.

This was no difference – I almost swallowed my tongue when he said, "We are going after a ship that is underway now. It will anchor tonight, seventy-five miles off the North and South Carolina coastlines. The Colombians and Cubans are betting we cannot stop it, because the DEA is on another mission in the Southwest."

He hesitated and the Chief asked, "How much of a load?"

We all must have gasped when the General said quietly, "We estimate five hundred tons. The ship is a cargo hauler and our information is that the holds are full and the desks are loaded."

Tolliver broke in and asked, "How many people will we be looking at? There are only seven of us if you are going."

The General answered, "I will be going, and we have some support from the CIA."

He looked at me expectantly and I said brusquely, "General, you know what I think about the CIA in this type of mission. Who do we have to guard against? I would trust the ship's crew more than them. Those clowns are only interested in their own agenda."

He answered, "I believe we can trust these people. They are the types we had some years ago. There is one of them, Leader, that may have been in Huntsville when you last passed through."

A soft female voice broke in, "Don't worry, Leader, I will shoot that son-of-a-bitch. I remember Baby and Cousin."

I looked over at George and she returned my gaze without a change of expression. We exchanged nods and turned our attention back to the General.

"Let's not get edgy now. To get this job done, we have to have cooperation from all hands, " Sheffield said.

I responded before he could say more, "With all respects General, if you knew we had a built-in problem, why did you call me? If I go on this trip, will I need someone to protect my back?"

He quietly said, "You will not need protection from this side. We have made it clear, old quarrels or vendettas will not be tolerated. Leader, your problem may come after we return, but by then you will at least know where you stand. You cannot back out on us because we need you. There are not more than twenty people in this world who can take a ship at sea, and we have four of them here."

He pointed out Tolliver, the Chief, the Tech Sergeant, and me. This caused a murmur from the others and they were briefly told about Detachment X-Ray going after the Russian trawler in the South Atlantic. That explained why the operation was planned with no training involved —Detachment X-Ray was trained for keeps.

The general told us more about the plans for the operation. We would be leaving Cherry Point Marine Air Station at about 2030. There would be one helicopter with a cover, as a security force for the unloading. There was no anticipated trouble from the steamer crew, but we had to be ready for a hostile meeting. One of the CIA people had a password to gain the confidence of the ship's captain. According to the information, the password had been worked out before the steamer had sailed from the last port of call. After the boarding we would take the crew in custody and would assume the roles of the crew. The General looked at George and Seaman, then told us that there were two women crew members, and they were both known by the boss of the pickup crews.

The pick up force would be coming out of the Little River, South Carolina area, with a mixture of boats from the fishing fleets and private owners. An estimated twenty boats could be expected to start arriving shortly after

0200 Saturday morning. One of our duties would be to capture these people as they come aboard for off-loading instructions. The instructions were emphatic that no one could be left on the pickup boats. It was important to the mission that we take custody of everyone. The ship's plans were to off-load about a third of the cargo to the locals from the Carolinas, and then the ship would steam up the coast for drop-off points in the Virginia Capes, Long Island, and Cape Cod. The General stressed we had to finish with our work before 0430. That was the time for the ship to check-in with the people in Virginia, and we were to back in New Bern before 0500. No explanation was given for the strict schedule. Someone asked how we would handle the ship's crew and the pick up force. The General was very firm; no one could be left as witnesses. We were to leave a mystery for people to discuss and try to solve, and with well-placed suppositions, it could be expected that the Bermuda Triangle would be given credit for the disappearance of the ship with all hands. The pick up crews would be another part of the legend, since they would be traveling through the Devil's Triangle in small boats. I had some faint thoughts about these people because I had relatives up and down the coast in both Carolinas. All I could do was hope that none of them had taken up the dope trade.

The General said, "O.K., I think that takes care of everything that we know for sure. As you can see, Detachment X-Ray always has good information before going in—we always knew where we were going and not much else."

After a few chuckles, he continued, "Are there any questions? If not, we will break until it is time to go. The cook has food for you, and your equipment is ready to be claimed and tested. Make sure everything is in working order. You probably should get that squared away before eating. We will leave here at 2030 sharp, so you have an hour to prepare for the trip.

Our equipment was already separated with our names on the stacks. The men were pointed to one door and the women to another, for dressing.

Everyone was quiet picking up the equipment, and I grumped, "Shucks, why do we have to dress in different rooms? I have been waiting all afternoon to see Seaman's bare ass—again."

There was no response until the hesitation before saying---again. Then things got back on an even keel when Coppage threw a bundle of trash at me. All hands started complaining about having to go back to the black uniforms. The equipment was a basic weapon for a mission such as the one we were heading. The only changes were the firearms – instead of heavy military weapons, they were light and deadly looking. When it came to the knuckle knife, I noticed them being picked up, examined, and returned to the table. We did not need that particular weapon, because we brought one along. There was no need to ask, the uniforms fit almost as well as they did when they were made to our specifications. It felt strange but exciting after dressing and looking at the reflection in the mirror. I stepped out after changing into the uniform and renewed acquaintances with the Chief, who walked out of the dressing room with me. The knives that were left on the table had disappeared. Chief had been teaching school, and we discussed the number of us who had gone back to school and graduated into the teaching profession. He told me that the Sergeant and Seaman had also been involved in education. Tolliver was the only one who had not gone to teaching, and he was a Colonel in the Marine Corps. As the others joined us, we gravitated to the kitchen where enough food for an army was laid out, buffet style. The General joined us with four other people. I came alert and felt George squeeze my arm. I knew I had backup, if needed.

General Sheffield brought the new-comers over and introduced them with code names. They were also dressed in the basic black. I looked them over and didn't recognize anyone.

I started relaxing until one of them said, "Leader? So you are Leader, I have been looking for you for a long time."

I looked at him with what I hoped was a cold stare and retorted, "O.K., now you have found me."

The General broke in and suggested we go through the buffet, because we only had forty minutes before leaving.

My antagonist growled, "We can finish this some other time."

"I am looking forward to it, Pal," I said, with some heat.

George had moved over near us and had taken her place slightly behind him, and out of my line of fire. While we were talking, the CIA Agent noticed her and tried to move to where he could see both of us. I would not allow it, by moving in the opposite direction. This tactic caused him problems because he couldn't see the two of us.

The General walked over after surveying the situation and said in a cold, firm voice, "I said earlier that personal problems cannot and will not take control of this exercise. All of you know that the mission is the only important thing directly ahead of us. Now break it up, and if you can't work together, stay away from each other."

I took George's arm and started for the buffet line. She began to relax when I told her that I had the most beautiful bodyguard in the world.

I whispered, "When you moved behind that jerk, you were flat out gorgeous."

Seaman joined us, with Tolliver, and whispered, "You two work together real fine. Can I tag along behind?"

Everyone began to loosen up when I said, "Nah. You are so tall that you would draw fire. You have to lead."

Tolliver said quietly, "That was pretty good team work. I had not noticed until Seaman pointed it out. What is that clown's problem?"

"Beats me, unless this is something from Detachment X-Ray days. I have never seen him before this afternoon," I responded.

The agent under discussion came over to the table and said, "Just so you know, my name is Bill Sweeny. Does that ring a bell?"

I thought for a second, and responded, "Mort Sweeny?"

He nodded and said, "Mort was my older brother."

I answered, "Sorry about that, but if you will check, I believe you'll find a pretty good reasons for what happened."

# Chapter 22

A carry-all was used to transport our team to a secluded area of the New Bern airport. A helicopter was ready for takeoff, and General Sheffield was the last to board. He did it with some speed and extra effort because the helicopter was beginning to lift, and he had to jump to the landing ski or be left behind. Detachment X-Ray pilots were known for not paying attention to tardy arrivals when it was time for the take off. The pilot lifted to tree top level and headed east. When feet wet was announced, the craft dropped to wave top, or that's what it appeared to the passengers. The General started a briefing session about our mission. We would approach the ship at approximately 0130, and our group would land by repelling lines. No opposition would be expected because we had the password. There was some discussion about the boarding, if the password wasn't valid to the ship's skipper. We were told in no uncertain terms that we would board the ship, even if we had to jump into the Atlantic Ocean first.

The senior man of the CIA contingent was in possession of the password and was certain that it would work, because the crew of the steamer wasn't of the highest caliber of seamen. He said that the ship would accept the signal because they wouldn't know how to refuse the boarding. The CIA operatives were to be under our leadership until after the boarding was complete. When aboard they would take over the operation of the vessel, until we were ready to depart. Detachment X-Ray would control and secure the ship's crew, and two of the CIA people would rig the explosion points that would be set with timers. The General told us the best way to destroy the ship would be to blow the bottom out of the bow and run the ship at full speed to its grave. This was similar to the actions taken against the Russian trawler in the South Atlantic. We were to wait until all the off-loading boats were secure alongside, with their crews aboard ship. They were to be captured and secured with the ship's force and all would be locked in the boiler room. This information caused a pause in the discussion because the boiler room would be a deadly place, when the explosions commenced taking the ship apart. The plan for setting the explosives called for a small charge that would take out the fresh water to the boilers. This plan of destruction would obliterate such a small ship. That was the plan—no traces of ship, or personnel.

General Sheffield made the assignments for the boarding. As soon as we were on deck, Tolliver would take the Chief, Sarg, George, and two of the CIA people down the port side and take over the bridge and other conning stations. I would take Seaman and one of the CIA agents and capture the topside deck's crew and then proceed to the engineering spaces. The General and the senior CIA Operative would lend a hand where needed, but would proceed to the bridge as practical and take control of the operation. We were told to expect to find the Captain and four-deck seamen topside; at least one seaman would be manning the helm, and the Engineer would be located in the engine room and two oil wipers would be in the same space or the adjoining boiler room. After the General finished with instructions, I motioned for Seaman to join me, as she moved over I asked Sweeny if he wanted to join my group. He indicated that he would by moving alongside Seaman. When he sat down I leaned over and caught his eyes, and we stared at each other for a long moment. He broke a faint grin and extended his hand that I readily accepted. The others in the team were surprised but there was a method to my madness—if he was working for and with me, I could keep a closer eye on him.

The general asked if there were specific requests, and I suggested that at least two men from the ship's crew be available to help with the unloading of the helicopter. There was some discussion about the need for two men. Sweeny had caught my drift and told them that we would take half the deck seaman before anyone knew what was coming down. He looked at me for conformation and I nodded in agreement. I asked for our group to be the last to off-load because with the confusion and lights we should be able to take the prisoners with no opposition.

During the planning portion of the flight, I told Seaman and Sweeny that they would make the captures under my guard. To hold down any confusion, which caused a general laugh, I told Seaman to take the shortest man and Sweeny get the tallest one. Seaman broke us up by stating that if both were the same height she would take the one who happened to get in her way. The other groups would be moving toward their targets before we cleared the deck. It was likely that the other two seamen would be with the Captain, but we had to be aware, in case he was on the main deck. The General gathered us around a blue print of the ship and I immediately found an unexpected bit of good luck. The landing would be at the bow, and just aft of the weather break on the port side was an escape trunk from the engineering spaces. This trunk most likely would be open and would give us immediate access to both the engine and boiler rooms. We could expect three men below decks and the Engineer would be my responsibility, and my two comrades would take the two wipers.

All hands settled back, after the plans were in place, and tried to relax. It soon become evident that Seaman knew how to relax. Her head dropped toward me, and a weak snore could be heard. Sweeny and I got up and straightened her out, and she snorted one time and went into a deep and peaceful sleep. Space was made and I took a seat by Tolliver, and Sweeny moved over to his friends. The Colonel asked about the problem between the CIA and me. He nodded his head in understanding when I told the story about Mort Sweeny. We spent some time discussing the plans for the coming mission, and agreed that if problems arose, we would support each other, but neither of us anticipated any problems once we were on deck. The move down the ladder from the helicopter was going to be white-knuckled because we had no way of knowing what our welcome would be on the ship.

General Sheffield called for attention at 0030, and told us to check and recheck all equipment, because we should be in visual range of the ship at 0100. The helicopter had already established voice communications, and the ship had accepted the password. The ship's captain was discussing the approach, and what was needed for the boarding. He sounded relieved that a security force had been employed. The General asked for suggestions and Sweeny said that the ship should be darkened, except for hand-held lights by the deck seaman. It was a great idea, and we all acknowledged the suggestion because that situation would keep us from being blinded by shipboard lights. The Captain agreed and said that all lights except for running lights would be cut when visual contact was established. We put on goggles to protect our night vision when the lights were turned on after landing. The pilot called tallyho and approached, so all of us could see the ship. It was a small inter-island freighter and from the bow, we would have to move about twenty feet to get to cover.

The shipboard lights went out at approximately one and a half miles. All of the equipment was checked and rechecked again, because we couldn't afford a hitch for any reason while we were in the air. The General called all to attention and explained what he expected us to do. He and the senior CIA Operative would be first on deck, and if there were more than two deck hands, an escort to the bridge would be requested. Tolliver and his force would leave the helicopter after the General was on deck and had signaled for them to come down. My squad would go on deck after the others had cleared the landing zone. The helicopter crew had been briefed to get as close to the deck as possible, and direct their lights downward, and when we started to leave, the lights were to be turned to highlight the deck line handlers. That would give us a great advantage, to have their night vision completely destroyed. A question suddenly popped into Tolliver's mind and it was a good one. He asked quietly, "General, how do we leave? Does this bird have enough fuel to wait for us?

Everyone had tensed and the General responded, "I hope so. If we don't get delayed with some unforeseen problems, we have enough fuel. So whatever you do on the ship, do it smartly."

We circled the ship at masthead height and spotted all but one of the deck crew and surmised that he was probably at the helm. Even with knowing the location, it's still a shock to watch the ship ghost into sight under the helicopter. The pilot circled one time and hovered about ten feet above the deck. The General touched the deck and signaled and Tolliver's unit started down before the CIA Agent had touched the deck. We watched them call the extra crewman and he led them at a trot toward the bridge. Tolliver's people hit the deck and were talking to the line handlers to break their concentration. After everyone trotted off, the line handlers looked up just in time to be blinded by the searchlights. Seaman hit the deck and grabbed the smallest of the crew, as Sweeny swung into the other one, as he landed on deck. The lights were turned off as I left the aircraft, and we hustled the confused sailors aft to the weather break. Seaman and Sweeny took both of them out, with well-planned blows to the side of the head. They were tied up and gagged, and dragged into the shadows—we had captured the two females in the steamer crew.

The scuttle was open on the engineering escape trunk, probably for ventilation. No noises could be heard from the engine room except for the hum of the blower system. There were ten steps to the lower deck, and I took them very slowly, to keep down the possibility of someone catching sight of movement. After carefully surveying the surrounding area, I moved out on the catwalk and could see the Engineer sitting with feet propped up and reading. The two wipers were nowhere in sight, and I signaled for Seaman and Sweeny. Each of them came down slowly and when they made the catwalk, I pointed out the Engineer. In whispered conversation they agreed to stay on the catwalk to make an entrance to the fire room spaces. We moved one step at a time to the ladder down to the control boards. I took three steps down and then jumped. The man froze and before he could turn or say anything, I took him out with a blow to the side of the head with the machine pistol. He slumped off the seat and a revolver clattered to the deck from his belt. I was glad that the *Playboy Magazine* had an interesting centerfold, which kept the man from hearing us or catching my movement down the three steps of the ladder. After making sure he was unconscious, I headed aft to the fire room hatch. It was standing open and I watched Seaman and Sweeny, as they pounced on their prey. We bound and gagged them and dragged the officer into the fire room and lashed him to his compatriots.

The telephone rang at the control board, and I answered it with a muffled voice.

The General asked, "Leader, did everything go as planned?"

I said, "Yes Sir. We have the engineering spaces secured with three prisoners. You can find the two deck seamen at the starboard weather break."

He replied, "Great, that accounts for all hands. Bring your people to the bridge."

We checked the binding and gagged our prisoners again, before leaving for topside. The weather was calm and a half moon with clear skies offered good visibility. We made our way to the bridge and were joined by Tolliver and his people who had taken the other prisoners to the fire room. They had tied the seven members, lashed them together and left them gagged. We should have no problem with any of them. The one unsettling factor was that a total of fifteen guns had been confiscated. This was a good reminder that more weapons would come aboard with the unloading boat crews.

The General told us that the Captain had related the unloading plans, before he realized that his ship was being taken from him. We could expect the boats to begin arriving somewhere around 0200. There would be seventeen boats and normally, two people would be on each craft. Women would man some of the boats and we could expect some teenagers. This gave some pause but with a collective shrug of the shoulders that became no problem. The planning called for the boat crew to come on deck and there could be no exception. All hands would be collected at the ladder, so that each arrival could be hustled down below before another boat came alongside. A boom would be rigged, so that the boats could tie up and no one would be allowed to stay with them. After everyone was aboard, the boom would be hauled alongside the ship and secured. The visitors would be taken into custody in the most expeditious manner. Once they were restrained, they would be taken to the fire room where the ship's crew was being held.

I interrupted and said, "General, you are aware that I grew up in this region. I doubt much has changed with the natives. They are independent thinkers. They are good old boys and love their coon dogs, pickup trucks, women, and their guns. We can expect a fight if there is a prior indication to them about what we are doing, because they would be fighting for all those things. After we get them on deck I would suggest that whoever hits them should hit them hard. If we miss one of them, we could be in deep shit."

This caused a free flowing discussion as to how we would go about our plans to carry out the mission. Many ideas were put forth and discarded as we went about our preparations to receive the boats.

The General finally said, "O.K., Leader is correct in his assessment.

Instead of an accommodation ladder we will lower a boatswains chair or a Jacobs ladder to bring them aboard. In that fashion, we will have immediate control of the boarder. I will remain on the bridge as Captain. Tolliver will control the quarterdeck, where our visitors will be brought aboard. Leader, you and Sweeny handle the captures, and the rest of you hustle everyone off the main deck, as fast as possible. No hesitation from anyone. If they resist, shoot them and drag their bodies out of sight."

We caught sight of the first boat before we could rig the boatswain's chair, so a Jacob's ladder went over the side for the boarding. We decided that this situation would be better for our operation because only one person could be on the ladder at a time, and we would be able to restrain one person without the other seeing the action. The first boat measured twenty-two feet and was built for the surf. There was some objection for both people to leave the boat, but we insisted, because everyone would be needed to handle cargo. They tied their boat to the boom line and one of them came up the ladder and did not see the start of Sweeny's swing. We handed the unconscious seaman over for movement off the deck. The second was handled the same way and we found five handguns on the two men. This give us no choice, each person would have to be rendered unconscious before they could step on the deck. The next was a fishing boat from Calabash, North Carolina, with a man and a woman aboard but we didn't pick and choose. The first one over the rail was the man and Sweeny took him, and I took care of the woman without a second thought. I remember thinking that it didn't take long for the mission to become the controlling factor of all our actions. There was some grousing about having to come aboard, but no real problems, until we received the seventeenth boat. One of the people in it refused to come aboard because according to him he was the "boss man" of this operation.

The General finally called from the bridge and bellowed, "You may be boss man in the boats, but I am the Captain of this ship and not a bale will be unloaded until you get your ass on board and count them, as they come out of the hold."

There were still some objections, but we were adamant.

Tolliver called down to the "boss man" and shouted, "You heard the Captain. Either you get up here and go to work, or I will throw this whole bunch over the side. We don't need any grief from a bunch of fishermen. You have five minutes. If you don't get your ass aboard we will send all your people back, and you can head for home, with nothing to show for your long trip."

That ended the argument and we allowed him to step on deck and look around to find that none of his friends were in sight. He started to protest and grab for a weapon; he didn't make it. Sweeny and I hit him at the same time. The CIA people started setting the timers on all of the explosives. Tolliver and I went below and made sure all of the captives were bound, gagged, and lashed to a piece of equipment.

We couldn't afford to have a body floating to the surface with hands and feet tied. The hatches were secured before we left the engineering spaces.

I waited for orders in the engine room and soon felt the ship change headings and knew that the course would be east to the open sea. The engine order telegraph rang full ahead. I opened the throttles, answered the bells, and headed for the escape trunk. Someone groaned but I didn't look back. The General was waiting for me on deck and as soon as we felt the ship come to speed we went for one of the ship's boat. We hauled out from the ship and headed westward toward land. The helicopter flew overhead and after a twenty-mile run hoisted us aboard. I had just scrambled aboard, when a terrific explosion was heard. We watched the freighter's bow rise from the water from the exploding charges. When the bow dropped back into the sea there was no hesitation, the full speed of the engines drove the ship directly to the bottom of the ocean. A second muffled explosion denoted the boilers blowing. The boat we took was scuttled, and with a turn over the area, there were little flotsam and jetsam to mark the demise of the ship and forty-four people. The mission had been carried out with little or no problems, and a cargo of narcotics slated for the eastern seaboard wouldn't be landed. There would be some notice when the ship didn't arrive at the next appointed off-loading sites. It was a general conclusion that the outcry would be minimal. There would be a hue and cry when the local seaman didn't return, but that incident would soon find its way into the legend of the Devil's Triangle.

The flight back to New Bern was quiet, except for some muted personal conversations. One of the conversations was between Sweeny and me. He said he had listened to the General and others tell the story about Mort Sweeny and someone called Leader.

He said, "Mort was my brother, but he shouldn't have been involved to the point that people were killed because of his actions."

I told him that it was too bad that the incident happened, but I was willing to stand by my part of the action. He looked at me for some minutes, and then said that he wouldn't forget what happened, but I wouldn't have to look over my shoulders.

I extended my hand and said, "Fair enough."

He took my hand and after few moments the handshake ended and we were finished with the conversation. He moved over to his friends and one of them slapped him on the shoulder. In my mind, Mort Sweeny was history, and I was glad that the present and the future wouldn't have anything to do with the past. One of the other conversations that were interesting to me was between Tolliver and George. They appeared to be oblivious to all of the surrounding.

I mused, "Have I missed something?"

The helicopter took us into the New Bern airport and landed some distance away from the public area. There was probably no need for such action, because the small town airfield was just beginning to come awake for the day. This was normal routine for Detachment X-Ray—stay out of contact with civilians while we were in the black uniforms. A carryall pulled through the gates and came alongside to disembark. There was no sightseeing as each person left the craft; we ran the few steps to the automobile. The driver took us back to the house where the mission had started, and we immediately changed into street clothes. There was a sideboard meal waiting, with all types of breakfast food. Tolliver tried to get something started because I helped my self to grits first; and then reached for the side dishes such as eggs, bacon, and ham. Everyone seemed to be in a normal state of mind—good friends enjoying good friends. Tolliver and I sat at the breakfast counter and were joined by George and Seaman. They stated that plans were being formed to go back to schools for a PhD and invited me to join them at a mid western school—University of Iowa. This had been another story; the two women had graduated from the same class, without knowing each other. I didn't mention John Silvers and refused their invitation and told them about my "big house down by the river." Seaman suggested that we stay in touch, because she always wanted to visit the "Wild West," and she lived all the way back east in Idaho.

I laughed and said quietly, "I am not sure Venture, Washington, could put up with all of us. But if you come, I will let you catch one of my salmons."

The housekeeper came over and told Tolliver that the General wanted to see him. He returned and told me that the General wanted too see me, too.

I tapped on the door and walked in and he smiled and said, "Leader, I am glad you finally surfaced. I have sent out search a couple of times. You must have taken me at my word and gone deep into the population. Now a warning, my friend, watch yourself, the Chinese aren't ones who wait to talk."

I saluted him and replied, "We are not planning to talk. Where did you pick up such information?"

"Can't say," he said, and came around the desk to shake hands.

I was a little shaken because other people had knowledge, and I knew that the General wouldn't blow smoke. He knew what was being planned for Long Ball Kwong.

I came back to the table and Tolliver said, "Buddy Boy, the Marine air force is at the field. Let us get back to the nation's capital."

The women stood and I hugged them and in the embrace, placed a card in their pockets. It was a simple card—my personal telephone number was the only information displayed.

I whispered to Seaman, " This is in case leeches come out to play."

At the door, I looked over my shoulder and was somewhat surprised, George came out with Tolliver and they were holding hands.

There was little interaction with the Colonel during the flight back to DC. The aircraft landed, we shook hands and promised to stay in touch.

I said, "I must have missed something—George is a great person."

He grinned and waved, as a Marine sedan approached. It was an unmarked vehicle, but it was Marine because the driver had a haircut anyone would identify as Marine.

# Chapter 23

The mission with the General had taken such a short time that I was not even missed.

When I walked into the apartment house, one of the FBI Agents asked with a wry grin, "When did you leave?" We didn't know you were out of the building."

He laughed when I told him that there were so many people following me that I could dodge through them without being seen.

"There are so many of you, no one can see what the other is doing. I was out for a short time for a walk and cup of coffee," I continued with the cover story.

He waved when I headed for the elevator and he promised to stay on guard for my protection. It was good to see an agent with a sense of humor. Most of them were so serious that they could only see what they were told to see. With the exception of John, my friends didn't know that I had been out of town. I spent the remainder of Saturday, outlining ideas to go after Long Ball Kwong. Silvers called and suggested we get together on Sunday to discuss our plans. He said that the week would be taken up with a lot of movement in and out of town to stretch the resources being used against the entire group. All of us were being tailed and we decided that Carpenter wouldn't be brought into the picture. That would give us a small advantage of his scouting and tracking skills. All of the open movement would be an advantage for meeting and planning without fear of discovery.

Our time was running short because the cocktail party for Dong Ping was scheduled for Tuesday evening. He was scheduled to leave for China January 2, and we still didn't have any information on the departure route.

The District Police Department was in such disarray that no one seemed to know what was going to happen. A disquieting rumor broke that crowd control would be carried out by a combined force of Maryland and Virginia State Police, while the District Police would form the escort. We knew that if the rumor had any substance there would be little or no chance of taking Dong Ping while he was en route to the airport. We suspected that pressure had been brought on the White House to offer as an affair of state, honoring the departure of a world leader.

Sunday morning, John Silvers called with the news that a chartered boat had been arranged for the day. We agreed this would be the best chance we would have to get everyone together, without the chasers having a chance of interfering. John and Samantha stopped by to pick me up and we met the Josephs' and Jacobs at the boat landing. While we were waiting for the boat we watched the CIA and FBI boats leave the landing and lay to watching our efforts. We talked quietly about the fact that the Carpenters wouldn't be on the river trip. The Dock Master signaled that our boat was next. There was some elbowing between us, as we watched a beautiful crewman jump lightly to the pier with a mooring line in hand. The coxswain of the boat was a tall, lanky seaman who looked like a mountain man. I don't know who did the teaching, but the Sniper was a pretty good boat handler. We made a leisurely trip down river and just inside Chesapeake Bay, tied up to a channel buoy and rigged fishing lines. This caused an immediate hardship for our followers because it was a half-mile to the next buoy, and they had to stay underway, to keep us under surveillance. We kept the fishing lines in the water but instead of fishing, we concentrated on problems at hand. A consensus decision was made that the Long Ball Kwong operation would have to be called off, unless we had at least twelve hours to plan. It was beginning to look as if Long Ball would elude us, because the tails were no longer hidden. They were active and made sure that we knew they were in the neighborhood. They wanted us to know that our planned mission would be impossible to carry out.

Chow Ling was waiting when we arrived back at the pier and invited me for a drink. John Silvers was invited also, when I mentioned that he would be attending the reception at the Chinese Ambassador's residence.

The Chinese acted as if surprised, but I knew that he wasn't when he said, "Oh yes, the famous Silvertip and his lackey, Navy."

He laughed as he said it, and I matched his attitude with, "Oh, it seems as if some may be coming clean and admitting his sins."

"No sin, my friend, that was war," Chow said quickly.

"The war isn't over, my friend," I said, and continued, "I promised a certain Chinese officer that I would gut him if I saw him again, but according to you, there is no such officer in the Chinese Embassy."

Chow said, "I came to tell you that you will never get to him. You may have had a chance until he started talking to the press and answering all questions. He now knows that Captain Silvers is coming to the party, so you can't surprise him."

"Are you going to allow us to be alone with him at the party?" John asked pointedly.

There was a long silence before the Chinese agent answered, "Only to talk. He says that you were once a friend, but we will be close during the conversation."

The party at the Chinese Ambassador's home was the ticket of the season. The Ambassador and his Lady, had very early in their posting, became the toast of Washington Society. John and Samantha made a striking couple. He had surprised me by showing up in Marine evening dress, including the sword. Samantha was, of course, the beautiful lady that she was, but for the party, she had outdone herself. She had color-coordinated with the uniform. I noted that John had left the Marines as Colonel. They were not the only ones in military dress, but they were the noticeable ones. The receiving line was just inside the door, and Susan turned toward it. as we were announced. All heads had turned as we moved to the Ambassador, and when I introduced John and Samantha, a veil of caution showed in his eyes for a fleeting moment. He was pleasant but not as friendly as at other times. Madam Hau was different. She was her delightful self, and hugged Susan and offered me her hand.

I leaned over the hand and said, "Madam Hau, my friends John and Samantha Silvers."

Samantha received a hug and John blushed when our hostess told everyone how handsome he appeared in uniform.

She said, "Now that is how you are supposed to wear a uniform."

I glanced ahead and Dong Ping was standing at strict attention and offered only an occasional word, as the guests greeted him. I stepped behind Samantha so John and I could hit him with both barrels. I stopped in front of him and said, "Major Kwong, I believe."

His interpreter started to speak when John stepped in, "Well now, my old school chum, Long Ball Kwong. How things change, don't they, Long Ball?"

The interpreter kept talking with a puzzled look and Long Ball didn't look at either of us, until I whispered, "I promised to gut you, you son-of-a-bitch, if I ever saw you again. Well now, I have found you right in my back yard."

"I warned you not to mistreat my men, Long Ball," Silvers said, as we moved away.

The look we received after the last exchange was one of fear, but he controlled it and tried to show contempt. I laughed with as much disgust as I could put forth in this company. We moved out into the room and were met by Chow Ling who guardedly greeted Susan and me. There was a long, speculative examination when he greeted John and Samantha. Pei Li joined us and extended her hand to Samantha and introduced herself before any of us could do the honors. She and Chow Ling stayed with us, as we moved across the reception hall. I noticed two other Chinese, who were pacing us from about thirty feet across the hall. Pei Li blushed when I asked if she was still a fearless news correspondent.

She smiled and arched her brow when I leaned closer and whispered, "I still can't see how you can carry a weapon in those clothes."

She laughed lightly, and replied, "Have you considered that the clothes are the weapon or maybe they are covering the weapon."

Chow Ling nudged my elbow and indicated the side of the room with outside doors. We stepped out into the open air and he said, "My friend, don't take any action tonight, which we might regret."

"Not tonight, my friend, " I answered, "This is to show Mr. Dong Ping that we know he is our Major Long Ball Kwong of the Chinese Army, whom we had the displeasure of meeting in Korea. He no longer can deny that fact because this is Long John Silvers of the University of Chicago. They were classmates and were on the same baseball team."

Chow Ling answered, "Don't you think he may regret his actions? In any event it was war, and those things happen in war."

"Yes, it was war and we could understand the Korean's actions, but my friend, you people hadn't entered the war at that time. As far as we are concerned, he had no authority, and we plan to punish him for his actions, so my advice is not to get in the way," I said, almost in a whisper.

In a like tone he responded, "I have to get in the way. It is my duty to my country."

"I can understand that," I said, "and I am sorry. Tonight is just-to-get-acquainted night. Besides, Madam Hau wouldn't put up with any crap on such an occasion as this."

We both laughed, as he said, "Just remember that or I will tell her."

There was a buzz of conversation when we rejoined the party. The Secretary of State had entered the hall and was soon followed by the Vice President of the United States. We had not expected the Vice President, but soon found out why he was there. A butler handed me a note. I glanced at it and handed it to John. It was an invitation to join Ambassador Hau and guests in the library. Chow Ling again became our escort and Madam Hau took over the women. We started moving across the hall and saw Long Ball Kwong entering the library with Hau and the Secretary of State.

John said, "OOPS," and motioned to the left.

The Vice President was moving to the library, also. He was with the Premier of the Peoples Republic of China. I hadn't heard that this person was in our country. It was beginning to appear that John and I would soon be in deep shit between high officials of two world giants. Someone from one side had to have balls and gall to approach the other side, with a suggestion as to what appeared to be happening. I was betting on the fragile-looking old man whom we had named the "Turnip Salesman."

We entered the library and Chow Ling asked us to step out on the balcony. He didn't come with us, but in a few minutes, another door opened and we were joined by Long Ball Kwong.

He came over and said, "Long John Silvers, it is good to see you."

John answered, "I wish it was a better time for me to see you, Long Ball. We have been looking forward to this for some time, but not with pleasure."

Kwong responded, "So I hear, and John, I am disappointed with you. You were a commander, in what your country calls the Korean War. So you know I had to do what I did. You were treated harshly in a harsh situation, but you were treated with respect."

Silvers answered, "What respect? You allowed the Koreans to beat and shoot our people, and you, yourself tortured this man."

"I was in a bad situation, John," Kwong responded, "And the situation dictated harsh measures, because we were on the move. He would not answer our questions. The other people were interrogated also."

John snorted in disgust, and retorted, "Long Ball, you knew damned well that he was nothing but a grunt. He was dressed differently from the rest of us, and that was all it took for you and your men to pound on him. Long Ball, you wouldn't have taken notice of him, had he been in fatigues rather than Navy dungarees. Then you, in all your wisdom as a Chinese officer, tortured him with the hot and cold measures. I saw you as you would force him to keep his hands in an ice bucket until they were almost frozen, and then you would force them into scalding water."

The Chinese official finally acknowledged my presence and said, "I believe you were called, Navy. So, Navy, what is your position in all of this? You were treated like any prisoner who wouldn't cooperate."

I didn't bother to respond to his comments.

Our eyes locked, and I forced as much anger as I could muster and snarled, "Think back, you son-of-a-bitch. What was the last thing I said to you?"

He was beginning to show some agitation by my insulting and threatening attitude, but he did not answer the question.

I reminded him, "I promised to gut you like a fish, you bastard."

The soldier in him evidently was aroused because he started for me.

Chow Ling's voice behind me was urgent, "Do not be stupid."

I turned and noted that he was talking to his future Premier.

He turned to me and said menacing, "If any gutting goes on here, I will do it."

I held his gaze for a moment, and said, ""Don't push it, Chow Ling. Don't push it because I have two sharp knives."

He didn't take it any further and after looking at me for a minute or so, said "The other guests want to see you now."

We turned to the door and Long Ball Kwong asked, "Long John, will you shake hands with an old team-mate?"

Without hesitation the hand was offered and John said, "I wish it could have been different, old friend. Remember we tried to talk you into staying in Chicago?"

There was a long silence and Long Ball Kwong turned away, and by the time he opened the door he was once again Mr. Hsu Dong Ping. The room had been arranged for an interrogation. Two chairs had been placed in the recessed portion of the room and would put us at a lower level than the others in the room.

I muttered, "John, I don't think so."

He followed me to the mantel and we took opposite ends.

A few mutters started but a soft voice said, "I don't blame them."

Chin Hau knew how to take command of a situation even in front of his Premier. He accepted my bow with a smile.

"John, watch yourself, " I quipped, "We are in the middle of a real power structure. The man behind the Vice President is a member of the White House Secret Service Squad. Likewise, the two men behind the Secretary of State are from the FBI. One of them is my old friend, Walter Swackhammer. The skinny guy off to one side is another friend—he is Cliff Grogan of the CIA. You know Chow Ling; he is the agent in charge of the Chinese Secret Service, here in Washington. The beautiful woman, in green, is Tsu Pei Li. She is Chow Ling's assistant, and sometimes Chinese television reporter. And I still don't know where she hides her gun."

A pleasant female laugh and a few chuckles around the room broke my dissertation.

I continued before anyone could interrupt, "The two gentlemen behind the Premier are strangers, but I assume they are on the Premier's security staff. The two guys in the button-down collars are members of the National Security Agency. And with a great deal of pleasure, Ambassador Chin Hau, whom I believe is the boss of all hands."

I received a bow and smile from the "Turnip Salesman," but the customary twinkle wasn't in his eyes. Instead, I saw something that made my shoulder muscles twitch.

There were a few moments of silence, as the agents sized up their opposition.

John Silvers took over, "Well now, what an august body. Tell us how we can be of service."

The silence dragged on for minutes this time. I shifted my feet and caught John's attention, and indicated for him not to say anything further. There was a lot of shifting, water sipping, and note passing. The Chinese were waiting for the Americans, and the Americans were waiting for the Chinese.

The Vice President was the one who broke.

He stuttered, "We have been warned that a group of dissidents are threatening Mr. Dong Ping. This is a warning—the entire weight of the United States will fall on anyone who tries such a dumb stunt."

He hadn't looked in our direction and John signaled for silence this time.

The Secretary of State then said, "This is no time for anything to happen, which could cause a breach in our understandings with each other's country."

"If anything happens to Mr. Dong Ping, whether it is insult or injury, there will be people who will see it as an act of war," the Premier stated somberly.

The Secretary and Vice President started to speak, when Chin Hau spoke up, "Now, now, now, are we threatening each other because of a private situation? I thought that was in the past."

He directed most of his comments at the Premier.

He continued with, "I thought all of you wanted to talk to these young men. Yet, there hasn't been a question directed toward them."

He looked at us and asked softly, "Will you stand for an interrogation?"

He had a kind smile and I looked at him and said, "No sir."

I turned to John, and he stood straight, as a good Marine would, and said, "Nor me, and especially, since no one has told us why we should be questioned."

There were some dissatisfied mutters but no one would actually make charges against us nor would they ask questions. The ambassador waited a few moments for someone to speak.

No one did, and he said, "Then let us join the other guests."

When I passed the old man, I was sure there was sorrow and regret showing in his eyes. We went into the great hall and found Susan and Samantha with Madam Hau.

As we approached, John said to me, "Let's choose up sides and get the hell out of here."

Then to our hostess he said, "Madam Hau, we thank you for your invitation. Now we must leave. It has been a great experience to meet you and your husband."

There was no hesitation from the women who turned for the cloakroom.

A soft, fragile hand took mine in a firm grip and a gentle voice said, "I am so sorry."

We left before the agents could get from behind a gaggle of officials. Our luck held, as a taxi pulled up to let off some late arriving guests. The cabby was pleasantly surprised to get a return fare from the Ambassador's home. We had already blended into traffic, when the first tailing car left the gate of the yard. It turned away from us, but the next one turned towards us. We watched Cliff Grogan pass without taking notice of a crowded cab. It wouldn't take them long to find us, so we decided to go where they would look last—my apartment.

When we started talking, it didn't take them long to appear and it answered a question—the apartment was bugged. I pulled the drapes from a window and could see the Chinese car, the CIA, and Swackhammer's beat up Buick.

I said, "Hey, Babe, you can't stay the night because our friends would be listening to me panting while doing other things."

Susan spoke up grinning, and as if she was disappointed, "Oh no, don't they have something more important to be doing?"

Then she took a dig, "Honey, move to the first floor so they can be peeping toms and really get their jollies."

I said loudly, "John, when you leave, there is a gray Buick across the street. It belongs to the Chinese. The green Plymouth is from the CIA. Oh yes, my friend Walter T. drives the Buick, which is so beat up you can't tell the color."

We watched from the window as the three automobiles pulled away from the curb. Samantha whispered an invitation for us to go with them to Georgetown. Susan didn't wait for me—she accepted.

# Chapter 24

Four days after Christmas, we had reserved a table for dinner at the Ambassador Hotel. We found three empty chairs at the table. The Carpenters and Charlie Daniels were missing. Doreen was worried because Charlie hadn't said anything about leaving, and didn't say goodbye.

Samantha said, "Don't worry, Honey. Carpenter probably decided to go home at midnight and Charlie is taking them. When Carpenter decides to go, he has no time for the telephone. Charlie will be back."

Darlene Jacobs laughed and said, "Yeah, we have never seen Charlie so smitten—all because of a dab of red hair."

During the afternoon the men discussed Carpenter's absence, and we agreed that he had probably gone home, after we had called off the mission against Long Ball Kwong. He had been concerned about being away from home for this period of time. We called around and couldn't find his route out of town. There were no worries because he could call up more security than the President. Josephs suggested that Charlie had flown them home in a helicopter. One thing that hadn't changed was the coverage on us by the different agencies. They had us covered like a blanket, and it was surprising they hadn't made Carpenter as one of us. Swackhammer and Grogan were on duty this day, but they played it smart and brought their families to the Ambassador. They were embarrassed, but turned down our invitation for them to join us.

There was some movement from a number of people while dinner was being served. Doreen came around and leaned her arms across my shoulder letting her hands fall down my chest. While we were talking I felt her put something in my shirt pocket. She remained in that pose for a few more minutes before regaining her seat. After a short time, I felt my pocket and found a note.

In a bold hand it stated, "If I can be of help. S. O."

S.O. had to be Seamus O'Halloran, I gave a slight nod to his daughter, when she next looked my way.

We had reluctantly decided that the attack on Long Ball Kwong would be impossible. As the time neared for his departure, we were being covered twenty-four hours a day, with double the agents from before. The departure route was the best-kept secret on the Beltway. Bucky O'Halloran had even asked his sergeant, a number of times, about possible routes from the Chinese Embassy to the airport. He was finally told that the route was on a need-to-know basis, and a traffic cop had no need to know, until the motorcade started the run. I told Bucky to back off before someone became suspicious of him. On Friday, we planned a mock run at the Chinese Embassy. We were stopped in a traffic jam more than ten blocks from our target. The vehicles in the jam were mostly from the three agencies that were concerned with our movements. It was probably the first time in history that the FBI, CIA, and the Chinese security forces were allies. There were a number of attempts made by us to close the target separately. We were stymied on each occasion. The closest any of us came to the Embassy gates was Josephs, who was turned away five blocks away from his destination. Long Ball Kwong had been completely removed from any danger from our group. It became apparent that the different agencies had learned of our intentions—the Chinese were the only ones with first-hand knowledge. We were frustrated and angry, but agreed that we wouldn't be able to get him in our sights. There was some talk of a future try, but that was so much bravado—we didn't believe it would be possible, even as we discussed it.

January $2^{nd}$ dawned with a heavy dark overcast and snow beginning to fall. We were no longer after the future Premier of the Peoples Republic of China, but weren't about to give relief to the authorities. At 0600, John Silvers would leave Georgetown in his automobile, and I would leave Alexandria near the same time, in my vehicle. Jacobs and Josephs were to leave Georgetown in different taxis that would go in different directions. That meant we would be converging on the airport from four different directions. There were four cars following me, and I wondered how much stress we were putting on the agencies. John was parking, as I pulled into the parking garage. As I was walking toward the air bridge, I saw Josephs entering the lower level of the terminal. Jacobs was waiting for us at the escalator. The four of us didn't speak or even look at each other, but we started for the departure gates with about fifty feet intervals between each man.

When we turned toward the VIP departure ramp plain clothes and uniformed policemen, FBI Agents, CIA Operatives, and some very dangerous looking Orientals immediately surrounded us. I spied Chow Ling and Pei Li at the entrance to the departure lounge; Grogan and Swackhammer were waiting directly in front of the door to the VIP lounge. I waved to them, turned toward a view-port and began watching airport operations when they walked up with my comrades.

"It would be dumb to start something here," Cliff Grogan growled nervously.

I laughed and said; "Don't we know it. If a fight started in here, half of your agencies would be wiped out. Besides, you guys convinced us to be tourists long ago."

"What were you planning?" asked one of the agents.

No one believed when Jacobs answered, "We were planning a great holiday period in our nation's capital until you guys started crowding us so closely. I am still trying to get the guys to join me in charging you with harassment."

There were some disbelieving snorts and a few relieved chuckles.

The future Premier of the Peoples Republic of China came in with a security force large enough to take on a small army. The local agents surrounded us until he was in the VIP lounge, and the airport activity took on a hurried, but careful mood. Airport police surrounded an unmarked airliner as it rolled into the boarding area. Four police helicopters came and took prearranged positions to offer covering fire if it was needed. We waited for half an hour, as security forces with dogs inspected the surrounding area that included the recently arrived aircraft. When the security detachment pulled back, the lounge door to the tarmac opened and an army of Chinese made up two massed lines to the airplane. They were so tightly grouped, the officials could only walk in single file to the plane. This act gave individual coverage to the officials by the escorting agents. The Premier's parties of about twenty were the first to board. Long Ball Kwong came out and looked around. He saw us at the window, and with the first smile of the morning from anyone, gave us a mock salute.

The agents surrounded us and crowded us together, so no one could make a move. Two of them actually grabbed my arms at the elbow. I could see Josephs was getting the same attention, and I surmised that Jacobs and Silvers were being restrained also.

We watched the second group of Chinese officials start up the loading ramp. Most of them were short enough to be covered by the escorts. Long Ball Kwong was a tall man and just as he appeared above the heads of his guard, something happened that made me think of other times.

I imagined that I heard the KABLANG of the Sniper's rifle. There was a real commotion, as one of the official's head exploded, and the body was falling into the massed guards. No one caught it, and as the body lay on the tarmac. I could see it was nothing more than a dead mass, as the ones on a long ago battlefield. The agents began spreading out, and the police helicopters immediately lifted and began a search. One of them moved around the hangar, and I didn't see it again. The shooter wasn't found and we had an airtight alibi. It was sort of a let-down when the word was passed that the victim was Mr. Dong Ping.

We were questioned over four hours before the FBI allowed us to leave.

We went to the parking garage, and as we stood at the cars, talking, Josephs asked, "Now what, are we going to keep in touch or is this the end of our friendship?"

There was no answer, until Silvers said, "Let's give it some time and we can see how things develop. We know a lot about each other."

We did not ask the question, "Who was the shooter?"

I stood and watched my three friends entered Silvers' car and left without further conversation. I walked over to my car and saw Walter Swackhammer approaching.

He leaned down and spoke through the side window, "We need a bunch of bad guys taken out over in Arizona."

I did not answer him and put the car in gear and brushed him as I was backing out. An airport policeman pulled me over at the tollbooth.

Cliff Grogan appeared and asked, "Would you guys like to work for the good guys against the bad guys?

I said, "Cliff, get the hell away from my car."

He started to back away, leaned down to my level, grinned and said; "You can't live forever."

# Praise for Jess Parker's "Detachment X-Ray"

WOW!!! Nice job, I haven't stayed so riveted to a book in so long…it is a great book and so believable—I am waiting for your next work of art.
 Larry Brown of Arizona.

Well done. Above and beyond expectations…. Continuously interesting, easy to relate to.
 Bert Brault of Florida

This novel is fast paced, readable, humorous, disgusting and heartwarming.
 Lynn Barry of New York

For readers who enjoy military action and covert operations, Jess Parker's novel, Detachment X-Ray has it in abundance.
 Jerry Mohrlang of Colorado

Printed in the United States
22960LVS00006B/88-135